Someone was coming....

A flashlight bounced a warning before the sound of shoes on the steps. Alisha pressed against the wall. Darkness might hide her.

There were four of them, the two in the lead blond. The fourth small and dark.

The third was the tallest, lean and black-haired, the stairway's dim lighting making warm, soft sheens on his leather coat. He swung around the final steps, glancing over his shoulder toward the cubby in which Alisha hid.

Nothing in his expression changed as Frank Reichart met Alisha's eyes. A lump of dismay held in Alisha's stomach, before Reichart looked away again. For the briefest moment she thought perhaps he hadn't seen her.

And then he did a double take, very deliberately. His eyes widened, just enough to suggest surprise, and the shock in his voice was unforced, as if there was no guile to it at all. "Alisha!"

Oh, yeah. Getting out was going to be a problem.

Dear Reader,

The months between *The Cardinal Rule* and *The Firebird Deception* have been exciting times for me. I've moved across the world—from Alaska to Ireland—and have been busy writing books in the midst of all that. All I need now to share Alisha's exciting lifestyle is a couple of gorgeous, dangerous men chasing me over the European continent. Well, that and a secret organization trying to kill me, which, frankly, I'd rather avoid.

Hmm. Now that I think about it, my husband might take exception to the gorgeous, dangerous men. Well, I won't tell him if you don't...!

I hope you have as much fun reading Alisha's continuing adventures as I'm having writing them. I'd love to hear from you on my reader forums at http://cemurphyfans.com, or at my Web site, http://catedermody.com.

Cate

CATE DERMODY

For Veronica & Pat (just to mix things up a bit. :))!

Love,
Cate

Published by Silhouette Books
America's Publisher of Contemporary Romance

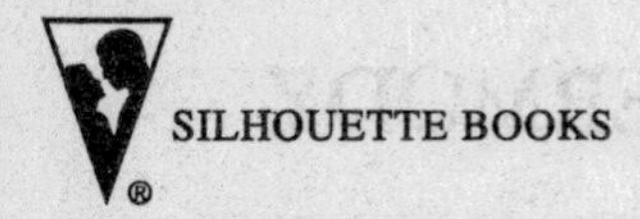

ISBN 0-373-51409-3

THE FIREBIRD DECEPTION

This edition published by arrangement with Harlequin Books S.A.

www.SilhouetteBombshell.com

Printed in U.S.A.

Books by Cate Dermody

Silhouette Bombshell

**The Cardinal Rule* #71
**The Firebird Deception* #95

*The Strongbox Chronicles

Books written as C. E. Murphy

Luna Books

Urban Shaman
Winter Moon
"Banshee Cries"
Thunderbird Falls

CATE DERMODY

is a born and bred Alaskan who returned to her ancestral homeland, Ireland, after years of talking about doing so. There, she has taken up walking the width and breadth of the country, which, after living in a state the size of Alaska, seems like a perfectly reasonable ambition. For those keeping track at home, although she still enjoys biking and swimming, she has not yet convinced herself that triathlons are worth the effort of running.

She lives with her husband Ted, housemate Shaun and a number of pets. More information about Cate and her writing can be found at www.catedermody.com.

This one's for Ma Lee and Grandma Reiffers

ACKNOWLEDGMENTS

My usual suspects, Silkie and Jai, were especially patient with me this time around, which I appreciate to no end. Lance Henry was once more helpful with Latin guidance (we're *pretty* sure we got it right!), and Ted, as always, deserves accolades for the care and feeding of a Kit. I'd survive on macaroni and cheese without him.

Chapter 1

A shadow separated itself from the darkness, black against the shaded grays and browns of a mountaintop night. Human in size, male in form, moving quickly and all but silently over stone and rubble. A dip in the craggy rock highlighted his profile against rich midnight-blue sky, the faint colors of stars glittering as if caught in his hair.

Alisha went absolutely still, muscles in her arms trembling with the strain of holding herself from a ledge, fingertips dug into the stone. As long as she remained motionless she would be no more than he had been, one undiscovered shadow amongst thousands. She could see the path he took from the corner of her eye, could watch him cross farther into her line of vision. In a moment he passed out of it, blocked from sight by her own aching biceps. Alisha curled her upper lip and cautiously lowered herself until her feet touched the earth, her weight barely disturbing the loose stone. She remained where she was for a few seconds, forehead pressed against her still-uplifted arm while she tried to find a curse that was worth mouthing in the silence of the Pyrenees night.

There was a promise of winter in the air, coming earlier to the mountains than to the Spanish lowlands beneath them. That promise made each breath crisper than it might have in warmer climes, chill settling into her lungs and spreading through her body until her fingers tingled with the rush of extra oxygen.

It would be easy to forget who she was in the silence of the mountain night. Easy to become nothing more than what she appeared, a young woman hiking and climbing alone. Sunset was hours past, the night sky blue with darkness. That she chose to climb alone at such an hour said things about her. An adventurer, or a woman so intent on earning solitude that safety was a secondary concern.

It would be easy to forget, at least, if there was not another climber on the mountain, moving as quietly and quickly as Alisha herself was. He had no more business there than she did, which meant it was extremely likely that his business was the same as her own.

Somewhere not far ahead of her lay the black box from a downed American military spycraft, injured by a hand-carried earth-to-sky missile and wrecked in the Spanish mountains. The CIA was not supposed to be spying on its allies, and outside discovery of the craft's remains would cause a furor at best. At worst it would reopen the breach made between so-called Old Europe and the United States. All she had to do was retrieve the black box. Any other remains were expected to be sufficiently cremated by the crash as to be unidentifiable.

It was supposed to be a routine mission, Alisha thought wryly. No complications. Get in, get the goods, get out.

What was supposed to be almost never was.

Alisha pushed away from the rock face, turning her attention to the shale and granite beneath her feet. This high up, there was comparatively little loose stone, which was good: it would allow her to approach her competitor with almost no warning.

She ran on her toes, gaze flickering from the ground in front of her to the shadows ahead of her, watching for the man's movements in the darkness. A pack hugged her back, what gear she required huddled there, muffled so metal couldn't clang and echo against the mountainsides, announcing her presence to whoever might be listening.

And someone was. Alisha hesitated at a sharp bend in the stone, calming her breathing before she cautiously glanced around the edge of rock. A runoff channel, left by millennia of melting snow water, bent around a switchback. It was the easiest course to take: her goal lay just beyond the switchback, only a little higher up on the mountainside. Had she been there first, it was the track she'd have taken. She could see the shape of her rival's body farther up that trail, and slipped behind the outcropping again, examining her other options.

The cliff that the switchback snaked around wasn't quite sheer. Alisha studied it from her vantage point in the shadows, then curled her lip again and slipped her backpack off. When she'd had all night and no competition, climbing with only the faint light of the crescent moon and her own judgment had been a challenge. With someone already ahead of her, it was wiser, if less thrilling, to rely on the technology she had at hand. Night goggles fit snugly over her face, little more than sunglasses in weight.

The world went vividly green. Alisha took a few seconds, waiting until she was confident of the oddly colored brights and darknesses. She didn't dare risk the metal crampons that were in her pack; the mountain wind shrieked noisily enough most of the time, but when it fell silent it was as if the world had paused to listen to every action she took. One clank of metal against rock would warn her predecessor of her arrival.

Alisha wriggled her toes in the boots she already wore. Formfitting, they were poorly padded, not intended for running in, but the rubber pebbles that covered the bottoms were made up of microfilaments that stuck, lizardlike, to surfaces. It was first-generation technology, nowhere near strong enough to hold a woman's full weight. The boots themselves would stick to the ceiling, and a rashly hopeful Alisha had found out the hard way that they wouldn't do the same when she was in them. Even so, they provided a surety that had given her enough confidence to free-climb this far.

Her gloves were covered with the same pebbled microfilament. Alisha shrugged her backpack on again, fastening it around her waist with a knot instead of the plastic clip meant to hold it. Another question of quietness over practicality, just as her choice to go radio silent hours earlier had been. Climbing steep mountainsides was not a place to be interrupted by unexpected voices in her ear. Alisha grinned a little and stretched tall to work her fingers over a ledge hardly deeper than her first knuckle.

It was enough to give her purchase; enough to allow her the slow burn of muscle in her biceps as she drew herself higher with upper-body strength alone. She liked to think of it as her gift, her secret weapon, a physical capability beyond most women. There were few enough opportunities to show it off: the point of a secret weapon was to only use it only when necessary. Crushing a contact's hand in a show of strength told him far more about her than it could tell her about him. But the mountainside would remain silent about her lapse into the sheer pleasure of physical exertion. Alisha jammed her toes into a crevasse in the rock, feeling the solid microfilament grip reduce some of the strain on her arms. Muscle trembled all the way to her spine, her core tightening to support her extremities as she pulled herself higher on the mountainside. Free-climbing, the riskiest way to climb.

Risky, but silent, no more sound to it than her deliberately controlled breathing and the occasional chip of rock falling away as her fingers or feet brushed rubble from a ledge. There were no pieces of metal that might catch an unexpected light and betray her presence to a watcher, no partner to converse with and warn about bad pieces of rock. There was only herself and the mountain, one determined and the other uncaring. Each incremental upward movement took all of her physical attention, eyes and hands focused wholly on the task at hand, feet always testing and supporting her weight.

It left her mind surprisingly clear for thought. She saw it as a kind of Zen, her body wholly occupied and her thoughts separated from that. It was an ideal she sought through the practice of yoga—the art that was at least partly responsible for her strength—and one which she found far more often in the midst of her job than any other time.

She hadn't waited to see if her handler had approved her going radio silent. Alisha found another faint smile in herself, rather than the stab of guilt she suspected her handler would have preferred. Agents were intended to be self-reliant, but Alisha thought Gregory Parker would rather she was slightly more concerned with his directions.

She had been, once upon a time. Not that long ago, she reminded herself; not more than fifteen months ago. A mission had gone badly, leaving Alisha uncertain of where anyone's loyalties lay, even her own.

Badly, she thought with a snort that bounced off the rock face, almost inaudible beneath the sound of the wind. More like disastrously, its final confrontation leaving more than one man dead and allowing a—

Alisha made another sound beneath her breath, more of a growl than she wanted to admit to. There were no words for Frank Reichart. *Scoundrel* was the kindest one she could think of, but it suggested a playful, lovable quality. There was truth to it: sometimes it seemed like only hours earlier that she'd been in love with him, found his roguish tendencies to be exciting and charming. But it had been over six years since they'd broken up—if Reichart shooting her qualified as something as mundane as "breaking up"—and now the term didn't seem strong enough. The others she came up with lapsed into profanity.

Alisha cast her glance up the rock face, watching stars edging against stone, and let out her breath with calm deliberation. At their last meeting Reichart had made off with a piece of valuable robotics software and then gone to ground so thoroughly that in fifteen months no one, not the CIA, not MI6 and not the Russian FSB, had verifiably reported his whereabouts.

Which might have been just as well, Alisha thought, not for the first time. As a CIA agent she was supposed to be emotionally distant from her missions and the contacts she made during them. Alisha only felt that distance in what she considered to be her worst moments: she wanted to feel. Anything else seemed to be a half life to her, dangerous as emotional involvement might be.

But to admit to that would be openly compromising her position as an agent. She'd found a way to deal with it, albeit a way that was far from Agency-sanctioned. The notebooks that tallied her own missions were locked in safety-deposit boxes around the world, emotional missives that gave truth to the woman behind the dry mission reports that the CIA expected. The idea that her personal journals of the espionage world as she encountered it might someday be discovered by someone else gave Alisha a peculiar satisfaction, for all that it was unlikely. The safety-deposit boxes were opened under her aliases, and she never returned for the journals once they were put away, but it felt like leaving her mark: a way in which she could let the world know she'd existed, and what she'd done with her time.

One of the more recent ones lay safely in Milan, and would tell any reader how much emotion had been revived when Frank Reichart had come back into her life.

Gravel slipped under her fingers, sending her jolting down several inches before her feet caught the last ledge she'd stood on. Alisha's heart rate soared, sending tremors through her hands and making her stomach sour with bile as she listened to the sound of rock bouncing against the cliff face she climbed, finally bumping and rolling to a clattering stop somewhere below her. She leaned into the cool rock face, trying to breathe steadily instead of taking gulps of air past the knot of panic in her throat. There would be no new "Strongbox Chronicle" if she wasn't careful. There would be no completed mission at all, especially with her radio already off and no way for her handler to trace her beyond the last location he'd had. And clumsiness like that would warn her rival that someone else was on the mountain.

Alisha turned her head just far enough to look over her shoulder at the drop below her. No more than dozens of feet, but the distance was swallowed by darkness, even with the night goggles on. A fall might finish her before morning came.

Look up, she whispered to herself silently. Focusing on the fall was a sure way to work herself into making it. Alisha turned her gaze upward again, examining the crevasses and juts of the stone. The cliff tilted inward a few degrees only several feet higher, the slope visible more thanks to the changing line of visible stars than to a real ability to see in the dark. *Nearly to the top,* she promised herself. *And then she'd see what there was to be seen.*

There wouldn't be much, from the briefing she'd been given. Alisha dug her toes into the rock face again and pushed herself up, searching for purchase for her hands. The surveillance aircraft had crashed into the mountainside through careless handling, but the box was thought to have survived, and was considered to carry critical enough information to retrieve it.

Besides, Alisha thought, humping over the tilt in the cliff face, it would be embarrassing if some Spanish intelligence agent or tourist happened on it instead of the CIA. The flyer was believed to have been destroyed in the impact, but the United States wasn't supposed to be spying on its ally, so the nearly indestructible black box still required retrieval.

Alisha pulled herself up the last few centimeters, using the edge of the ridge as her cover as she studied the ground below. The brilliant greens lent to the scene by the night goggles made it look like an alien landscape, glowing softly with scattered pieces of wreckage.

Scattered pieces, but not enough. Caution crept down

Alisha's spine and over her skin in a series of prickles that settled in her stomach, curdling into a warning nausea there. Too much was wrong with the scene below her. Skid marks blackened a stretch of mountain stone, the ancient tumble of erosion undone by a man-made object leaving its mark. A fire had scored the mountainside where that object had stopped, but the aircraft's crescent was lodged in the wall, only partially damaged.

Nor was it the blunt-winged aerial surveillance design she'd expected. The machine, even half wrecked, was sleek and brilliantly white in the peculiar light afforded by the night goggles. The curve of its wing was as much artistic as functional, bringing the idea of a death glider to Alisha's mind. The technology behind it was clearly not from any CIA- or U.S. military–sanctioned specs or programs.

But she recognized it with a painful jolt, a familiarity that made her heart feel as though it'd been yanked lower into her chest. The damaged blasters that dangled from the aircraft's wings brought visceral memory to mind, blood-pounding fear and excitement of facing those same lasers on a ground-based combat machine called an Attengee. That drone had been the handiwork of Brandon Parker, her handler's son. The Attengee drones had a frightening life-likeness to them, not in their spherical metallic bodies or the long ratcheting legs that propelled them, but in the artificial intelligence that drove them. The AI had been built for the purpose of warfare, and was remorseless in its dedication.

The smashed glider in the mountain gully below was younger brother to the Attengee drones, the next generation of intelligent combat machines.

Alisha's fingers cramped against the cold stone, making her aware she was holding on to the earth as if she might fly away from it. Brandon Parker had been taken into custody over a year ago, pending an investigation of his loyalties. Greg had never mentioned Brandon's release from custody, or that he might be working again. Had never mentioned the outcome of the investigation, even though his own allegiance had been in question. His resumption of his duties as her handler indicated that he'd been cleared, even if Brandon, whose purported mission was much deeper than Greg's, hadn't yet been. Bureaucracies moved slowly, so Alisha hadn't pressed the point.

Bureaucracies moved slowly, she thought now. Military tribunals—which was much more like what Brandon would have faced—often moved very quickly indeed. It was possible it had been concluded months ago.

More than possible. The shattered drone in the gorge told her it was almost a certainty. The only other possibility was that someone else entirely had developed the new robot. That someone might be the man whose trail had forged ahead of hers, and her mission cover might be nothing more than that: a cover, because she didn't need to know. Alisha flattened her mouth in annoyance, then let it go with a shrug. It was one of the prices paid for working in espionage. She didn't always know the truth behind what she did, and had to put her faith in the hierarchy she belonged to, trusting that her actions were for the greater good.

And for the moment, she had a mission. She drew herself over the ravine's edge, muscles relaxing in a moment's relief for the change of position. Even slithering her full length down the canyon's side left her several feet above its floor. Alisha cast a glance over her shoulder, judging the texture of the rocky earth. A boulder was lodged near the mouth of the gully, a few smaller stones scattered around it, but no shale; perhaps winter runoff had taken all the broken rock away long ago. Alisha gave a brief nod and pushed back from the wall, making a jump to reach the ground. She grunted out a soft breath as she landed, absorbing the impact with her knees, and took another instant to study the gulch.

She was alone. The switchback trail must have been longer than she'd guessed it to be: the man hadn't yet reappeared. Alisha pressed her lips together, deciding on a course of patience. Whatever her rival wanted, she didn't like the option of leaving her back to him as she scavenged the aircraft's remains. She could keep the element of surprise by hanging back now, and disable him once he'd gotten what he wanted from the glider. If it was delicate, all the better: he'd react like someone with something to protect, making it easier for her to achieve victory.

Footsteps, almost noiseless against the rock, sounded behind her. Alisha faded farther into the shadows, hidden behind the boulder. Peering out afforded her a view of most of the canyon. It was only moments before the man appeared, dark haired and broad shouldered in the green vision of Alisha's night goggles. He hesitated just beyond the boulder, studying the ravine as Alisha had done. She drew in her next breath slowly, deliberately, as if doing so might turn her invisible to his gaze and ears.

Instead he turned toward her more fully, still examining the canyon, as if she'd betrayed herself with that breath.

And she did, as his profile came into focus, pale against the dark green sky and mountains. Good sense and training were thrown away in a wash of anger and disbelief. Alisha stood, yanking the night goggles off and throwing them to the side in pure outrage.

"Reichart."

Chapter 2

Reichart startled gratifyingly, jerking toward her even as he first reached for a weapon, then aborted the action in almost the same movement. "*Alisha?* Jesus Christ, what are—" The question, too, was cut off, as he flicked a look over his shoulder at the ruined aircraft. For an instant the fight seemed to go out of him, his shoulders loosening as he dropped his chin to his chest. More quietly, though still loud enough to echo against the gully walls, he repeated, "Jesus Christ."

Alisha stalked toward him, deliberately stopping far enough away that she couldn't reach him, not trusting her already balled fists not to take on a life of their own and punch him in the nose. Feelings that should have been buried—feelings that should have been *gone*—bubbled to the surface, frustration and anger and exasperation so powerful she couldn't form words.

Way to compartmentalize, she congratulated herself.

Very professional. Her feet took her one more step forward and she threw the punch that her muscles were aching for, a wholly telegraphed act of violence that Reichart, almost to Alisha's relief, blocked easily.

The solid connection of bone and flesh broke the dam clogging her ability to speak, letting her burst out with, "You son of a *bitch!*" She fell back a step, exhaling hard, and turned her shoulder to Reichart, breathing through clenched teeth. New frustration knotted her stomach as she recognized what her own body language said: that she did not believe Reichart would strike her from behind. That, in essence, she still trusted the bastard.

"It's nice to see you, too," he said mildly. Out of the corner of her eye, she could see him rubbing his wrist where he'd knocked her punch aside. It gave her a bloom of satisfaction that took some of the edge out of knowing how her body language betrayed her. "How've you been?" he asked, still mildly. As if there weren't oceans of bad blood between them, Alisha thought, and tilted her face up to the stars glittering beyond the canyon walls.

"Fine, thanks. You?" There was an acid edge to her response that she didn't bother washing away. It helped to prevent her from turning and trying to deck the man again.

"Busy," Reichart admitted. "Saving the world, all that. You know how it is."

"I never had the impression saving the world was on your list of things to do," Alisha said through her teeth. "I thought you were more of the *he who dies with the most cash wins* philosophy." She could still see him from the corner of her eye, short waves of his dark hair knocked askew by a mountain wind that the gulch protected them from. His expression was as neutral as his voice, no hint of concern or curiosity in his eyes. Keeping the mask on,

Alisha thought. As she ought to have done, though even as she thought it she dismissed it with an almost imperceptible shrug. For better or worse, Reichart pushed her to do things she shouldn't.

Pushed, or provided the excuse. Alisha looked over her shoulder at him, then beyond him at the downed glider. "That thing yours?"

Surprise darted through his eyes, a slight widening as he, too, looked back at the aircraft. "It's yours. Didn't they tell you?"

"Yeah, but who can trust the Agency?" Alisha exhaled and looked up at the stars again. "I saw somebody—you—on the other side of the switchback. Made me wonder what they'd really sent me after, that's all. Then when I saw the flyer I knew I could be dealing with something built from the plans you stole from me."

Irritation filled Reichart's voice. "They were corrupt. Useless. You saw me?"

"Oh," Alisha said, filling her voice with brightness. "Didn't I mention that part? Jesus, Reichart, did you really think I'd offer functional AI software up to the black market?" She glanced at him, watching his expression sour, and breathed out a smile. "You did. How flattering. You didn't rub off on me that much, Reichart."

"Evidently not." The sourness was in his voice, too, the emotionless mask he'd had in place allowed to slip. And it was allowed, Alisha had no doubt. She preferred to permit herself the dangers of sentimentalism, but she could certainly keep it off her face and out of her voice when she chose to. Reichart's control wouldn't be undone by a chance meeting in the mountains, no matter how complimentary the idea of being able to affect him that much might be to Alisha. "How'd you get past me?"

"I came up over the ridge." Alisha lifted her eyebrows. "If I'd known it was you I would've dropped a rock on your head."

"You would have, too, wouldn't you?" Sourness was replaced by wry admiration. Alisha exhaled another smile.

"Probably. Shooting you would be too loud up here. What are you here for? The glider?"

"The box."

There was no point to schooling her features; doing so would be as much betrayal as the resignation that slid across Alisha's face. Reichart saw it and pursed his lips. "Does this mean we have to start fighting?"

"You could be a gentleman and let me have it."

"No," Reichart said. "Not really."

"How much are they paying you, Frank?" Alisha shook her head and finally turned back to him, to walk past him toward the ruined aircraft. "Better yet, who's paying you? The FSB says you weren't on their payroll for the Attengee auction." She crouched by the glider, putting one hand on its cool silver surface. "Grab my night goggles, will you?"

"Yeah." Reichart did, as Alisha examined the glider. It was partially lodged in a crevasse in the gulch wall, metal edges smashed and sharp against the stone. Alisha slid her backpack off, rooting through it. She hesitated at the butt of her gun, fingers caressing the roughened texture of the grip, then sighed and left it alone as she continued searching for a pair of heavy gloves. They reminded her of a chef's cutting glove, puncturable but difficult to cut on a sharp edge. She slid them on, flexing her fingers inside the gritty material, then took her goggles from Reichart and pulled them back on again, as well. "You need a hand?" he asked. Alisha shook her head.

"I've got it." She heard Reichart step backward, taking

her at her word, as she worked her fingers into a gap between shredded metal and blackened stone. She put one foot against the gulch wall for extra heave, then drew a long breath of the crisp air through her nostrils, feeling oxygen flood her bloodstream. Her fingers tingled with it, making her feel lighter and less connected with her own body.

Breathing is the center of yoga. The words ran through her mind like a mantra, allowing her to focus more fully on her breath and the oxygen she felt preparing her muscles for a moment's overexertion. *Breathing is the center of yoga, and yoga is the center of my strength.*

Metal edges made pressure dents against her fingers even through the protective gloves. Alisha could envision the red depressions in her skin as muscle in her arms fired, popping and burning with glorious physical intensity. Oxygen-rich muscles along her spine worked together, bunching and straining. Alisha was overly aware of her posture, of keeping her stomach solid and her shoulders open, encouraging the easy breathing that allowed her to haul back on the glider with unexpected vigor. Rock and steel alike shrieked protest as she used the canyon against itself, feeling the solidness of her foot braced on its wall as if she was drawing strength from the core of the very earth.

The aircraft came loose with a shudder and a crash that echoed through the mountains. Alisha leaped back, the craft's weight barely missing her toes as it smashed to the stone floor, rocking a few seconds before it settled there. Alisha allowed herself a little puff of breath and a grin at the glider before she looked up.

Reichart's gaze was unexpectedly soft, the gentleness in it made vividly obvious by the night-vision clarity the goggles lent her. His smile quirked a little further at some minute change in her expression and he shrugged one shoulder. "I love watching you work. It's been a long time."

Alisha felt her stomach muscles tighten again, this time keeping her from stepping toward the man. After nearly seven years and more wrong turns than she could count, the impulse to take up the challenge that Frank Reichart presented was still there. "Yeah, well, don't tell anybody I was showing off."

She crouched by the glider again, glad of the opportunity to act instead of further regarding Reichart. She *had* been showing off, taking advantage of a rare moment to use the strength she usually kept hidden in front of someone who already knew about it. Now she could feel the muscles in her legs trembling, their moment of exertion over.

The exposed innards of the glider were far more densely packed than Alisha had expected. Wiring, no more than differing shades of green through the night-vision goggles, lay tightly bound against solid black—metal; Alisha prodded a stretch with her finger, feeling none of the give she'd expect from plastic. Of course it was metal. Plastic would have melted in the fire that'd scored the ravine wall. She shed her heavy gloves, reaching for her backpack again. Climbing equipment was the least of what she carried, and she hesitated over the gun again as she dug through the dark material, looking for a tiny soldering iron.

"You're just going to cut it out for me, then?" Reichart asked. Alisha pushed her goggles onto her forehead, shooting him a brief glare before igniting the soldering iron.

"Hadn't really been my plan, no. On the other hand, I see you're perfectly willing to let me do all the work."

"I'm a feminist," Reichart said with sufficient aplomb to earn a quiet chuckle from Alisha.

"Just remember this femme kicked your ass last time she

saw you, and she'd be happy to do it again." There was remarkably little sound to the burning of metal, Alisha's hands steady as she cut an arc down the glider's width, then a second across its breadth, muttering, "Always be prepared."

"I know you weren't a Boy Scout, Leesh."

Alisha cut the heat from the iron, consciously choosing to pull back instead of press forward. Deliberate actions, too deliberate; Reichart would see it, but there was nothing to be done for it.

Leesh. It was the nickname she had for herself, a nickname that only Reichart had ever landed on. Most people shortened her name to *Ali,* until Alisha herself was able to define different parts of her personality as belonging to one name or the other. Ali was the softer, pretty side of her; the girl who could work her wiles and get men to do what she wanted. Leesh was the strong, competent woman who risked her life for the Agency. That was the person Alisha more thought of herself as being. Ali was the sugar coating over Leesh, and nobody but Reichart had ever seen it clearly.

"You don't like it when I call you that, do you." Reichart was watching her too closely, picking up on things she didn't want him to. Alisha glanced up at him, then back down at the cooling steel on the aircraft.

"You're the only one who does. Find something to pry with. I'm not much of a Boy Scout after all." Her handler had considered the soldering iron and the work gloves overkill. According to the mission, there should only have been wreckage at the site, not a damaged but significantly intact glider.

Reichart slid his own backpack off, zipper loud in the quiet night as he opened it. "Never understood that. I think *Leesh* comes a lot more naturally from *Alisha* than *Ali* does." He handed her a crowbar that ratcheted out to full length, clicking into place so it wouldn't collapse again. Alisha pulled her face in a look-at-that moue, and stood to haul one of the quarters she'd cut into the glider's surface back. It creaked loudly enough to send goose bumps over her arms, even beneath the long sleeves of the close-fitting microfiber shirt she wore. Reichart rubbed his hand against the back of his neck, making Alisha smile a little.

"Ali's a softer name," she said, as close as she ever intended to get to confessing the deeper connotations she saw associated with the nickname most people chose to call her by. "Guess people like that better." She pulled another quarter back, feeling the shiver of metal in her biceps. Reichart grunted and edged forward. Alisha raised the crowbar, vaguely threatening, and glanced down.

The black box—undamaged, unsurprisingly, given the condition of the rest of the glider—lay settled into the rest of the wiring and metal, directly between the aircraft's two major thrusters. Alisha sighed and straightened. "All right, now what? We thumb-wrestle over it?"

"I know how strong your hands are." Reichart gave her a faint smile that faded when Alisha didn't return it. "No, we don't thumb-wrestle. You're just going to give it to me."

Alisha changed her weight just slightly, settling into her center, more than prepared to fight over the topic. "Or what, Reichart? You'll shoot me again?"

"No." Reichart's gaze flickered up to the edge of the canyon wall. "But *she* will."

Chapter 3

Emotion tied a knot in Alisha's belly, dread and dismay, but mostly self-disgust. She looked toward her backpack, where the gun still lay safely tucked, and behind her, a woman clucked her tongue. "Don't be silly, sweetheart."

The cocking of the woman's weapon sounded like nails being driven into a coffin. Alisha closed her eyes out of irritation rather than fear, then carefully lifted her hands away from her body, fingers spread. Only then did she dare to turn and look up at the gulch's lip.

A lovely Asian woman stood highlighted by the crescent moonlight, her full mouth curved in an anticipatory grin. "I've reconsidered," she said. "Be silly."

"Shooting me won't undo me giving you the slip in Zurich," Alisha said, keeping her voice steady.

"No, but it'll make me feel better."

"Helen," Reichart said, tired note of warning in his voice. Alisha looked over her shoulder at him.

"Helen?" She looked back up at the woman, a little startled. "Sorry. I was expecting something like Young Lee Ha."

"This from the Hispanic girl with the Irish last name?" Helen demanded. "Get over yourself, sister."

"If I get the chance," Alisha muttered, glancing back at Reichart. "You know, I always wanted to have the cavalry show up on the cliff top at the critical moment. It never occurred to me that I might not be the army when it did. She your girlfriend?"

Reichart gave her such a flat look Alisha grinned as she walked to the canyon wall and spread her hands against the cold rock. "Fine. Just leave my backpack so I can get out of here without killing myself."

"Take it," Helen said without missing a beat. Alisha tilted her head to stare up the rock wall at her.

"What exactly did I do to you?" She suspected the answer was *dated Frank Reichart,* but Helen only glowered down the gully wall and didn't answer.

"We'll leave it," Reichart said drily. "First because there's no reason for anyone to get killed here, and second because there's probably a tracking device in the pack. Nice try, Alisha."

Alisha shrugged. "It was worth a shot." She could see him out of the corner of her eye again, cutting the wires that held the glider's black box in place. "At the risk of sounding like a bad movie, Reichart, you know this isn't over."

Reichart straightened, box in hand, and gave her a rakish grin. "I wouldn't have it any other way. Hel, cover her until I'm out of the switchback."

"Then can I shoot her?"

"Helen."

"All right, all right, fine."

"You know where to meet me," Reichart said. Helen's affirming huff of breath sounded beneath the slap of his footsteps against the stone. Alisha put her forehead against the wall and counted to ten, then looked up.

"He's fast," she said brightly. "Probably out of the switchback by now. You should head on out."

"Shut up."

Alisha lifted her eyebrows and leaned her forehead against the rock again, grinning again despite everything. Her heart rate was quick, but didn't have the sickening thud of fear to it. It was more the excitement of a chess game, jockeying for the best position on the board. She was in a terrible position at the moment, but things could change very quickly. For now it was about steadying her breathing, and most especially about focusing on what her senses could tell her in the silent dark night. She closed her eyes, fingertips spread against the stone as if it might whisper secrets to her. Nothing else, for the moment, mattered.

It felt like a camera lens zooming in on something, Alisha always thought, the way her hearing kicked into overdrive when a situation went bad. Zoomed in and slow motion, each sound overly precise and warning her of things to come as if she had a sixth sense. There was nothing so esoteric about it; it was combat training and perhaps a little of her yoga practice, combining together to tell her—

—that Helen had taken an almost-silent step back from the cliff edge. Then another, moving slowly to hide the sound of her movements. Alisha smiled against the stone, counting Helen's steps until they faded. She waited another five interminable seconds before she shoved back from the wall and snatched up her backpack.

The gun went into her waistband; she would need both hands to rappel down the cliff wall she'd scaled, but she wanted the weapon easily at hand. A grappling hook with a line already attached was all she needed to scramble up the shorter canyon wall. Everything else she left behind, trusting that she'd be able to come back for it later.

The hook clattered with unholy loudness as she tossed it over the stone ridge and dragged it back until it caught. Alisha wrapped her hands around the rope, wincing even though silence was no longer critical.

A gunshot, far louder than the grappling hook, rang through the mountains, stone shattering where the bullet hit. Alisha went absolutely still for a few seconds, then flashed a bright grin at the wall. Good. Let Helen think the noise was Alisha following her. It'd make her watch behind her, and Alisha intended to come out in front.

She pulled herself up to the top of the ridge in a few long steps, the rope making her ascent much easier. Show-off, she couldn't help thinking. It would have been faster and easier to scale the entire mountain using equipment in the first place, and that might have put her at the glider long before Reichart and his cohort arrived.

Hindsight was twenty-twenty. Alisha pulled herself over the top ridge, lying low and giving her arms a quick shake, though there was nothing of the strain in her muscles that she'd felt coming up the longer ridge. She tugged her night goggles on, searching the ridge for a place to lodge the grappling hook, then wound the rope around her arm in quick tight loops.

The cliff behind her fell farther down than she'd remembered. Alisha stared into darkness that extended beyond the goggles' ability to enhance her vision, then inhaled a quick breath that was as good as a shrug. The rope would be long enough or it wouldn't. She gave it one more good tug, making certain the grappling hook would stay in place, and dropped into the green-laced darkness.

Each jolt of her weight hitting against the mountain wall made the rope tighten painfully around her arm. Making use of a shunt would have been more practical, but also more time-consuming to set up. Instead, Alisha paused between backward jumps, braced against the mountainside as she jerkily unwrapped enough rope for the next leap down, a primitive form of rappelling. It was exhilarating in its own way, even the uncomfortable feeling of blood caught in bulges between the rope wrapped around her arm. It made her right hand itch, pain burning along the ulnar nerve as it was pinched, until she wanted to stop and crack her knuckles, like doing so would release all the unaccustomed pressure in her arm.

The rope ended before the cliff side did. Alisha glanced over her shoulder, surprised at the distance she'd traveled: climbing the wall had seemed shorter than the downward journey. At least the ground was in sight now, some twenty feet below. Too far to drop wholesale. She sought ledges and crevasses with fingers and toes, almost jumping from one brief edge to another. Her right arm, already abused from the rope, didn't want to support weight, and her fingers tingled numbly as she forced them to use. Breathe, she reminded herself. All the hurrying in the world would do no good if she lost strength and slipped and fell to the waiting rocks below.

The final jump to the flat surface sounded loud in her ears, though she knew the pebbled flats of her shoes absorbed most of the noise. She pushed out of the crouch she'd landed in, running on her toes before she'd quite recovered from the impact. If the sound of her landing had carried, she'd already lost the element of surprise. Alisha slipped behind the stone outcropping she'd sighted Reichart from, gun drawn and held in both hands as she waited.

And waited, chin tilted up, gaze half focused on the green stars as she listened for the telling sound of footsteps. She would have to explore the switchback later, to see how far out of the way it took her before coming back around to the canyon.

Either that, she thought, or she'd missed Helen entirely. The idea made her curl her lip with irritation, fingers tightening around the gun's butt.

There! Finally, the soft pad of shoes against stone. Alisha waited for them to pass, then stepped out of the outcropping's shadow, gun leveled. "Let's try this again."

"How the—?" Helen lifted hands knotted into angry fists even as she let go the outburst.

"I'm just that good," Alisha said. "Where are you supposed to meet Reichart?"

"You'll have to shoot me."

"Don't tempt me. Where are you meeting him?" Alisha edged forward, gun still held ready. "You can tell me now or you can come back to Langley with me and tell lots of different people while you're under the influence of a truth serum."

Helen barked a laugh. "You expect me to believe you're not going to drag me back there anyway?"

"No," Alisha said, "but that's not the point." She hesitated out of Helen's reach, unwilling to close the distance until she was certain of what she had to do. "Last chance, Helen."

"Go to hell."

Alisha shrugged and reversed the .45 in her hand, taking a swift step toward Helen with the weapon raised as a bludgeon.

A gun cocked, loud as Gabriel's horn, and with the sound came Reichart's voice. "Don't do it, Alisha."

The muscles in Alisha's arm yowled protest as she halted the downward swing with the pistol's grip, her shoulder wrenching with the effort. Reichart spoke again, his voice coming from above the stone outcropping Alisha had hidden behind. The words were tinged with regret and old weariness. "You shouldn't have told me how you got to the canyon first."

Helen's fist connected with her jaw like a pile driver.

Pain, bright and piercing, slid through Alisha's eyes and into the back of her brain, taking up residence there with what felt like an eye toward permanency. Alisha groaned, lifting a hand to her head, and found the night goggles still in place. She fumbled them off and the pain receded, purity of light no longer blazing its way into her skull. She flopped her hand to the side, goggles clattering against stone, and for a few long moments lay without moving, face crushed into a wrinkled frown.

Her jaw hurt, the taste of blood lingering thick and sweet at the back of her throat and pooled in the hollows of her cheeks. Beyond that there was the usual pleasant ache of well-exercised muscles and the considerable stiffness of a body left to lie on hard rock for several hours.

Alisha opened her eyes again, staring at the white ball of sunlight overhead. Too high for morning, especially on this side of the mountains. She walked her hand back over her chest, finding the neck of her close-fitting shirt unzipped a few inches. Beneath the opened fabric lay a bump, sensitive to touch. She winced and relaxed again, grunting under her breath as doing so made her more aware of the shape of rocks beneath her back.

If there was a silver lining, she thought, it was in that it had taken a drug to keep her unconscious for hours, rather than Helen's punch being that powerful. Alisha sat up with another groan, then rolled over onto her knees, stretching forward in an asana to pull some of the kinks out of her back. Forehead resting against the stone, she inhaled a careful breath, then let it out in a sigh. Second silver lining: Reichart and Helen had left her in the mountains, instead of taking her comatose body back to whoever was employing them.

Alisha set her teeth together and finally turned her radio back on, muttering, "Cardinal reporting in. Anybody there?"

"Christ, Cardinal." Greg's voice came through instantly, sounding exhausted. "Where the hell've you been? I didn't approve you going radio silent!"

"Had a little situation," Alisha said. "Lost the box. And the aircraft is largely intact," she continued, deliberately talking over Greg's sharp inhalation, hoping to cut off the questions she knew were coming. "I can babysit, but I can't pack it out of here."

Silence met her comment, before Greg inhaled again. She could all but see him nod, pushing away the questions he wanted to ask in favor of dealing in the moment. "Damn it. We expected the glider to be destroyed. We thought only the box would survive. All right. We'll send in somebody on what looks like a search and rescue. You'll have to get off the chopper in a leg cast, all bruised up, probably."

Alisha touched her throbbing jaw. "Won't be a problem."

"What happened, Cardinal?"

Alisha pressed out of her asana, holding herself in downward-facing dog for a few long moments before she walked her hands in to her feet, bent her knees and straightened to a tree pose, hoping it would give her the strength to answer. It seemed to. Her voice was composed, if tired, as she said, "Reichart happened. Again. Of course."

Another long silence echoed in her earpiece, before Greg's voice came through, flat and displeased. "We'll talk about this when you come home. A chopper's being sent to your position. Kremlin out."

Alisha winced and dropped her chin to her chest. Once upon a time the code names they shared, Cardinal and Kremlin, had been a joke, a way of signing off that always left her feeling part of a close-knit secret family. Now Greg's clipped sign-off made Alisha think of the heartless Cold War that the Clancy novel had been written during.

Alisha, weary, stiff and thoroughly chastised long before the official admonishment would come down, slunk up the switchback to await extraction.

Chapter 4

"I'm recommending you for psychological evaluation, Alisha." Director Richard Boyer's deep voice was gentle, but the words fell like an assault against Alisha's skin. A blush fought to burn her cheeks and she took a deliberate long breath through flared nostrils, dragging more oxygen into her bloodstream and slowing her heartbeat. She didn't dare move her hands from where they lay relaxed against the leather armchair in Boyer's office; in stillness she could retain the pose of tranquility, but her hands would betray tension if she allowed them to move.

"Sir, I really don't think that's necessary," she began, then stopped the words at Boyer's brief, tolerant smile.

"Obviously not, Alisha. That's why other people do the recommending. Alisha, you're a good agent, but this Reichart thing has gone too far. I know you were close once—"

"We were engaged, sir," Alisha said. If she was going

to be hung out to dry, she wanted the whys to be explicitly clear. Boyer's eyelashes flickered.

"Engaged," he said after a pause. "I was trying to be delicate."

"That isn't necessary, sir." Alisha tried to dredge the ice from her tone, leaving calm neutrality in its place. Based on the second tolerant smile Boyer graced her with, the attempt failed. Alisha put her tongue between her teeth to keep from grinding them.

Boyer sighed and sat back in his chair, spreading his hands in a gesture of openness. "Very well. You were engaged and he shot you, a situation which I now believe has never fully been resolved in your mind, Alisha."

"I saw a psychiatrist for three months after that incident, sir," Alisha said, working to keep her voice steady instead of allowing it to give in to angry desperation. "Time off was recommended and I took it. I was given a clean bill of mental health after the break."

"And the situation has changed since then," Boyer said patiently. "Alisha, I'm willing to allow you to continue working while you attend therapy sessions, but I have no problem with suspending you if it's the only way to get beyond this recalcitrance."

Alisha stared across the desk at him, then pressed her lips together as she glanced away. "Well." She looked back, eyebrows raised. "That puts it in perspective, doesn't it."

"I thought it might. Now, I realize that the nature of your job may well prevent you from daily therapy sessions, but I want you to understand that I fully expect you to attend regular meetings with Dr. Reyes whenever you're available to do so. Starting this afternoon."

"This—!"

"Or I put someone else on the Firebird mission," Boyer

said, overriding her without having to lift his voice. "And you've been specifically requested, so I'd rather not do that."

"Firebird? Requested? By who?"

The air pressure in the room changed as she fired off her questions, a cool breeze stirring the hairs at the back of her neck.

"By me." The voice was wry and familiar, but wholly out of place. Alisha stood, turning toward the door with a frown.

Brandon Parker, in rolled-up shirtsleeves and with his hands in the pockets of khaki pants, gave her a pleasantly apologetic shrug. "H'lo, Alisha. It's been a long time."

Men kept saying that to her. For a few long seconds, that was the only clear thought in Alisha's mind. Brandon was still talking, the words registering distantly; she would be able to look back at the moment and hear every word he said, as clearly as if she was paying full attention now.

The fifteen months since she'd last seen Brandon had treated him well. Maybe it was hard for them not to have: the last she'd seen of him was his unconscious and bleeding body being carried out of a safe house on a stretcher. There was no sign of that trauma now, his broad shoulders lifting and falling as he said something self-deprecating and looked at her in hopes of earning a laugh. Alisha managed a brief, meaningless smile that took some of the pleasure from Brandon's blue eyes, though he forged ahead with his speech.

He would never have Reichart's edge, the *here comes trouble* look that was so appealing—and unfortunately accurate—in the other man. Brandon was corn-fed Iowa, blond hair showing a tendency to fall in his eyes even when tidily cut, as it was now. He never looked less than comfortable in the clothes he wore, or more than a slightly rumpled professional. Sporty, Alisha thought, even in a white-collar dress shirt. Brandon had none of Reichart's polished bad-boy look or his slightly dramatic fashion sense.

Which was part of his attraction.

But if his surface reflected brightness, it did so to hide the darkness beneath.

"The glider's your work," Alisha said, too loudly and too abruptly, cutting off Brandon's cheerful stream of talk. His eyebrows shot up and he gave her a crooked grin, spreading his hands.

"The Firebird? Of course. Did you ever have any doubt?"

Alisha shook her head. "A little. Not really." Not really: there was one of the keys. She had an inherent impulse to believe in Brandon Parker, to believe in her own hunches when it came to him. That those hunches and beliefs had turned out very badly once already made her spine itch with discomfort. "I didn't know you were working again."

Brandon rocked back on his heels, putting his hands into his pockets again. "Apparently my genius is too great to be ignored, especially when Director Simone provided all the paperwork authorizing the Sicarii mission."

"Director Simone." Alisha found herself leaning forward on her toes, as if making up for the distance Brandon had rocked back. "The European theater director? She sanctioned your infiltration mission?"

"The paperwork's in order, Alisha," Boyer agreed, deep voice filled with a soothing rumble. "Brandon and Greg were both involved in a covert mission that only a handful of very high-level people knew about."

"And you weren't one of them." Alisha turned toward Boyer, her words somewhere between a statement and a question. She'd trusted Boyer out of desperation and an odd belief that a man whose voice was as deep as his was must be as solid as he sounded. Her trust in him had nearly gotten him killed, but even now she sought the reassurance that she hadn't been played by her director, too.

"When I say high-level I'm talking about senators and generals, Alisha. A mere CIA director doesn't rate." Boyer chuckled as he spoke, though his eyes remained cool.

"I wish you'd told me," Alisha said.

Boyer inclined his head, acknowledging her desire if not apologizing for having failed to fulfill it. "You didn't need to know."

Alisha nodded stiffly and looked back at Brandon. "You asked for me on this mission?" She barely waited for his nod before asking, "Why?"

Brandon's eyebrows lifted a little. "Because I trust you, Alisha. You know me and you know my work, and just as importantly, I know you and yours. I haven't been a field agent in a long time. I need someone I can rely on if I'm going after the box."

"You?" Alisha asked incredulously. "You're a scientist, not a—"

"Doctor?" Brandon put in, grinning. "Your geek is showing again, Alisha."

"So's yours." Alisha felt a smile curve her lips, though it faded quickly. "Brandon, I know you're physically fit, and I know you had field-op training when you first joined the Agency, but it's not something you decide to do on a lark. I'm not sure this is a good idea." She glanced at Boyer, hoping for support, and found his expression utterly neutral. There would be no help from that corner.

"Alisha, these AIs are my life's work. I don't want anything associated with them in Sicarii hands, and Reichart is—"

"Oh, for Christ's sake!" Alisha burst out. "Don't tell me he's working for the Sicarii, Parker. Not after what you did to me." She fought the urge to clap a hand against the back of her neck, where a lump of scar tissue was all that remained from an explosive that the Sicarii had planted to make her their proxy. An explosive they'd planted, Alisha reminded herself violently, after Brandon Parker had turned her over to them.

"Alisha, I had no choice," Brandon protested, desperation coloring his voice. "They'd realized I was working with you. If I hadn't brought you in they'd have tortured and killed me."

"That's a choice, Parker," Alisha snapped. "A lousy one, but a choice. There were better ones. You could've come in instead of keeping up with the game, so don't give me that bullshit about having no choice. You damned near murdered me."

"I can see this is going to go smoothly," Boyer said mildly. Alisha flinched guiltily, looking toward the man she'd forgotten about. Boyer gave her a brief smile. "If it wouldn't be too much trouble, perhaps you two could take solving your differences out of my office. Alisha, you have a two o'clock appointment with Dr. Reyes. I expect you to be there." He left unspoken the reminder that she would be suspended from duty if the appointment wasn't kept. Alisha put her shoulders back, all the more aware of the warning for it not having been said.

"Yes, sir." She marched past a tight-lipped Brandon and into the hall with the scientist on her heels.

"Alisha—"

Alisha turned on her heel, stopping so abruptly that Brandon came up short and was forced to take a step back, out of her personal space. "Don't," she said. "I'll work with you because Director Boyer seems to think it's a good idea. I'll keep you from getting your ass shot off.

But don't think I've forgotten Rome, Brandon, because I haven't."

Brandon smiled, quick and regretful. "You have a lot to forget about Rome, don't you."

"Go to hell, Parker. Just go to hell." Alisha turned and walked away.

"Alisha. Ali!"

Alisha pulled her lips back from her teeth in a snarl, head ducking before she forcibly lifted it and turned toward the voice. Gregory Parker, her handler and Brandon's father, was a small, dapper man, the curls in his graying hair kept barely under control by a short-clipped haircut. He grimaced at her expression and drew to a stop beside her. "I take it you've been to see Boyer."

"When you said we'd discuss it, Greg, I didn't realize you meant the we that included a psychoanalyst. Silly me." Alisha didn't try to hide the bitterness in her voice. Greg heaved a sigh and slid his hands into his pockets as he shrugged. Alisha's mouth flattened with recognition as she realized he shared that piece of body language with his son.

"Alisha, I had to discuss the matter with Director Boyer. No one, least of all you, can afford for your personal life to affect your job."

Alisha closed her eyes, front teeth set together as she inhaled, waiting until she trusted her voice enough to speak. "A variety of people were holding guns on me, Greg." She opened her eyes again, meeting her handler's gaze. "What exactly was I supposed to do? Getting shot wouldn't have achieved anything except six weeks in traction. It certainly wouldn't have brought the box back."

"Your report suggests there were at least a few minutes when you were alone with Reichart. You could have acted then."

Alisha groaned. "Except I thought I was alone with him. Reichart and I are pretty evenly matched. Mano a mano, I figured I could take him. From that perspective there was no harm in not acting immediately."

Not even she believed it. Greg's sideways glance told her he didn't, either. Alisha pinched her mouth, looking away. "Psychological reevaluation just seems a little harsh for one mistake."

"What about last June?"

"Greg, I kicked his ass!" Alisha protested. "I thought he was down for the count. I did not deliberately allow him to make off with the Attengee software."

Greg sighed. "I'd like to believe you, Alisha."

Bitterness filled her tone again. "But you won't until Dr. goddamned Reyes does. You can go to hell, too."

Good sense told Alisha that waiting calmly in one of the doctor's comfortable armchairs would make the best first impression. Impatience dictated that she pace the office, avoiding the chairs and stopping to read the certificates of accomplishment that decorated one wall. Dr. Margaret Reyes.

"I prefer Peggy."

Alisha turned from the wall of diplomas to look at the woman standing in the doorway. An inch or two taller than Alisha herself, Dr. Reyes wore her hair in dark cornrows, the ends highlighted to warm blond. Half-moon glasses were nestled in her hair, and she carried a long coat over one arm. She was at least a decade younger than Alisha had expected, and smiled as she came forward with an offered hand. "Peggy," she repeated. "Peggy Reyes. It's nice to meet you, Alisha."

"You, too," Alisha said automatically, then felt a flicker of irritation cross her face. Peggy Reyes saw it, too, and flashed a grin.

"Or it would be if you weren't being sent to be brain-drained against your will, right? Well, there's no getting around it, I'm afraid, so we might as well get started. Coffee?" She flung her coat across one of the chairs and looked over her shoulder curiously at Alisha.

Alisha wet her lips and found a crooked smile waiting. "I don't drink much coffee in this country. You're not really what I expected. My last psychoanalyst was..."

"Stodgy?" Reyes suggested with a grin. "Old? Solicitous? The truth is, Alisha, nobody likes being sent to a shrink. Volunteering to see one is one thing. Being sent is something else." She stuck her head out the office door to ask for two cups of coffee, adding, "Just in case," to Alisha as she came back in and closed the door. "So I make it a practice to try to do away with underlying resentment and sullenness by being as up-front about the whole process as I can be."

"What does that accomplish?"

Reyes dropped into one of her own armchairs, kicking her feet onto the coffee table. "Makes me seem more human, more likable. People are usually more willing to talk to people they like."

Alisha breathed out a laugh. "I think it's working," she admitted wryly. Reyes lifted her hands, palms out, giving them a revivalist shake.

"Glory be. So tell me about this ex of yours. Is he really all that and a bag of chips?"

The secretary came in with coffee. Alisha accepted her cup without sitting down, inhaling the scent as she looked for a way to answer without betraying her own secrets.

Chapter 5

"How'd it go?" Brandon jogged across the tarmac to catch up with Alisha's long strides, her attention focused on the plane ahead of her.

Not focused enough, she thought drily, or Brandon was determined to not be put off by a cold shoulder. She glanced over at him, watching him match his stride to hers, and shrugged. "Not so bad," she acknowledged. "I never thought I'd meet a psychoanalyst I liked, but she was nice."

"They're all nice," Brandon said. "It's their job. They're supposed to be. But Reyes is interesting."

Alisha did a double take at him. "You've met her?"

"You really think they'd let me back on the job without scouring the inside of my head first? Even with Simone's paperwork all in place, after three years working for the Sicarii they weren't taking any chances."

"I'm sure you won't take it wrong if I say that makes

me feel better." Mostly better, Alisha amended silently as Brandon fell back a step or two and gestured her up the plane stairs ahead of her. It might have made her feel much better, had she not been vividly aware of the things she hadn't told Peggy Reyes in their session that afternoon.

"I'd be surprised if it didn't," Brandon said from behind her. "I know you're angry, Alisha, but I'd really like to talk about that incident in Rome."

Alisha stopped in the plane door and turned to look down at Brandon. His expression was open and hopeful, no guile in it. "You know what? I'm not ready to do that yet."

Disappointment washed the blue out of his eyes, leaving them gray in the afternoon light. "All right," he said quietly. "Maybe you'll tell me when you are."

"Maybe." Alisha ducked through the plane door—unnecessary; there was plenty of headroom for a woman her height—and made her way into the passenger area. It was a military flight, the amenities lacking, but it was leaving immediately, which was all that mattered to Alisha.

"Who are we meeting?" Brandon asked as he sat down across from her. Alisha looked up sharply.

"I am meeting an asset in Paris. *You* are not meeting anyone."

A pained smile crossed Brandon's face. "What's wrong, Alisha? Don't you trust me?" He turned his gaze to the window, watching military personnel on the tarmac, clearly knowing her answer and not wanting to hear it spoken aloud.

And so she didn't say it aloud, studying his profile in silence instead. It was more than not trusting him; experience had taught her not to reveal any of her assets or the places she'd be meeting them. Alisha's hand drifted to rub beneath her left collarbone, the edges of a gunshot scar more noticeable in her memory than they were on her body. Frank Reichart had put that bullet into her six years ago in Rome, and she still wasn't certain if he'd also murdered her contact that day, a cardinal in the Roman Catholic Church. She'd told Reichart where to find her, and it was very possible the cardinal's blood was on her hands as figuratively as it had been literally.

Not again, Alisha promised herself. She wouldn't compromise another asset that way. CIA policy was based on need to know, and Brandon Parker didn't need to know.

And this is what those of us in the business would call a long shot, Alisha thought half a day later. She wrapped her hands around a coffee mug nearly as large as her head, watching the Seine whisper by just to her left, on the far side of a thick, waist-height wall. The water reflected the gray skies, but in her mind's eye it was black, bouncing street light back up toward the café she patronized.

The river's rush was a backdrop to French voices raised in laughter and greeting now as it had been then. Alisha braced her mug against three fingers of her left hand, brushing her thumb against the base of that ring finger. Frank Reichart had proposed kneeling next to this table, and fifteen months ago when he'd wanted to talk to her, this was where he'd said to meet him.

It was a very long shot. Alisha put her coffee mug down and pulled her cell phone from her purse, using it as the timepiece she'd opted not to wear. Evening would have been a better time to try this stunt, she thought, but she wasn't sure she was up to facing the café under circumstances that similar to the night Reichart had asked her to marry him.

Three-fourteen in the afternoon. Pi, Alisha thought with amusement, and put the phone facedown on the table, picking up the mug again. Dr. Reyes would get more mileage out of Alisha's being at the café than she wanted to think about.

Maybe they were right, Alisha thought. Maybe her judgment really was that bad when it came to Reichart.

She breathed out a laugh. If it was, it wasn't just about Reichart. The clandestine journals she kept, the mistrust she felt for Brandon Parker—if Reichart was a problem, it was only because he was the linchpin to the whole house of cards that was Alisha's life. She couldn't afford for the psychoanalyst to be right. It would take her life apart at the seams.

The phone rang, beeping out the *Mission: Impossible* theme. Alisha grinned at it as she always did, picking it up to put it to her ear with an automatic hello that was less a question than a statement.

"You're completely mad."

Alisha's heart rate leaped as relief and vindication swept over her, leaving goose bumps on her arms. She slid down in her chair with a quick laugh, pushing her coffee mug away. "Where are you?"

"Close enough to know where you are," Frank Reichart said acidly. "*Are* you completely mad?"

Alisha closed her eyes, still smiling. "You've spent too much time with Brits, you know that? 'Completely mad.' 'Lovely.' The first word you ever said to me was 'lovely.' If we'd been in America I'd have thought you were gay."

"You wouldn't have been the first. Is there a purpose to this little trip down memory lane?"

Alisha's smile faded and she straightened up in her chair again, watching the river. "I'm expecting an asset who can give me some kind of information on where the black box has gone."

"And you chose here as your meeting place?" Enough

strain came into Reichart's voice that Alisha couldn't stop herself from glancing around, as if she might catch a glimpse of the man. She wouldn't see him, she knew, but he was closer than she thought if he used *here* instead of *there* to define the café.

"I figured if he was paying any attention, this place would flush him out of the woodwork. And I was right. So who'd you sell it to?"

"You *are* completely mad," Reichart said. "Me? An asset?"

"It's got too many syllables to be the first word that comes to mind," Alisha said with a faint smile. "But it'll do."

"Why the hell would I tell you anything?"

"Because you don't want me to lose my job," Alisha suggested.

Startled silence followed, before Reichart let out a swift curse. "I'm sorry, Leesh." Then he hung up, leaving Alisha to study her phone with pursed lips. It had been a long shot, she reminded herself with a shrug.

"Alisha."

The man who spoke from a few feet behind her wasn't the one she'd hoped it would be. Alisha turned her head toward him, sighing. "You're not supposed to be here, Parker."

"I know. But we've got a problem."

"It'd better be a doozy."

"It is." Brandon sat down across from her, sliding an envelope toward her. Alisha arched her eyebrows.

"Is this okay to open in public?"

Brandon looked at the empty tables and chairs around them. "I think it'll do. You won't need much of a look anyway."

Alisha's hands stilled in the process of opening the envelope. "Is somebody dead?"

"No." There was no surprise in Brandon's voice at her question. "Not yet, anyway."

"Jesus," Alisha said mildly. "You've filled me with confidence." She tilted the envelope, sliding photographs out of it. She was too aware of Brandon's gaze on her as she rifled through them, no more than brief glances before she slid them back into the envelope and leaned back, eyes closed. "Ah." The quiet sound was all she could trust herself to make for a few moments. Then she pressed her lips together and opened her eyes to meet Brandon's as steadily as she could. "Whose are they?"

Brandon shook his head slightly. "The satellite was over Russia."

"The FSB? Not possible." Alisha gave a short, sharp jerk of her head. "He wasn't working for them."

"They say he wasn't," Brandon said. "He said he was. Somebody's lying."

"Besides." Alisha dumped the envelope's contents into her hand again, looking at the top picture. A satellite photograph, taken only twelve hours earlier, according to the time stamp. It showed a field scattered with silver-domed drones, the machines at rest in the first photograph. Chaos ensued in the later pictures, one army of combat drones fighting another. Splashes of color indicated the kills. Alisha rifled through the photos again, watching the fight play out like a flipbook: from one picture to the next, each side of the drone army regrouped, moved together and attacked. There was a single machine left in the final picture, the sole survivor of the mock battle. Total annihilation, Alisha thought.

"Besides," she repeated, bringing voice to thought again, "the software didn't have the drone schematics in it, and these look like yours. I don't think it was Reichart, Brandon. It had to have been someone else." *It could have been you.*

"At least three FSB officers saw the Attengee that you disabled—"

Alisha's eyebrows shot up. "Disabled?"

Brandon grinned faintly. "Destroyed. Credit where credit is due, eh?" Alisha huffed a satisfied breath and he went on. "The drone you destroyed. They may have built their Attengees according to description."

"The software was corrupted," Alisha said.

"Did you check it?"

"I wouldn't know how," Alisha admitted. "But Erika wouldn't have let me down." She smiled at the memory of the technical geek shooing her out of the hotel room so she could work in peace. "Even if I wasn't able to score her the German guy."

"What?"

Alisha refocused on Brandon, then chuckled. "Nothing." Erika and Brandon had dated once upon a time. He hardly needed to know the details of his ex-girlfriend's love life.

He gave her a curious frown, but let it go. "Even assuming you're correct and the software was corrupted, a decent programmer would be able to extrapolate and rebuild from what was there." He fell silent a moment, then amended, "A brilliant programmer."

"Credit where credit's due, eh?" Alisha gave him a faint smile that he returned wholeheartedly as he leaned forward.

"Alisha, listen. You could be right. They could've gotten the Attengee software and schematics from elsewhere. But will you accept that I could be right, too?" His smile turned into a small frown, a wrinkle appearing between his eyebrows. "I know this crap with Reyes and Reichart's got you antsy right now, and I don't blame you. Just…make sure you're not having knee-jerk reactions in the opposite direction because of it, okay? Is that fair to ask?"

Alisha looked down at the photographs, then put them face down on the table as she picked up her coffee mug again, inhaling the sweet scent. "Yeah," she finally said. "Yeah, it's fair." More than fair, she thought, and gritted her teeth before putting the mug down and meeting Brandon's gaze. "You're right." The words came hard-won, but she tried to make them gracious instead of simply angry. "Normally Reichart would be number one on my list of usual suspects. I'm just too pissed off to see straight right now. And…" She drew in a deep breath through her nose, tightening her hands around the mug. "I appreciate you believing in me."

Brandon's smile went wry. "I hope someday you'll return the sentiment."

She should have seen that coming, Alisha thought, and gave him a faint smile in return. "Help me save the world from the FSB Attengees and Frank Reichart, and I just might."

"Any idea how to start?"

Alisha lifted her chin, looking around at the low Paris buildings until high-rises took the horizon away. "Yeah," she said thoughtfully. "I think we use you as bait."

Chapter 6

Rain pooled in the small of Alisha's back, a constant cool pressure against fabric that had not, as yet, allowed the water to seep through. She squirmed forward a few inches, feeling the water shift and run down over the curve of her waist as she dislodged it, then begin to collect again. She hadn't known there was enough depth between hip and rib to make the tiny reservoir, and, she thought with an inaudible sigh, she could have gone her whole life without finding out.

She suspected she'd been inside the building she lay on top of, a building Brandon Parker had entered only a few minutes earlier. Suspected, but couldn't prove it: she'd been a captive at the time, never seeing more than a single dark room. Brandon hadn't told her anything about where he was going. She assumed he had the wit to know she'd follow him.

Alisha curved a brief smile, peeking down over the roof's edge toward the ground three stories below. If he didn't know she'd followed him, all the better. She'd fully meant it when she'd made the plan to use Brandon as bait. Dragging him to Rome and sending him back to the Sicarii safe house he knew best was the first step of that. But it could go both ways. Trailing him gave her the opportunity to discover if he was genuinely loyal to the Agency, or if he'd been waiting for a chance to betray them all again.

To betray me again, Alisha amended wordlessly. Her stake in the matter was personal, and she felt no apology or remorse for that. She slid a rope over the building's side, the black slithery snake of it invisible against the darkness and the rain. A few good tugs made sure it was secured on the rooftop, and she slipped over the edge, rope wound around one thigh and calf as she lowered herself a few inches at a time.

There'd been no guards to disable on the Roman town house grounds. No dogs, no surveillance cameras; nothing to alert neighbors to the building being anything other than strictly ordinary. She'd come across rooftops to this house, making quick use of her pitoned rope to gain access to the more difficult slate-covered roofs. By the time the rain-muffled noise of the piton hitting stone alerted anyone, she had gone on to the next house, lithe and quick in the wet night.

The first darkened window was to her left now. Alisha pushed off from the building wall, swinging a little so she could glance inside. Her own reflection came back to her: a close-fitting black hood, keeping her hair dry. Water tangled in her eyelashes and dripped off her nose; wetness on her cheeks gave a sheen of good health and attractiveness even in the darkness. Strong shoulders and a slender black-clad form, and through the mirror of herself, an undisturbed bedroom. Alisha stopped her bouncing swing and tested the window, mildly exasperated to find it locked.

Who needed to lock third-floor windows? It wasn't as though anybody habitually gained entrance at that level.

Nor, Alisha thought a moment later as she slid a thin piece of metal between the sill and the frame, would an ordinary window lock stop anyone who genuinely wanted to enter through a third-story window. The catch inside slid aside with a tiny flaking of paint, and Alisha levied the window open a few centimeters before returning her wedge to a narrow pocket on her suit's outer thigh.

She hesitated on the windowsill a few seconds, long enough to ascertain that there were no pressure sensors beneath rugs strewn across the stone floors, then slipped all the way inside. Water spilled off her shoulders, pattering down to the floor in splats that sounded much louder to her ears than they really were. Alisha unzipped the throat of her jacket to tug a chamois cloth out, running the soft absorbent material over her body, then over the floor, wiping up evidence of her arrival. She twisted the extra water out the window, then closed it behind her, sliding the chamois back into her jacket and pulling a face at its clammy coldness.

A light blazed at the end of the hallway outside the door, but there was no glow from beneath other doors; the third floor as a whole appeared to be as deserted as the room Alisha had entered through. She ran through the hall and down the stairs on her toes, keeping to the outer edges, where any dampness she left behind would be less likely to be found by stockinged feet.

Not until the ground floor were doors open and lights on, incandescent light spilling into the hallways from the kitchen, dining room and well-appointed living room. But there were no voices, no footsteps beyond Alisha's own, despite having watched Brandon enter not ten minutes earlier.

A sheen of water, almost dried, caught the corner of her eye. Alisha turned her head, watching it fade away as she looked at it directly. A quick smile curved her mouth and she glanced away again, watching it reappear like a star too dim to be seen outside of peripheral vision.

A second wet mark, a man's stride farther away, made a slightly darker spot on the narrow carpet that lined the hall. Alisha darted forward, matching her steps to the marks on the carpet and stone, and stopped outside the kitchen door, pressed against the wall as she listened. Still no voices. The facade of an ordinary household was a thin one, here. Alisha slipped inside the kitchen door, taking in the Tuscany-colored walls and counters with a glance, though her focus was on the drying footprints that led to a pantry door. If there were guards at all, they'd be beyond that door, she thought, and for the first time she hesitated.

It would have been vastly easier to bug Brandon, but utterly pointless. The Sicarii would never trust him, not openly, not immediately, and sending him into the situation carrying a wire of any sort would spell his death sentence out in low-level transmissions. Alisha might not trust him, but she didn't want his blood on her hands, either.

If there were guards, the Sicarii would be alerted to her presence, and Brandon would be compromised. Alisha mouthed a curse and crossed the kitchen, pressing her ear against the warm dark wood of the pantry door. For a few seconds her own heartbeat echoed back at her, but it faded into unimportance as she drew a slow, steadying breath and focused her hearing.

Nothing. Nothing she could hear, at least. Alisha eased the door open, wishing it opened inward instead of out, although out was a much more reasonable choice for a pantry. A grin flashed across her face and she shook her head minutely. The odds were better than even that a fight was waiting beyond the door, and she was making silent architectural commentary. *You're jaded, Leesh.*

The only thing waiting beyond the door was the heady scent of spices, garlic tangled with the sharper smells of tarragon and sage. Alisha took one deep appreciative breath, holding the door to let light into the pantry as she searched the floor.

Round spots of water, the remnants of drips, spattered the floor at the far end of the pantry. Alisha squinted, taking one step back to consider the depth of the spice closet, then clucked her tongue inaudibly. *Very nice,* she mouthed, unwilling to speak aloud. The false wall at the back of the pantry was very likely as old as the house itself, stone appearing naturally aged. Had she not been looking, she might never have noticed the slight shortness to the pantry's depth. Even knowing it was there, it was easy to doubt her own sense of spatial relations, figuring the width of the house in accord with the depth of the rooms she'd been in.

But one stone at knee height had a smooth spot worn into it, almost unnoticeable. Alisha crouched and pressed her black-clad fingers against it, lips pulled back from her teeth in a grimace that anticipated the noisy scrape of stone against stone.

Instead, an entire section of the wall slid backward several inches, stopping a finger's width deeper than its neighboring stone, and slid to the left without a single sound. Alisha found herself grinning in astonished delight at the workmanship involved in the hidden door: the door itself would never be scraped up by the wall it hid behind when opened, thus making it all the more likely to remain secret.

The real wall behind the false was carved with handholds, making a ladder that descended into darkness. There was perhaps as much as fifteen inches depth between the walls; even Alisha, whose frame was slender and strong from yoga practice, found herself holding her breath as she clambered down the ladder. No one carrying extra weight on his body would be comfortable entering the hidden passage, and anyone with a tendency toward fat simply wouldn't fit at all.

Thank God for modern clothes and fabrics, Alisha thought as she dropped to a stone floor. She couldn't imagine making her way down that ladder in the clothes of the house's era, five hundred years earlier.

Of course, as a woman, she'd have been extraordinarily unlikely to have the option to explore such passages, five hundred years earlier. Let's hear it for women's lib, she thought irreverently as she turned her back to the wall, pressing herself into shadows so she could examine the hall she'd come out into. Damp, cool air smelled faintly, but not unpleasantly, of moss and mold; the house almost certainly had a wine cellar, separated from this passageway by thick stone walls. Electric lamps, spaced wide apart and filled with dim bulbs, scattered handsful of light down the unguarded hall in front of her. It angled away, cutting deeper into the earth than Alisha had expected.

A faint click sounded above her. Alisha looked up to see the faint light from the pantry disappear as the door closed again. She crouched, back still to the wall, and examined the stones at knee height there, finding none with the telltale smoothness that suggested a lever or a button that would trigger the door. A cursory search of the rest of the wall found nothing, either, though Alisha was certain it had to be there.

Maybe not, she scolded herself. Maybe the entrance was so easily accessed because it couldn't be used as an exit. Maybe getting out was going to be the problem.

She scowled into the dim hall and began a loping run down its slow descent. If leaving was going to be problematic, she might as well learn everything she possibly could before tackling that issue. Brandon Parker was somewhere in the dark in front of her. She'd learn what she could from his behavior, and worry about escape later.

That attitude, Leesh, is going to get you killed someday.

At least it would be interesting. Though why getting killed only qualified as *interesting* was a thought better pursued another time. The passage took a sudden sharp turn, its downward slope becoming a staircase cut out of earth and stone, spiraling deeper into the ground. If this was indeed the same building she'd been held at fifteen months earlier, there had to be another passage out. Alisha couldn't imagine someone bothering to carry her unconscious body down the pantry ladder, or this tight-wound stairway. She took the steps quickly and silently, listening for voices or movement ahead of her.

"You've taken a long time to return with your hat in your hand." A woman's alto, speaking Russian, echoed so suddenly that Alisha went still, unable to pinpoint the speaker's location. She stayed where she was, hand against the round wall, her head tilted in concentration as she listened.

"I've been in custody," Brandon said in the same language the woman used. His Russian was marred by a slight American accent, unlike the woman's. "I came as soon as I could."

"But not soon enough." Venom slipped into the woman's voice. Venom, and something familiar. Alisha frowned, trying to place it, but the recognizable note was lost in the woman's liquid accusation: "The CIA must also have Attengees, now. Our advantage is lost."

"They do." Brandon sounded steady and calm, not like

a man bargaining for his life. "They also have the next generation of my combat drones, the Firebird aerial models. I'm coming back to you with those schematics and that software. Openhanded."

"And you expect us to believe you." A murmur of agreement washed up the stairwell, two or three more individuals, at least one of which was another woman. Alisha began her passage down the stairs again, hesitating between each step to listen and try to ascertain Brandon's position.

"I'd be surprised as hell if you believed me. On the other hand, I've been cavity searched and swept for electronics, so if I'm here on behalf of the Company or any other agency, I'm sure as hell not doing them any good. Assuming I walk out of here at all, I won't be walking out with anything like proof." Chagrin crept into Brandon's tone as he spoke. Alisha grinned at her feet as she made her way farther down the stairs. She hadn't been sure they'd subject Parker to the indignities of a complete body search. Just as well for her, she thought. It had put off Brandon's conversation with the Sicarii long enough for Alisha to trail him into the catacombs beneath the house.

The clarity of sound cut off as Alisha stepped out of the stairwell, still pressing herself to the shadows between electric lights. Her lip curled, as much of a curse as she could allow herself, and she darted a few steps higher again, until the voices were no longer muffled.

"—king with?"

"Agent MacAleer."

"Alisha MacAleer," the woman said. She sounded unexpectedly comfortable with the name, and a thrill of nervousness spliced through Alisha's stomach. Brandon hadn't stepped outside the boundaries of what needed to be said, but still, she could have done without the Sicarii being reminded of her existence. "Of course," the woman breathed. Hairs lifted on Alisha's arms, familiarity niggling at her again at the softness in the voice. "Perhaps if you deliver her to us I'll consider the rest of your proposal at face value."

"How long do I have?" Brandon's response was steady, uncompromising. Just as it had been when he'd turned her over to the Sicarii once before, fifteen months earlier. Alisha allowed herself the luxury of fisting her hands, then flexed the fingers wide in a deliberate release of tension.

"Three days," the woman said, so carelessly Alisha could imagine the shrug that went with the words. "If you haven't delivered, you'll be terminated. You should have stayed in hiding, Dr. Parker."

Brandon's voice dropped so low Alisha could barely hear him. "Even the power behind the throne has to come out into daylight sometimes."

"Don't flatter yourself." Dissonant harshness came into the woman's voice. "Positions of that much power are reserved for players who've been in the game far longer than you have, Parker. Be sure your reach does not too far exceed your grasp."

"Else what's a heaven for," Brandon said. "I didn't think you had any poetry in your soul, Phoenix."

Phoenix. The English word leaped out of the conversation, making a frown wrinkle into Alisha's forehead. A code name, not nearly as useful as it might have been. But then, it was better than nothing, and if she was careful she might be able to work the Phoenix's real name out of Brandon.

Enough, she decided, and took two quick steps back up the stairs, deciding on the wisdom of escape over further intelligence. She'd heard enough to be able to check anything Brandon said to her in his report against what had really been said. It was enough.

A flashlight played on the stairs above her, light bouncing down in a warning that came before the sound of soft-soled shoes on the stone steps. Focused dread sent a cold wave through Alisha's stomach, tightening the muscle there, and she jumped silently to the bottom of the stairs, abandoning any hope of listening to Brandon's conversation as she searched for a hiding place. The hall bent back, a cubby beside the round stairs, or went forward, descending farther into the ground. Alisha cursed again, silently, and took a few long steps into the cubby, pressing herself against the cool stone wall. Darkness might hide her, especially if the newcomers were intent on reaching their destination.

Please, God, let this not be another false wall behind me. That would be the price of arrogance, discovering that her hiding place was the very door that the men above her wanted to enter. Alisha banished the thought, then inhaled one last soft deep breath and went utterly still, letting the centering she'd learned in yoga relax her and make her as one with her surroundings as possible. Even her gaze was half lidded, disguising the whites of her eyes as she watched the men coming down the stairs.

There were four of them, the two in the lead so blond their hair almost glowed in the flashlight's bounced-back aura of light. The fourth was small and dark, the sort of man whose thin frame often hid wiry strength.

The third was the tallest of them, lean and black haired, the stairway's dim lighting making warm sheens on the soft leather of his coat. He swung around the final steps with an easy, long stride, glancing over his shoulder toward the cubby that Alisha hid in.

Nothing in his expression changed, not even a flicker of surprise to betray her presence as Frank Reichart met Alisha's eyes. A lump of dismay held in Alisha's stomach, before Reichart looked away again. For the briefest moment she thought perhaps he hadn't seen her.

And then he did a double take, so deliberately she could all but see the thought that commanded his head to turn. His eyes widened, just enough to suggest surprise, and the shock in his voice was unforced, as if there was no guile to it at all: "Alisha!"

Oh, yeah. Getting out was going to be a problem.

Chapter 7

You absolute son of a bitch.

Alisha didn't think she'd said the words out loud, but a thinness came into Reichart's smile. Not apology, and not surprise, but some regretful cousin to both of those things. The expression held long and clear in her mind, much longer than the instant in which it flickered across Reichart's face and was gone. He took a single step back, breaking the moment, and sound that had gone unnoticed, muffled by the intensity of meeting Reichart's gaze, shattered into Alisha's awareness.

A warning lingered on the air: "We've been compromised. Get Phoenix out of here." Spoken by the small wiry man, Alisha thought; he was the one coiled and ready to spring, watching her predatorily. The first of the two blondes was already gone, presumably acting on the smaller man's order. The other moved up to fill the space Reichart had vacated, an enormous pale shadow to the wiry man.

"All right," Alisha breathed. "Who wants to get his ass handed to him first?" The wall was at her back, an advantage she had no intention of giving up. Thought filtered down slowly, like dust in sunlight: the Sicarii had to be disabled and Reichart neutralized before Brandon was killed. It was no longer a question of compromise. Alisha had no doubt that if Phoenix believed that Brandon had double-crossed her, she would execute him without hesitation.

The wiry man lunged, a feint meant to see how she'd react. Alisha barely flinched, and he gave her a snarling smile that showed crooked teeth. Neither of the men had drawn weapons: a good sign. It probably meant they wanted her alive, whereas she had little compunction in terminating them.

Terminating. Another euphemism to help compartmentalize the duties of the job from the person doing them.

Then time stretched and slowed, leaving no room for individual thoughts, only action. She could hear her own heartbeat, slow and steady, and between the long breaks between beats, the harsh breathing of the men approaching her.

The blonde was to her left, large and clumsy-looking to Alisha's combat-heightened senses. She could see the muscles twitch in his arms, widening his grasp in precursor to action; could see the tension in his legs as he prepared to spring forward. He would grab her in a bear hug, crushing her arms to her sides and squeezing the air from her lungs. That, for the moment, was the real danger the two men presented: she had an equal reach on the smaller one, but couldn't possibly match the bigger man's advantage.

Alisha stepped into him, barely moving away from the wall, but gaining momentum and preparing the weight of her body to flow through the punch she threw. She was inside the blonde's space before he knew she was attacking, slow surprise darting across his face. Either he didn't expect aggressiveness from a woman, or he lacked training: the block he flung up was clumsy and slow, Alisha's hit already slamming home before he reacted. The heel of her hand drove hard into the xiphoid process, the tiny spur of bone at the bottom of the breastbone. It was a shot she liked, though it could easily be fatal. Not this time: she didn't hear the pop of bone breaking, or feel the give of it squishing back into his diaphragm.

He wheezed out a breath too harsh to have surprise in it, the air knocked from his gut. The threatening bear hug collapsed as he dropped to his knees, arms dangling uselessly as he curled over, trying to suck oxygen back into too-empty lungs. It would be at least thirty seconds before he recovered. The fight would be over in that time, one way or another. She could leave him to gasp and face his companion—but even as the idea was born, combat instincts brought her into a vertical leaping kick that ended with her heel cracking into his jaw. His head snapped back and he followed it, crashing to the floor with a trail of blood creeping from the corner of his mouth.

Time resumed its normal speed for an instant, thought intruding on her actions: *two hits: me hittin' you, you hitting the floor.* It was the rule of genuine combat; rarely did a real fight last more than a few seconds. Alisha turned to face her second opponent, who flanked her now, his position greatly improved in the moments it had taken her to bring down his partner. Neither of them spoke or feinted, both watching for weakness or a sign of readiness to act. The wiry man held his right hand as if he was accustomed to carrying a knife in it, fingers curled too loosely to make a fist.

But his lunge came from the left, when he made it. *His*

left, Alisha's right, and her weaker side. A shot of admiration crashed through her, warmth in the midst of cold combat. He was good, maybe as good as she was, able to learn from two blows thrown at another combatant where her strengths and weaknesses were. Alisha flung herself to her left, throwing herself into a dive that nearly tangled her in the prone blonde's legs. She caught herself on her arms, surging through the dive on pure adrenaline and strength, and rolled out of it ten inches from Frank Reichart, who looked down at her without expression. The urge to spit "You could help" made her tongue feel stiff and ugly in her mouth, but he'd betrayed her presence. There would be no support from that quarter. If she was lucky, there'd be no hindrance, either.

Alisha drove the heel of her hand forward again, hoping to catch him off guard, but there was no chance of it with Reichart. He knocked her hit to the side easily, then moved back into the hall that the voices had echoed from, removing himself from the fighting zone. Alisha curled a lip and turned on her heel, crouched and prepared to face the wiry man again.

He was already in action, making a low, lean line of himself as he rushed her. His right hand was still curled, and though there was no knife blade curving away from his fingers, the attitude made Alisha that much more cautious. She dove to the side again, less for distance than the opportunity to come in low with a sweeping side kick. He hurdled it and twisted to face her again as he landed. Alisha rotated her weight onto her arms and spun another kick out, feeling dirt grind into her hands even through the gloves she wore.

The kick connected with his knee. Alisha felt ligament slide and pop out of place, the kneecap suddenly no longer where it was meant to be. The wiry man went down with a gagged grunt of pain. Alisha came out of her spin in a jump, intending to bring her full weight down on the man's torso.

Silver glittered in the stairway lights, arching up from the wiry man's right hand. A curved blade fit against his forearm, his fingers wrapped easily around the hilt. Irritation sliced through Alisha's belly, a pang of admission that came nowhere near the alarm she might have felt outside of combat. She had expected the knife, and had still opened an opportunity for him to use it. With her weight already off the ground, Alisha could only go forward, landing knee-first in his abdomen. He was prepared for her, muscles knotted in expectation of her weight, and while air grunted from him, he wasn't knocked breathless.

She flinched back as she landed, quadriceps taking the strain of her weight as the knife skinned past her thigh-hip-stomach, leaving a thin line of pain behind. Experience told her the cut was superficial: bloody, painful and messy, but not debilitating. Tension tightened the skin around the wiry man's eyes and nose as he completed the knife's arc and reversed it into a straight-armed back-blow that would gut her if it landed.

Knife fights were dangerous on a level different from any other kind of battle, tending to bring out caution in the combatants. Attempts to avoid surface injuries frequently led to the opportunity for the opponent to strike a killing blow. Winning a knife fight wasn't about walking away unhurt, and the only way to do it was to override the body's instinctive wish to avoid danger. Alisha reached inside the attack, moving too quickly to allow herself thought or fear even as she felt skin part again, a score struck along the soft skin of her upper inner arm. This strike was deeper: she could sense the need to give in to a shriek of shock and pain.

Instead she wrapped her arm around his, bloody triceps pressed against his forearm so his hand and weapon were half captured between her arm and body, his momentum stopped. She seized his triceps with clawed fingers and forced his arm up, locking his elbow.

Grounding herself took no effort, the floor beneath her knees offering her a sensation of physical sturdiness that went far beyond even her own considerable strength. As always, the midst of combat seemed an odd place to most fully appreciate and feel the centeredness of yoga that made the universe seem to flow and ebb around and through her. Odd, but appreciated.

Alisha slammed the heel of her left hand up into the man's locked elbow, using power that felt like it was taken from the earth itself. Bone shattered, muscle and sinew popping upward at a horrible wrong angle. The man let out an aborted scream and turned ashy gray before Alisha curled her fingers in his shirt and pulled him up far enough to smash her fist into his jaw, rendering him unconscious.

Pain flooded through her as she dropped him again. The jab in her arm had caught muscle, though not deeply enough to render her arm useless. Alisha peeled the edges of her jacket away from the wound, giving it an investigative glance; it was clean, bleeding freely, with no obvious fibers caught in it. A field dressing would help, but would also waste precious time, and she had none to spare. She came to her feet, fingers exploring the cut that sliced over her hip and abdomen. The waistband of her pants had caught the knife's brunt, leaving the rest of the injury shallow. *You were lucky, Leesh.*

Reichart was gone, disappeared in the eternal seconds it had taken to disable the wiry man. Alisha closed her hand over the cut in her shirt and belly, then crouched and picked up the knife the wiry man had carried. Reichart would have to wait. Alisha sprinted down the hall, concern lending strength to her run. Brandon had proved himself an able fighter once upon a time, but she'd sent him into the disintegrating mess that now surrounded him, and trust aside, she wasn't going to lose a man on her watch.

She wasn't going to lose Greg Parker's son, no matter what the cost might be.

The room she burst into had a sick familiarity to it, the stone walls scarred and crumbled in the corners. Stone, Alisha thought distantly. Not concrete, like she'd thought when she was held here. Then again, she'd been drugged out of her mind. And there were old stains in the floor, brownish red residue from blood never properly cleaned. Maybe her own blood.

No: there had been a hall behind her then, short, with a sharp corner at its end. She hadn't found the room they'd held her in. Alisha shook off the memory, letting awareness of the situation in front of her roll over her. Five people, all men; the woman Parker'd been talking to was missing. Three hung back, watching—

—watching Frank Reichart strangle Brandon Parker. Brandon's eyes bulged as Reichart snapped him against the wall, cracking his skull against stone. Brandon sagged, the grip he held on Reichart's wrists loosening as he lost strength. Alisha reversed the knife in her hand, holding it in her fingertips by the blade. Its weight was wrong for throwing: too much curve to the blade and the handle too heavy, but it would do.

It thunked into the meat of Reichart's hamstring like God had called it home. He howled and dropped Brandon, who gagged in a single breath before smashing his fist into Reichart's face as Reichart fumbled for the knife in his thigh. The dark-haired man toppled and Brandon kicked him in the ribs.

Alisha went down under the weight of three men and for a few long moments saw nothing but muscle and fists, heard little more than the sound of her own heartbeat and the labored breathing of the men she fought. She bit down on something—a wrist, a cheek; she wasn't sure what—hard enough to tear flesh, earning a gratifying scream of outrage and pain for her efforts.

A gunshot shattered the air, echoing and rebounding endlessly off the stone walls. Everyone scattered, Alisha scrambling to her feet to find Brandon standing over Reichart's prone body.

Fire sank inward from the slice across her belly, a burning sickness that lifted hairs all over her body as she fought back bile. Her ears rang with the sound of the gunshot, leaving no room in her hearing for her own heartbeat. She thought it might have stopped entirely, suspended for all time between one beat and the next. Her chest hurt, a throb that she finally recognized as the ache of lungs gone too long unfilled. Alisha dragged in a breath, harsh and cold and filled with dust drifting from the ceiling. It was the dust, nothing more, that turned her vision misty and obscure.

Brandon stepped away from Reichart, bringing the gun around to the remaining Sicarii. "Hands up. Against the wall. Do it! Alisha, go. I'm with you."

Alisha cast one more look at where Reichart lay, then ran for the door, Brandon on her heels.

Chapter 8

Wet cobblestones gleamed in the streetlights, ten stories below. Raindrops made ballerina patterns in the puddles, visible even from the height. Alisha tightened the blanket she'd dragged from the hotel suite's bed around her arms, keeping it well away from her torso. She'd applied a butterfly bandage and taped the long, shallow slice that ran across her hip and belly. Even the smallest movements made the edges twinge with discomfort, and she hadn't put a shirt on over the injury, not wanting to feel the constant brush of fabric against raw skin.

The puncture in her arm was deeper than she'd thought at first. It could probably use stitches, though for now it had simply been cleaned and bound with what had once been part of a blouse. The pressure from the blanket wrapped against the wound both ached and felt good.

At least it felt. Her body was cold to the touch; she

knew it intellectually, but the chill didn't seem to matter. Goose bumps stood up over her ribs and made prickles of discomfort along the cut on her stomach, warnings of worse things to come. A thin bra and low-cut jeans were nothing to be wearing as she stood barefoot on the rain-spattered balcony. Warmth would be better for her.

But warmth might play up the cold blankness that had settled inside her, a dullness that defied emotion. It was better to be numb outside and tell herself that it caused the emptiness inside than to remember Frank Reichart's still form lying on the stone floor.

She'd left Brandon outside the Sicarii stronghold, their paths diverging to mislead anyone who might follow. Her injuries had driven her back to the hotel room sooner than she might have otherwise chosen. There were supplies there to patch herself up with, more discreet than staggering wet, bleeding and clad in snugly fitted clandestine wear into a drugstore or market that might carry bandages and disinfectant. Now dampness clung to her hair as she watched the quiet street below, the genuine wetness long since dried in the hours since she'd returned to the hotel room. Bells somewhere in the city had announced the passing of the three-o'clock hour, dawn closer now than sunset.

A wash of warm air through the open balcony doors heralded Brandon's sodden arrival as the suite's main door opened and closed. He paused long enough to take off his shoes, then squelched across the carpet in wet socks. "You made it." His voice was rough and sore sounding, the after-effects of strangulation.

Alisha turned her head toward him, watching his shadow catch in the reflection of the glass balcony doors as he came to stand in their frame. "So did you. I was beginning to be concerned." She couldn't taste the truth in her own words, didn't know if they were honest or not. Concern seemed remote, as far away and unattainable as any other emotion.

"Beginning to be." Brandon squeezed water out of his hair between his fingers, sending rivulets down his cheekbones. "I'm glad my welfare is of such concern to you. What the hell were you doing there?"

Alisha looked back at the street. "Spying on you." There should have been guilt in the admission, she thought, but she felt none.

"Jesus, Alisha. You nearly got us both killed."

"And I did get Reichart killed." The words could have been spoken by someone else, so distant did they sound. "Not that he didn't deserve it, I suppose. The son of a bitch." Neither heat nor pain in the insult. Alisha closed her eyes, drawing in a breath that did nothing to center her. It was nearly inconceivable to her, that Reichart was dead. Betrayal after betrayal, Alisha thought, and still she expected that somehow he would prove to be one of the good guys.

"Not unless you hit the femoral artery."

"What?" Alisha turned her head back toward Brandon, eyebrows drawn down.

"He's not dead unless he bled out," Brandon said.

"You shot him." The aftereffects of the gunshot rang in her ears again, making her close her eyes in remembered pain.

"I shot the ceiling, Alisha."

"What?" Alisha pushed away from the balcony wall, staring at her erstwhile partner.

"I shot the ceiling," he repeated wearily, then muttered, "but I did not shoot the deputy," before saying, "or Reichart, either," aloud again. "I was trying to get everybody to stop fighting so we could get out of there. That's all."

"But I saw—" Alisha put her hand out to the balcony railing, the muscles in her biceps protesting as she made use of them. No, she thought, she hadn't seen. She'd heard. One gunshot. Had seen Reichart lying motionless on the floor. Had *concluded,* not known.

Memory assailed her, the flavor of grit and aged stone drifting from the ceiling drying her tastebuds. Alisha put her hand over her mouth and, without the railing's support, sank down into a crouch that pressed her thighs against the slice across her belly. Pain sparked through her, a real and honest feeling that made her shudder and let go a rough, shaking laugh behind her hand. Her eyes, wide-open and unfocused, burned with dryness that wanted to be tears. She could feel tremors starting in the core of her, and tried to force her hands to be still, though she knew she couldn't betray any more relief if she tried. Exposed and vulnerable in front of someone she didn't dare trust. *Dangerous, Leesh,* she warned herself, but her muscles wouldn't respond when she tried to stand up again so she could compose herself.

"Why?" She forced the word out from behind her fingers as she jerked her gaze up to Brandon.

He sighed and pushed his hand through his hair again. "Don't think I didn't want to," he muttered, then sighed again, more explosively. "I figured it was the one thing you'd never forgive me for."

"What?" She'd asked that question more times in a minute than she usually did in a week. Her mind felt as if someone had stirred it with rain-scented fog, making it thick and drowsy, unable to make connections with its usual alacrity.

"The human heart can forgive a host of evils," Brandon said with a faint smile. "I'm just not sure yours could go so far as to forgive someone for killing Frank Reichart." He touched his throat, where even in the darkness bruises were visible. "Not that he didn't deserve it," he agreed.

"He was trying to kill you," Alisha said thinly.

"Yeah. I noticed that."

"And you didn't shoot him because of *me?*" The idea seemed ludicrous. Alisha touched her own throat in sympathy. Brandon let go a puff of laughter that had little humor in it.

"Yeah," he repeated. "Although right now, what with you spying on me, I'm not sure you deserved that courtesy."

Alisha drew her lower lip into her mouth, accepting the reprimand. Then she straightened, hands on her thighs. Her biceps and stomach protested as she moved, and Brandon hissed at her expression, stepping out onto the balcony. "You're hurt."

"I'll live. Brandon." Alisha knotted one fist in the blanket she still had draped over her shoulders. "You shouldn't have known I was there. I was going to use what you told me in comparison to what I heard to make certain you were trustworthy. I think you understand why." It took effort to prevent herself from lifting a hand to touch the scar at the back of her neck. The act of stopping the movement telegraphed the desire to do it; Brandon curved his hand at the back of his own neck, lips pressed together tightly.

"I don't like it," he said after a moment.

"But you understand it."

"Yeah. Look." He stared at her, expression intent without quite being a frown, then walked past her to lean heavily on the railing, looking down at the street below. "I don't know where you came in, so I'm just going to start from the top. They want me to turn you over to them as proof of my loyalty." He barked out another humorless laugh. "They did before you showed up and went medieval on their asses, anyway. I don't know what the hell they're going to think now."

"What were you going to do?" A time-wasting question, Alisha thought. A way to avoid the one she should really ask. Brandon gave her a sharp look.

"I was going to drug you again and see if they managed to blow your head off this time. I don't know, Alisha." Sharpness filled his tone, replacing the sarcasm. "Using me as bait was your plan. I don't know what I would have done if I had to use you as the price of admission. Used you," he admitted, "and trusted you to get out of it. Just like I did last time."

"I still don't know if I believe that's what you really thought last time," Alisha said quietly, then shook her head. That argument was as fruitless as the question she'd asked. She lifted her chin, watching Brandon's profile. "Do you have any idea what Reichart was doing there?"

Brandon glanced at her. "You're not going to like it."

"Will I like it less than being used as a trading piece to get you back into the Sicarii?" Alisha tilted her head at the hotel suite, watching her reflection bounce off the glass doors. She looked ghostlike, the tangle of tight curls unrestrained, and making a shadow of her face. "Let's talk in there. It's secure."

"A lot less." Brandon followed her into the suite, pulling the doors closed and the drapes over them before he went on. "Reichart was one of my interviewers, Alisha. He's working for them."

Alisha stopped at the end of the couch, arms folded into the blanket as she wet her lips, then swallowed. "One of your interviewers." Of the scenarios she'd run through in her mind, that hadn't been one of them. She closed her eyes, holding herself still while the idea and its ramifications sank into her. "You're sure?" Another useless question. Maybe Greg and Boyer were right. Maybe she genuinely couldn't see clearly when it came to Reichart. If that was the case, she didn't belong on this assignment and she needed the time with Dr. Reyes a lot more than she would ever be happy admitting. Alisha wet her lips again, then walked carefully into the suite's bedroom to replace the folded comforter at the foot of the bed before returning to the living room.

"He came in after me," she said then, just barely trusting her voice. "How could he have been one of your interviewers?"

"*Interviewer* is a little strong," Brandon admitted. "He was the one standing around looking bored while they strip-searched me." He leaned against the suite's bar, watching the microwave count down as a cup rotated inside it. A package of instant decaffeinated coffee lay behind his hip where he leaned on the counter. More for the warmth than the awakening properties, Alisha thought. She wasn't tired, either, for all that the small hours of the night were growing larger.

"Strip-searched," she said drily. "How about we skip the details of that. I'll just have to imagine it." A thread of humor had worked its way into the words, like life returning to her veins. Reichart wasn't dead. Alisha went into the bedroom, an excuse to move so that her expression couldn't be seen, and came back with a blouse she shrugged on over her shoulders. It bulged around her biceps where the bandage was knotted, and she didn't button it, but instead traced her fingers over the cut on her stomach.

Brandon arched an eyebrow at her, then reached out to pop the microwave open before it beeped. "I want you to know that walking into a Sicarii stronghold with a price on my head isn't something I'm eager to repeat."

"Too bad," Alisha murmured, but Brandon went on without hearing her, stirring crystals into his hot water.

"There're a half-dozen strongholds I know about. I chose the one in Rome because it's where a woman they call Phoenix works out of most often." Brandon glanced at her. "She's an American agent, Alisha. I figured if I could see her, I might walk out of there alive."

The words thudded into Alisha's heart like cannonballs. *An American agent.* That could explain the itching familiarity the woman's voice had triggered in Alisha's mind. A chance encounter, or a meeting once upon a time. "Do you have independent verification of her loyalties?"

"Through Director Simone, yes. I told Phoenix as much of the truth as I could. That I'd been at Langley, that I was working with you. I'm sorry about that, but it was something they'd be able to verify, and starting out lying seemed like a bad idea."

Alisha shook her head minutely. "It doesn't matter." It did matter, but she agreed: it was a choice that he'd needed to make. Alisha might well have made the same choice herself. "I understand. Go on."

Brandon bent his head over the cup of hot coffee, inhaling the sweet scent without drinking. His hands were wrapped around it, leeching heat into fingers pale with cold. "I don't know if you've been back to the Vatican," he said after a few long seconds. "To examine other Sicarii records."

Alisha spread her hand across the couch cushions, feeling not the nubbly fabric, but instead ancient embossed leather. The memory of scent overwhelmed the richness of coffee for a moment, replacing it with musty pages and dry, dusty halls.

Below the Vatican's secret library were other, older, more carefully guarded vaults of treasures. Alisha had only been privy to a single room, where handwritten records kept by second sons consigned to the church traced royal genealogies more thoroughly than any public records had ever imagined. Bastard children, many of them by-blows their royal fathers never dreamed existed, were traced down through generations, father to son and mother to daughter. Some were marked off decades or centuries past, annotations beside the names admitting mistakes in the lineage. Others came down through a thousand years of history, until a single parent had begotten thirty or fifty direct-line descendents. They seemed, for the most part, to concentrate on the oldest child born to the line; anything else, Alisha thought, would soon be overwhelming. Almost all of them were sons of kings or princes. Almost, but not all. Verifying a bastard child carried by a wedded queen was more difficult, but not impossible, and the church was thorough.

Frank Reichart's name had been one of the last in a line tracing back to Henry VIII's youth. It had been his records that Brandon had bribed Alisha's way into the Sicarii vault in the Vatican to see, his intent to make Reichart's loyalties clear. Alisha could still feel the parchment beneath her fingertips, tracing out a history that the Sicarii believed meant the divine right to rule still lay in the blood of ordinary men.

Alisha pulled in a sharp breath, lifting her head. "I tried," she said. "I didn't have the pull to get in there again. I didn't know where to begin."

Brandon nodded over his coffee cup, still not drinking. "My family is in there, Alisha. Descended from William of Orange."

Alisha smiled faintly. "So why aren't you king?"

Brandon returned the smile just as thinly. "Because he died childless, according to any official records. It doesn't matter. I thought it'd be enough to start with, actually being of Sicarii descent. Wanting to be remembered as more than a computer programmer. Ambition makes it easy to deceive."

"Are you really that ambitious?"

Brandon looked over at her, putting his coffee cup aside, though he kept his fingers looped through the handle. "What if your name was in there, Alisha? Can you tell me the temptation to play God—or at least queen—wouldn't be there?"

Alisha snorted. "Me, the royal descendent of what, Brandon? A Greek-Hispanic-Irish-Hawaiian princess? I don't think they made them that much of a grab bag."

"But each one of those cultures had its own royalty," Brandon pointed out. "And at least two of them have enough ties to the Catholic Church that if there's royalty in your genes, the Sicarii will have records of it."

Alisha shook her head. "Even if they do, so what? Sure, some days I think I could do a better job of ruling the world than most people, but I don't think any individual's capable of it, and any situation where you put the government above the laws of men can only benefit the government. I don't believe in divine right. I can't believe you do, either."

"Mmm. Not as such. I don't think God intends for certain people to rule above others. But if you have the education, the intelligence, the compassion to rule well, does it matter if you're put there by a group of madmen?"

"Yes." Alisha heard the hard note in her voice and did nothing to try to temper it. "Because you owe them, and you'll either die defying them—rendering your stance moot—or you'll be forced to destroy them, which almost certainly makes you no better than they are." She drew in another sharp breath through flared nostrils and lifted a hand to stop Brandon's argument. "Not that it's not a fascinating discussion, but you're not done with your report. What happened with Reichart?" Double-crossing, scheming, bastardly Reichart. Calling him names didn't hide her relief that he was still alive. There was still a chance to get answers out of him.

Not that she'd ever had much luck with that in the past.

"He told me," Brandon said over the rage of her internal monologue, "that he hadn't known he was a Tudor until you told him, during the Attengee mission."

"He volunteered that?"

Brandon frowned at her. "I didn't have anything else to do while they were stripping me naked and probing me. I asked him what the hell he was doing there."

Alisha pulled her mouth long in a *fair enough* moue and gestured for him to continue. Brandon frowned a moment longer before letting it go and shrugging. "He said he always goes where the money is. I get the impression that's true."

"Heh." Alisha nodded. "If he's got one predictability, that's it."

"Yeah. So a mercenary with royal lineage thinks the Sicarii are a sure thing. Is it that much of a surprise, Alisha?"

"No," Alisha said quietly. Not a surprise. Just a disappointment.

"You expect him to be better than he is, don't you?" Brandon's question followed her own thought so closely Alisha pulled her shoulders back to keep them from hunching defensively.

"Hope springs eternal," she answered. "Even after all these years it's hard to accept I was so completely wrong about him." She turned a faint smile on Brandon. "After all, I'm supposed to be a good judge of character."

"So how do you judge mine?" Brandon's voice lowered, his gaze both intent and shy; after only a few seconds it skittered away, as if he was uncertain about hearing Alisha's appraisal.

"Poorly," Alisha said. "I trusted you when I shouldn't have because I wanted you to be something you weren't. I wanted to protect your father from what you could be, and that was a mistake. If you earn my trust, Brandon, then you'll deserve it, but I'm not going to make that mistake with you again."

"You make it repeatedly with Reichart."

Alisha felt the cords in her neck stand out and waited long seconds before she was able to force a smile. "Everyone has a fatal weakness."

"The soft spot in the dragon's hide," Brandon half asked. Alisha's smile softened a little.

"I'm not Smaug, Brandon. And you're not Bard, so don't get any bright ideas."

"Bard killed the dragon, Alisha. That's not what I'm after." Brandon's expression shadowed and he picked up his coffee cup, leaving the counter behind to approach the couch. "Alisha…"

"Whatever you're going to say, Brandon, don't," Alisha said, tone flat. "I don't want to hear it."

Brandon gave her a very thin smile and spoke sotto voce. "There's someone on the balcony."

The windows exploded inward.

Chapter 9

Concussive force slammed into Alisha's back, knocking her off the couch and sending her flying across the living room floor. Shattered glass rained down, the thick drapes torn and shredded with the force of the blast. There was nothing in her ears but ringing pressure, no way to pinpoint anyone's location. Brandon had disappeared from her line of sight. There were wood splinters in her palms and hot coffee cooled rapidly as it dripped down her face. Her vision had gone wrong, unable to pick out details in the aftermath of the explosion. Alisha lifted her head, feeling the muscles of her neck protest with pain and stiffness that hadn't been there a moment earlier.

One glass panel in the curving hotel bar in front of her was still intact. It reflected the suite behind her in shambles, furniture and scraps scattered everywhere. A smoldering, stinking fire rose from the arm of the couch, making one thing evident: there was nothing wrong with her vision. The lights had been blown out, leaving the tiny fires scattered around the room and the rain-dampened streetlights from below as the only source of lighting in the darkness.

Alisha turned her head very slowly, looking over her shoulder toward what had once been the balcony doors. There was no longer a balcony, wind whipping the remains of the drapes in silent snaps. No one, as yet, had entered through the gaping hole in the building's side. Seven seconds since the explosion. She didn't remember beginning the count, the first numbers lost to her unconscious mind, but more than a decade of training told her to trust the internal chronometer. If the blast itself was meant to kill, there might not be a follow-up team to make sure the job was done. Nine seconds.

Alisha planted her hands against the floor, drew herself into a somersault and rolled behind the bar at the tenth second.

The snap of glass breaking came through the ringing in her ears, a single warning sound. The follow-up team. Ten seconds after detonation. It was when she would have come in, had it been her gig. Alisha felt the small of her back, as if the gun she knew lay in the bedroom might somehow have materialized there. Her shirt was torn beyond recognition, and without thinking Alisha stripped it off, winding it around one fist as she considered her options. Time was slow, the seconds counting off in her head seeming very far apart.

They would have night goggles, rendered slightly less effective because of the fires than they might have been, but a dash for the bedroom wouldn't go unnoticed. Alisha slid the bar counter doors open slowly, silently and without conscious thought. A dozen bottles of alcohol lay knocked on their sides. Alisha shifted a bottle of vodka out, trying not to disturb the others, and used her shirt-wrapped hand to twist the stiff top off. The temptation to take a swig hit her so unexpectedly she found herself grinning as she shifted her feet under herself and prepared to stand.

One chance, Leesh.

Not a problem, she assured herself, and with smooth confidence surged to her feet, making herself a painfully visible form in the darkness for anyone wearing night goggles.

She swung her arm wide, spraying vodka in an arc across the room. A voice barked as she was noticed, and two figures, barely lit by the stench-ridden couch fire, whipped to face her.

The arc of alcohol splashed over the fire, and a sudden new burst of flame shot up. Bullets spattered, flying high as her assailants scrabbled to remove the blinding goggles. Alisha was in a dead run long before her conscious mind could send *move!* signals to her muscles, the bedroom door reached in a few desperate strides.

She came through the door in a roll, feeling her neck muscles protest again as she hit the floor at full speed. Agony seared along her belly as small bandages and tape pulled free, opening the cut again. Bullets whined above her head again, hitting the wall with puffs of dust. Tiny beads of plaster crumbled down the wall and came to rest in the carpet. They'd need to be cleaned up soon, Alisha thought distantly, or they'd be ground into the carpet and their chalk would be difficult to remove.

She came out of her roll at the head of the bed, hand sliding under the pillow for her gun. She popped up to her knees in one fluid movement, taking a precious second or two to track before squeezing the trigger.

There was only one Sicarii—they had to be Sicarii,

Alisha thought—in the bedroom, no doubt intending to sneak up behind Alisha and Brandon, should they survive the initial explosion.

Brandon. In thirty seconds Alisha hadn't spared a thought for him. Nor could she now, as she squeezed off three shots: center-center-head. There was no time for delicacy or disabling. The first bullet slammed into the mark's shoulder, spinning him around. The second crashed into his spine, and the third missed as he dropped to the floor, the sudden stink of violent death permeating the room. Alisha ducked forward again into another roll, bringing herself back to the bedroom door.

Smoldering fires were alight everywhere now, the shrieking wind from the torn-out wall whipping acrid smoke through the room. There were three figures she could make out in her quick glimpses around the doorjamb, all of them with the telltale sleekness of operations clothing. Brandon wasn't among them. Alisha gave a little nod, driving home that knowledge, then leaned around the door again to take another three quick shots. There were thirteen rounds in the fully loaded .45. She couldn't afford to miss, nor did she. The second man went down even as Alisha launched herself out the door, seeking different cover and hoping the night goggles were as useless to her assailants as normal vision was to her.

Bullets shattered the wall she'd hidden behind, making her painfully aware of the difference between *cover* and *concealment*. A wall bullets could smash through so easily was only concealment; it would never protect her from those bullets.

The bar counter, made of solid, heavy wood, made much better cover. Alisha dove behind it, landing on her stomach and rolling to her back before she had time to catch a breath. No one approached in the brief moment it took to switch positions a second time, pressing her back against the cupboard she'd left open. A bottle of alcohol curved against her back, and the urge to open it and take a swig hit her again. Maybe later, if she got out of this alive. She'd deserve a drink, if she lived.

The concussion of bullets firing faded from her ears, letting the preternatural hearing that she relied on in combat settle into place. Even her own breathing fell silent, though she wasn't sure if she'd stopped breathing, or if the sounds of her body had become so irrelevant as to be utterly ignorable.

The softest footsteps possible, the only thing to betray them the crunch of shattered glass grinding into the carpet. One to her left. Good, Alisha thought; that was her dominant side. An attack to her strength was always good.

And the other *above her.*

Alisha surged to her feet, turning as she straightened, and fired without taking time to find her targets. First shot to the left at center-mass height, and then as her twist brought her around to face the counter she brought her weapon up, firing toward the ceiling.

There was an instant of surprise visible on her assailant's face before the kinetic force of the bullets knocked him backward off the counter. Alisha snapped back to her left, pulling the trigger again, but the third man was gone. She dropped to the floor and crept around the end of the bar, eyeing the body there. It moved, and she edged forward to get in position to pull the trigger again, or better still, keep him alive long enough to discuss the attack. Interrogation would have to wait a few minutes, if it was possible at all; her hearing rang with the sound of the shot she'd fired. But better to wait and question than to have no answers, she thought.

A gun pressed into the base of her skull. For the first time since the windows had exploded, emotion slid a cold knife of fear through Alisha's belly. "You're good," a man said in lightly accented English. "Better than she said, even. But not good enough."

Alisha's shoulders rose in slow tension. "Who's she? Where'd you come from?"

"The front door," he admitted with a tiny shrug that shifted the gun against her skull. "Anticlimactic, but so effective."

"Yeah." Alisha heard the hoarseness in her own voice. She'd been so busy looking for enemies from the shattered windows she'd never looked behind her. "Good job."

Surprising warmth came into the man's light chuckle. "Do you think complimenting me will cause me to spare your life?"

"No," Alisha said honestly. "But if somebody's going to kill me, it's nice that it wasn't some jerk getting lucky."

He stepped to her side without taking the gun away from her head. "I'll pass your regards on to the appropriate persons," he promised. "Say good night, Gracie."

Alisha lifted her chin a little, staring across the wind-ripped room out into the wet Roman night. The fear in her belly was gone, replaced by silent expectation. It was good, she thought, not to be afraid. She even turned her head toward her murderer, feeling the gun's muzzle press harder against her temple. She couldn't quite see him as she looked up, his form slender and tall but unremarkable in the smoke. She took one last breath and exhaled it slowly, then gave a minute shrug and whispered, "Good night, Gracie."

Brandon appeared out of the smoky mess like a war-torn god, barely on his feet but with the zeal of a madman in his eyes. He had no weapon, but raised his fists locked together in a hammer. Bone snapped in the Sicarii's neck as the blow landed, weight of the hit smacking the man to the side. His gun fired, muzzle flare so close Alisha felt its heat across the bridge of her nose. The bullet drove into the floor just beyond her.

She jerked her gaze up, staring at Brandon in wide-eyed silence. He gave her a shaky smile in return, then said, "Damn," and collapsed into the rubble on the floor.

Alisha lurched forward, too late to catch him in his fall. A cursory examination in the poor lighting suggested no bullet wounds, though his clothes were more badly damaged than Alisha's, and his skin was littered with fragments of glass and larger scrapes. Except for his throat, there was no bruising yet visible, but as Alisha pulled his eyelids back to examine his pupils, she could feel the tenderness in his skin that said bruising would come soon, and badly. There was likely a Brandon-shaped dent in one of the walls.

And now there was pounding on the door, raised Italian voices full of concern. Alisha left Brandon's prone body in favor of examining the one Sicarii she thought was still alive. His breathing was shallow, blood bubbling at the corner of his mouth; she'd put a bullet into his lung. Alisha swore and knotted her hands into his shirt, the close black fabric almost too slippery to grip. "Who sent you? Who's 'she'? Who are you working for?"

The man turned his focus on her with clear effort, then offered a faint, bloodstained smile as he rasped, "From the ashes comes the phoenix to destroy you." His last breath was a coughing laugh before he became dead weight in Alisha's hands.

"Goddamn it!" Alisha dropped him and straightened to deliver a kick to his ribs. Then she stepped over his body, ignoring the pounding on the door to return to the bedroom and lift and activate her earpiece. "This is Cardinal," she snapped. "I have a situation in Rome. Four bodies and an agent is down, I repeat, an agent is down. Please send in authorities. Cardinal out." She flicked the earpiece off and scooped up a bottle of alcohol, taking a long dredge without looking to see what it was. Whiskey burned down her throat, bringing tears to her eyes and somehow clearing her mind. Then, bottle in hand, she stalked out to deal with the hotel staff.

Only later did it strike her how she must have looked, confronting the terrified staff. Scraped and bloody, wearing nothing but a dusty, torn bra and half-shredded jeans, the remains of her shirt wrapped around her right hand and a bottle dangling from her fingertips. With smoke billowing and the wind in the room tangling her hair around her face, she might have been one of the dead answering the door.

But it lent her an air of authority, and no one balked or protested when she said it must have been a terrorist attack, and that an ambulance was needed. By the time the paramedics arrived she'd swept the room of anything Agency-owned, and walked down to the ambulance under her own power, taking the stairwell instead of the elevator in order to avoid any media that might have arrived. She joined Brandon in the ambulance and pulled an orderly's vest over her torn clothing, then yanked the doors shut and pounded on the vehicle's side to let the driver know they were ready.

A woman in the passenger seat turned to look back at her as Alisha made her way toward the cab of the ambulance. "Will he be all right?" The woman spoke American English, her accent tainted with transatlantic vowels.

"I'm not a doctor." Soreness was catching up fast, and

Alisha's voice reflected her discomfort, though she took a slow breath and added, "I think so. Just banged up. A few days' rest should do it. Who're you?"

"My name is Susan Simone," the woman said coolly. "You may have heard of me."

"Shit." Alisha took a better look at the woman, who was in her fifties and less aging gracefully than successfully fighting the battle. Her graying hair was tinted blond except at the temples, and her gaze was sharp and steady in the predawn streetlights. "Director Simone. Sorry."

"I won't hold it against you," Simone said, still coolly, "as you've just been blown up."

But don't do it again. Alisha heard the warning as clearly as if it'd been spoken around, and ducked her head. "Thank you, ma'am. When I said send in authorities I didn't think I'd be going all the way to the top."

"The president is the top, Agent MacAleer. I'm merely a waypoint."

Under the circumstances, Alisha thought, it was wiser to withhold the "Bullshit" that was her first response. She drew breath to say something else, but Simone continued on. "Your current alias will have to change. No one's yet thought to ask who you are, but that will happen soon enough, especially when it becomes clear that the bodies in that room were not killed by an explosion." She cast a glance at Brandon. "He'll be brought to a private hospital. You, Agent MacAleer, will leave Rome immediately."

"Director Simone—"

"Immediately, Agent MacAleer."

Alisha pressed her lips together and lowered her chin to her chest. "Yes, ma'am."

Chapter 10

"Cardinal, this is a bad idea." Greg sounded tired over the staticky cell phone connection. "You're under orders."

"I want them countermanded." Alisha had made it as far as the coast, miles outside of Rome, and stood on the roadside now, watching the sun rise over the Apennine Mountains. She'd been given new clothes, more ammo for her gun, all the things she'd need to leave not just Rome, but Europe, including a new passport. She flipped it open and held it up to the sunrise, studying the name. *Karen Buckner,* an American grad student traveling in Europe. Alisha closed the passport again and turned her attention back to the conversation. "I'm going back in, Kremlin. I've still got my mission to reacquire the Firebird's black box, and Reichart was last seen in Rome."

"Reichart." Greg said the name through his teeth. "I'm more convinced than ever that you—"

"If Boyer takes me off the case I'll step away." Alisha

put steel into her voice. "But I want it from him, Kremlin. I'm playing ball here. You want me to see somebody local for my shrink session? I'll do it. I'd rather talk to Reyes, but I'll do it. If I'm off this case, it's Boyer who's taking me off. He's the one who agreed to put me on it."

"And waltzing back into Rome after the European director's thrown you out?"

Alisha shrugged without the slightest apology. "She said leave. She didn't say anything about staying gone."

"Not exactly the letter of the law, Cardinal."

"Fuck the letter of the law, Greg." Alisha turned in a tight circle, grinding earth under her heel. "I just got blown up. Your son's in the hospital. Reichart's got this Sicarii question to answer to, and even if he didn't there's the box, so excuse me if I'm not real goddamn concerned with the letter of the law."

Long silence met her impassioned speech, before Greg sighed. "When did you develop this problem with authority, Ali?"

Right about the same time the authorities around me started looking like they might be working for the bad guys, Alisha thought. "I don't know," she said aloud. "Maybe you could suggest I talk it over with Dr. Reyes."

"I will," her handler said without a trace of humor. "Alisha, do not do anything foolish. I'll call you back with Boyer's decision within the hour."

"Fine. I'll be waiting." Alisha hung up the phone and put it in her back pocket, then crouched to pick up the backpack of hiking gear and general supplies she'd been provided with. Rome was barely an hour's walk away. She would be waiting. Just not where Greg expected her to be.

"*Arrivederci.*" Alisha's curt goodbye was the first word she'd spoken since hanging up on Greg. She hadn't even spoken to order coffee in the back-street café she'd entered on the edge of Rome. It was well past dawn now, though still far earlier than most European cities began to function at full speed. Not like New York or Los Angeles, Alisha thought. Not like D.C. Six a.m. meetings were the stuff of jokes in those cities, but their humor came from a thread of truth.

Prickles walked up her spine, a warning that someone approached from behind. She sat facing west, with the sunrise and open streets behind her, not because she wanted to, but because there was a pattern to be kept here. Her preference would have been the corner table in the little café, where she could watch people come and go without ever being approached unexpectedly. A chair scraped at the table behind her, then creaked with the weight of someone sitting in it. The muscles between Alisha's shoulder blades tightened, but she didn't turn.

"*Arrivederci* and hello," the person behind her murmured. His English was heavily accented, even within just a word or two, though Alisha had heard him drop the accent and sound like he was from Nowhere, California, when the need arose.

"Carlos." It was the name she'd last known him by. "It's good to see you again." She didn't need to turn to see the man, her mind's eye building the picture for her. He was in his late forties, maybe older, a corpulent man who built his business around the reputed genial nature of fat people. It was a facade; Alisha had watched him put a massive hand over a man's face and smother him, the cheery smile never slipping.

"Carlos, who is this Carlos?" he asked, another part of his ritual. Everything she'd done since entering the café, even the refusal to speak for over an hour and her first word finally being *arrivederci* was part of Carlos's game. Alisha had no idea what his real name was, nor had she ever tried to find out. "Not that a wise man argues over the name a beautiful woman wants to call him."

Alisha pulled a little smile at her coffee cup. "But a man should be accorded the respect of his name," she replied. "What should I call you, then?"

The chair creaked again as he leaned back, and an explosion of cracks sounded, his knuckles popping expansively. "Jon, I think. Today I am a Jon." Alisha could all but hear him shake his head, as dismay and gloom filled his voice. "Ah, but then the beautiful woman will write me a 'Dear Jon' letter, and my heart will be broken. But come, why do you sit with your back to me? Is that any way to greet an old friend, little bird?"

Little bird. He had called her that since the first time they'd met, long before she'd taken on the code name Cardinal. Alisha's grin became full-fledged and she finally pushed her chair back, scooting it in a half circle to Jon's table without getting out of it. Coffee sloshed onto her fingers and Jon offered her a napkin with a physical grace that reminded her of Marlon Brando in his later years. "*Grazie.* You look good, Jon. Have you lost weight?" The question was part of the ritual, too; she said it every time to flatter the man, but this time there was some truth to it. He would never be small, but he seemed slightly less mountainous than he had in the past.

"Ah, the doctors," he said with a liquid shrug that showed the same grace as offering up the napkin had. "They think my heart is strained, my knees are bad, and they make me eat only fish and vegetables. They take the joy out of life, little bird. Do not go visit the doctors."

Alisha laughed, then grimaced as her injuries protested. "Only when I have no choice," she promised. Jon's expression went wise, though his smile never faded.

"Perhaps last night you had no choice, hmm? There are

terrorist bombings in my city, and the next morning my little bird arrives at the roost to speak with me. I think it is not a coincidence, hmm?"

"You think correctly," Alisha admitted.

"You want to know who sets explosives off in hotels?"

"I think I know." Alisha hesitated, eyebrows lifted. "If you have evidence to the contrary I'd be glad to hear it."

Mirth spilled through Jon's eyes. "A businessman does not offer up such information for free, little bird. And if it is not what you come seeking, perhaps it is not what you wish to pay the price for. If not this, then why are you here?"

Alisha drummed her fingers on the table twice, then looked up. "I need to know where Frank Reichart is staying."

"You would not like it if I told Frank Reichart where you were staying," Jon said, mock-severely. "This is no lovers' spat, hmm?" His eyes narrowed, smile becoming sly. "Ah, little bird, you seek to fly beyond your cage bars, I see it now. This is why I have the pleasure of your company, and not some other fortunate fellow. Mere money will not do in this case, Alisha."

Alisha's chin came up, as much in surprise at the use of her real name as in preparation for negotiations. "You're right. I'm walking a thin line." She glanced over her shoulder at her backpack, half guilty. It was well past an hour since she'd spoken to Greg, but she'd turned the phone off, making it impossible for him to reach her. Jon saw the glance and his smile grew ever more sly.

"I think perhaps you are off the line and searching for it again, little bird."

"No." Alisha slid down a few inches in her chair, then winced and straightened again. There was no part of her that didn't ache, except the ones that actively hurt. "I know exactly where it is."

"Out of reach?"

"No," Alisha said again. "But let's say I'm not stretching for it, either."

Some of Jon's smile faded away, leaving crinkles at the corners of his eyes that could have been joy or concern. "Things have changed since last we talked, I see."

"They have." Alisha shifted in her seat, aware the small movement betrayed discomfort. She was oddly unconcerned about that. What she knew of Jon tied him directly to Europe's underworld, where he traded in information like it was cash. Sometimes it proved to be. He was a wealthy man, known for trafficking on both sides of the law, and willing to take money from either. That he survived playing the game was testimony to his skill.

And, no doubt, testimony to blackmail files on anyone who might conceivably damage him. But she trusted him enough to be fond of the nickname he'd given her, and to be unworried about showing small weaknesses in front of him. It was partly because he never lied about what he was or what he did. It was also that she had no doubt he could ferret out any secrets she wanted to keep hidden, anyway, and so playing her hand close to her chest seemed like a waste of energy around the enormous information broker.

"You will tell me how things have changed," Jon said abruptly, breaking up her thoughts. She frowned at him and he waved a hand, graceful large movement. "Not now. I see that it weighs too heavily on you now to speak of it. But someday, little bird, I will ask and you will tell me. You will tell me everything. And for this, I will find your former lover for you. Do we have an agreement, little bird?"

"I'm in a hurry, Jon."

He fluttered his fingers again, reminiscent of the little bird that he called her. "By noon, pushy child. Three hours and you will have your lover. If we have an agreement."

"Why do you want to know?" The question was purely curiosity. Jon tilted his head, almost a bow of reverence.

"Because, little bird, information is priceless." The answer meant nothing, but from this man, it might also mean everything. Alisha held her breath a moment, then nodded her head in return.

"We have a deal."

Alisha pulled the cell phone out of her hip pocket, flipping it open without turning it on again. The backpack Simone's people had given her was abandoned in the café under the reluctant gaze of the owner, whose preference was to fail to see Jon and his business associates. A handful of euros had purchased new clothes when the shops opened, from a do-rag to tuck her hair beneath to cheap tennies that she could run in, which was all that mattered. The T-shirt was larger and more shapeless than she liked them, but it didn't brush the slice on her stomach, which had begun to throb and itch. It took conscious effort not to scratch at it, and so the jeans she bought were low-cut enough to barely stay on her hips, which kept them from scraping at the lower end of the cut.

The clothes she'd been given were stuffed into the unlocked trunk of a rental car, one that Alisha hoped would drive out of the city. She hadn't found a surveillance device anywhere in the clothing, but it wasn't paranoia if they were really out to get you.

So long as the right hand didn't know what the left was doing, she was in the clear. Turning the phone on, finding whatever message had been left, would compromise that freedom. Might compromise it, she corrected herself. Boyer might give her the go-ahead to continue the mission.

Might. Alisha folded the phone closed again, and slipped into a bakery to get another cup of coffee and a biscotti. The baker's wife clucked at her, said she was too skinny, and double-dipped the biscotti in chocolate before handing it over. Alisha grinned her thanks and retreated to a table in a dim corner of the bakery to eat and think.

Her hand itched for a fountain pen and the thick parchment paper she used to write her journals on. There was no point in hunting the materials down; she never wrote the chronicles until after a mission was complete. Still, the impulse was there as a way to clear her thoughts.

After a mission was complete. Alisha stirred the biscotti into the coffee, watching the wall opposite her without seeing it. *That's the crux of the matter, isn't it, Leesh?* She wasn't sure it made much difference what the phone message said. A message from Shrödinger's cat, she thought with a quick smile. It neither confirmed nor denied her permission to complete the mission until it was listened to.

Going renegade was an ugly thought. She'd made a play at it a year earlier, to draw the Sicarii into an auction for the Attengee drones. A surprising number of people, even her own handler, had believed it was possible she'd really done so. Alisha shook her head, still watching the wall.

Her own self-perception was that she was a rule follower. In a decade of working for the Company, she'd been largely content to not always understand the bigger picture. It wasn't her preference, but she'd long since accepted that working for the greater good often had to be done on a need-to-know basis. She was pleased when she did know what the bigger picture was, and able to trust that her superiors were making the right choices when she didn't know.

Discovering the Sicarii and both Greg and Brandon Parker's involvement with them, no matter how white-washed it now appeared, had shattered much of that trust. Not necessarily because of the Parkers themselves, Alisha realized, though that was unquestionably a part of it. More, though, was that the existence of the Sicarii put a spin on the clandestine world that went outside the boundaries of what she'd known. Governments, in her experience, were involved in the world of espionage. Even known organizations like the Mafia were easy to grasp in that picture. But a group as silent as the Sicarii, whose purpose was to yank the world back into an era of god-kings and divine right, threw what she knew out of perspective. Profiteering was one thing. World domination was something else, and it unsettled her. If Frank Reichart was working toward that end, she needed to do more than just accept that. For her own sense of well-being, she had to find a way to stop it. Even if it meant going against direct orders.

The chocolate had all melted off the biscotti. Alisha took a bite of the coffee-laden bread, catching a drip before it fell to stain her new T-shirt. It didn't matter what Boyer had decided. She was going after Reichart.

Chapter 11

"The hotel security is *pssht*." A graceful wave of Jon's big hand dismissed it. "He is like you, little bird. Only when it is necessary does he step into the bright lights of expensive surroundings. He does not wish to be noticed or admired, hmm? Only forgotten. Like you," the enormous man repeated. Alisha shook her head.

"If he's like me it's because we're in the same business, Jon. Nothing more."

"Mmph." Jon's black-eyed gaze was calculating, though he dismissed the conversation again with another wave of his fingers. "There is his own surveillance in his room. A sound recorder, not visual. Very sensitive."

"I didn't ask for this much detail, Jon," Alisha said warily. "Only where he was staying."

Secrets came into the smile that rarely faded from the

big man's face. "But someday you will give me many details," he replied. "I do not like to be beholden to."

Alisha shook her head again. "I don't understand why you're interested."

"Because, little bird. There are no greater stories than love stories."

"This isn't a love story," Alisha said, and repeated it now, under her breath, as she slid a pick into the lock on Reichart's door and heard the tumblers fall open. She pushed the door open, lifting a tape recorder from which the maid's voice called, "Room service," in Italian. The recording had taken only a moment to make, and the maid hadn't yet come through Reichart's room. She wasn't meant to at all; his room was marked on her hotel map as one that wasn't to be cleaned until the guest had checked out. The woman would probably get in trouble, for which Alisha felt badly.

But not badly enough to cease operations. Alisha crossed the room to the window in a few quick steps, dropping a white-noise generator there. It sounded surprisingly like a vacuum cleaner, and would reverberate off the glass panes, making any sound that might cut through it that much harder to distinguish. Early-afternoon sunlight bounced off the fire escape outside the window, making Alisha blink as she turned away.

There was no chance the black box she wanted would be in Reichart's room. It would be stored somewhere safe, off-site, assuming he hadn't yet made the drop that would deliver it to whoever was paying him.

And that, above all, was what Alisha wanted to know. Cut off the snake's head, she thought with grim determination, and crouched beside the bedside table, rifling through newspapers there with a quick, light touch. Different American papers, in order of printing thickness. It was one of Reichart's quirks, borderline obsessive-compulsive behavior. He would keep them for weeks, turning them to the crossword pages and folding back the corners until a full quarter of the page was hidden. The habit had driven Alisha crazy. Folding the pages back usually hid half the clues, and sometimes half the puzzle, as well. She, every bit as obsessively, would fold the pages back the way they belonged in a game of endless one-upmanship.

It was as well they'd broken up. They'd be divorced by now, or one of them would've killed the other. Alisha overrode the impulse to rub the surgically hidden scar beneath her collarbone, and took a too deep breath, pushing away the memory of a bullet knocking her askew. *Breaking up* was such an innocuous phrase, disguising a world of truths.

A pair of gray sleeping shorts Alisha was certain Reichart had never worn lay tucked neatly beneath the pillow. The man was a furnace, throwing off covers until only in the coldest nights did he sleep beneath more than a sheet. Alisha had woken up from overheated nightmares more than once, buried under an entire bed's worth of blankets. But keeping a pair of shorts on hand meant that even in the worst circumstances, he'd be able to grab at least one article of clothing before bailing out the window. At night, a gun would sleep there, as well; Alisha's trained eye could see faint impressions of the weapon in the cotton fabric of the shorts, though most people would never recognize it.

Several changes of clothes hung in the closet, denim and silk, a pair or two of good slacks and some highly polished leather shoes. The very picture of a metrosexual man's wardrobe, Alisha thought, though the soft thigh-length black leather jacket that Reichart favored wasn't there. She cast a brief grin at his belongings. To her, the tidy hanging and the neat row of socks in the dresser drawer drew a picture of a man who wanted certain assumptions to be drawn. And the picture drawn wasn't necessarily an inaccurate one. Reichart was a clotheshorse, as vain about his appearance as any woman Alisha had ever known. But the very materials his clothes were made of suggested a softness about the man that was dangerously deceptive. Like pitching a panther as a house pet on its sleek black fur and rumbling purr, without mentioning the hidden tooth and claw.

Alisha finished her circuit of the room and came to lean against a small desk opposite the bed. Nothing more in the room than he might want to be found. Of course not. It would be too easy if there was a computer with an open file saying, "Here be dragons, please come visit." She smiled faintly at her own whimsy, gaze returning to the tidy stack of newspapers. It was a peculiar habit for Reichart to allow himself to keep, seeming like a single admission of neuroses that a mercenary in the spy game couldn't afford.

The thought hung in her mind, almost visible words, the rest of the world detaching from the idea. Alisha inhaled and held it, studying the concept sideways, afraid if she put too much direct thought behind it, it would evaporate. Frank Reichart was not a man to allow himself follies like the collection of old newspapers for their crossword puzzles.

Alisha crossed the room without knowing she'd done it, going through the papers again, memorizing the dates, editions and periodical titles. These ones scattered back only a week, a drop compared to some of the collections she'd seen him keep. Two copies of the *Seattle Times,* one from the previous Monday and one from the day before. The *Atlanta Journal-Constitution,* the *Minneapolis Star Tribune;* Sacramento, Boston. Alisha restacked the papers, straightening the edges, and reached for her white noise generator.

The silence as it shut down hit the small bones of her ears, raising hairs on her arms and making her overly aware of the city sounds beneath her and voices in the hotel's hallway. Greetings exchanged, the maid's thin, polite voice rising and falling with what Alisha imagined was a nod that bordered on a curtsey, and then a man's response, little more than an acknowledging grunt.

There wasn't enough clarity to be certain of the male voice, but alarm shot through Alisha's body, turning her fingertips cold and raising more goose bumps. The window locked from the inside; there was nothing she could do to fix that in the moments she had. She turned the noise generator back on, feeling static wash over her as it began to hiss, and popped the lock open. The window opened with more ease than she'd expected, for which she was grateful as she rolled out onto the fire escape and slid the pane shut behind her. The scent of rusty, sun-heated metal filled her nose as she ran a dozen steps to the nearest ladder and scrambled up, pulling a face at herself. It drove her crazy when the fleeing heroes in movies ran for the rooftops instead of the streets, but it was human nature to look down first. If it'd been Reichart approaching his room, the extra seconds might be all she needed to escape unnoticed.

She pulled herself over the edge of the roof moments later, the punctured muscle in her right biceps protesting. Alisha held her stomach taut, trying not to drag it over the building's edge, then rolled onto her back, heedless of smearing dirt on her new T-shirt and jeans. She could feel blood gathering beneath the bandage on her arm, though the shallow slice on her belly didn't seem to have reopened. "You know how to have a good time, Leesh," she muttered.

A cautious peek over the building's edge assured her that the rust on the fire escape hadn't been disturbed by her passing. She drew back a few centimeters, still watching as a window banged open beneath her and Reichart poked his head out. Alisha retreated, certain he hadn't seen her, and ran on tiptoe to the building-access door on the roof. The lock was older than she was and came open with an easy click. A moment later the door shut quietly behind her, leaving no trace of her passage across the building top.

Less than an hour later, Alisha elbowed her way into her own small hotel room and dumped newspapers and a thick, squat book onto its desk. The room was paid for in cash and the clerk was discreet enough that he hadn't required identification, exactly what she wanted. She'd paid for a full night, and taken the clerk's faint smile as acknowledgment that like most of the business's patrons, it would be pretended she actually required the room for more than an hour or two's service. Assuming no undue pressure, she had a reasonable alibi for the next twenty-four hours.

The cell phone had fallen out of the bag of papers and lay next to her elbow, accusingly silent. Alisha pressed her lips together, then pushed it aside, letting it thud back into the canvas tote. It wasn't breaking rules until she knew what the decision had been, she reminded herself. She would call in soon. As soon as she'd gone through the papers. It was a promise to herself, but Alisha didn't know if she would keep it.

She pushed a small lamp to the back of the desk so she could open the papers to the puzzle pages. Black-and-white squares and cryptic clues looked up at her, making her lift her shoulders and put her teeth together. Muscle knotted in her neck, bringing with it the memory of grumpy headaches in elementary and junior high school whenever "fun" extra credit like crosswords was handed out. Even now, twenty years later, the prospect of struggling with wordplays and inside jokes made her grind her teeth with preemptive frustration.

She would fold the pages back later. Flipping back and forth to see the clues she'd folded under would be infuriating, and she was already annoyed. Reichart had come into their relationship with the crossword habit already, Alisha reminded herself. He couldn't have chosen crosswords because she hated them. She sat down heavily, breaking the binding on the fat cheat book she'd bought along with the newspapers, and switched the lamp on. Yellow light made a weak flood over the papers.

There were patterns she remembered, numbers that Reichart was superstitious about. No, not necessarily superstitious; that had been her word. She'd teased him for only half filling out the crosswords, always starting with forty-two, whether it was down or across. "It's the answer to everything," he'd said once, with the rakish grin that got him both in and out of trouble with equal ease. There were numbers he liked because they carried cultural superstitions: thirteen, four, three; others because they were snippets of dates that were important to him. Nothing so obvious as his own birthday, but she'd watched him fill out three lines in a row more than once, the hexadecimal version of her own birthday. Another series of six numbers was, she thought, his mother's birthday. That had delighted her, though she'd never teased him with *mama's boy,* much as she'd wanted to. She scribbled letters into boxes for all the numbers she could remember, then went back and began again, using the cheat book to try to figure out the jokes and puns written into the puzzle.

Not until golden sunlight pierced the corner of her eye did she realize she hadn't moved from the table in hours. Straightening made her spine protest, and a familiar childhood headache took up residence in the back of her neck, tendrils of pain reaching toward the top of her skull. Most of the squares were filled, though she'd written the atomic weight of boron down as being "fat" and no longer cared enough to try to correct it.

She sank into a yoga pose, twisting her torso and spreading her arms, feeling muscle stretch and loosen, then rolled onto her hands and knees to arch her back dramatically in a cat pose. The worst effects of the headache receded as she came to her feet again, stretching into a sun salutation. She'd begun the practice of yoga as a teenager, and now couldn't imagine doing her job without having its ancient fundaments to strengthen and relax her body. She felt more centered, and even the idea of reapproaching the crossword puzzles didn't annoy her as much. She returned to the desk, smiling wryly at herself as she began folding the crossword pages back. *You should have done asana before starting, Leesh.*

For a few seconds, the folded-back crosswords looked like nothing more than that, newspapers with bent pages. Alisha unfocused her eyes, studying them without real focus, and suddenly the pattern became visible. She switched the papers around, puzzlelike, until three sets of two fit together, folded-back pages making a string of letters that ran from one page to another, utter gibberish. She sat down again and began copying out the letters in a hurried scrawl, her mind still only half engaged with the task. Focusing too fixedly on what she was doing would lose her the ability to do so, like walking on a high wire. It required all of her concentration and none of it at the same time; a slip was too deadly to contemplate.

There was no sense to the letters she wrote out. Alisha's mind floated as she looked down at them, a sure sign that blood sugar was low and she needed food. Gibberish; encoded. Or sheer nonsense, she warned herself, the thought feeling soft and distant. She might have made a mountain out of a molehill, seeing something in Reichart's behavior that wasn't there.

One letter replaced for another. It was a simple enough code, in view of such things; its cleverness was in breaking it up across multiple crosswords in multiple publications. Reichart's newspaper habit was too thorough to easily pick out the ones that might be carrying instructions or notes for him. Signal hidden in the noise, Alisha thought. As much as she didn't like crosswords, she knew people who enjoyed the wordplays enough to build them. The prospect of adding in hidden messages like these must have thrilled the faceless creators behind Reichart's communications.

The usual way to break this code was to take the most ubiquitous letter and assume it was *E* and work from there. Alisha rewrote her lines of letters, substituting and notating until her fingers were tired and cramped from writing. The dim pool of yellow illumination over the desk was the only light in the room, the sun long since set. Alisha looked up once, cracking her neck as she glanced to the ceiling. There was no overhead light in the cheap room, and the darkness seemed oppressive. She needed food. Alisha sighed and sank down into her chair, pressing her fingertips against her eyes tiredly. The crosswords were still encoded, even if she had the letters right. "You're out of your mind, Leesh." Her voice croaked, warning that she hadn't so much as had a drink of water in hours, and she got to her feet wearily, willing to trust the hotel water over being parched.

Leesh. The nickname hung in her mind, ringing hollowly as she turned back to the string of letters without having gotten her water. She counted out eight letters, writing the *M* she met there on a new piece of paper, and scratching it off the list. Five letters, twice each from the beginning as she scratched more out, netted her *E E,* and nineteen brought her a *T.* Another *T* at the eighth letter in. Alisha sat down again, beginning the count over and writing more quickly, her need for water forgotten.

Tyler. No fate. Les Deux Magots. Two seven ten three.

Alisha stared at the deciphered letters, thought and body both gone still and cold with surprise. The last snippet of conversation she'd held with the fat information broker came back to her, his words sounding as clearly in her mind as if he stood beside her, speaking them now.

"We do the things we do for fear, for money," Jon had said, and then his voice had gone gentle. "But most of all, we do them for love. All stories are love stories, little bird."

Alisha took the orders that her nickname broke and left the hotel room, dizzy with success and a desperate need for food.

Chapter 12

Alisha turned her phone on as she left the hotel room, grimacing as the display flooded with announcements of missed calls and messages. She ignored them and thumbed in a number, gaze focused down the street as she waited for the pickup.

After several rings a woman's voice answered with a groan. "This better be good. I'm leaving work in two minutes, and I've got a hot date waiting." The vowels were slightly stretched out, remnants of an Upper Michigan accent.

Alisha turned her wrist up before remembering she'd abandoned her watch along with the backpack of equipment Director Simone had provided for her, and grinned at the street. "It's me, E. Hot date? You? I thought you were procreating strictly by way of Stanford's sperm lab."

"Procreating's one thing. Sex is something else entirely. Do you have any idea how much trouble I'll be in if I don't report you calling me? Man, if you're not dead, you've got a lot of explaining to do, Ali. Everybody's in a froth." Her voice dropped, sly confidentiality slipping into it. "You got something I could get in trouble for?"

"Only if you get caught," Alisha promised, and the woman on the other end laughed.

"I never get caught. That's why they pay me the big bucks. Tell me what's going on, Ali. And seriously, if you don't have a real good reason for me not to, I'm gonna have to report this call to Boyer. He's been purple all day, and that's not easy for a man of his complexion."

"I swear to God I'm gonna call him as soon as I'm off the phone with you," Alisha said.

"Promise?"

Alisha took a deep breath. "Yeah."

"Do you have your fingers crossed behind your back?"

Alisha laughed. "No." She looked down at her free hand to be sure, and repeated, "No. Look, E, I cracked a code and—"

"That's my job!" Protest came through the line loud and clear, making Alisha pull the phone away from her ear a little. "What're you doing, horning in on my territory?"

"As if I possibly could, Erika. My brain is little and smooth compared to yours, and I know it."

"Okay." The technical geek sounded mollified, and Alisha grinned again. Erika had left high school at fourteen and finished a master's in mathematics by twenty-one, with what she had once airily referred to as "a year or two of headspace," between the degrees. She'd been recruited to the CIA even younger than Alisha herself, though Alisha had a year's seniority on her. "Talk fast, Ali. The guy I'm meeting is hot, *H-A-W-T* hot. Like Feynman's brain in Brad Pitt's body."

"I think I've figured out how to trace Frank Reichart's activities over the last several years," Alisha said.

"Shit," Erika said after long seconds of dead silence. "Call me back in five minutes."

The first message was from Boyer himself, his deep voice apologetic. "I'm sorry, Alisha. I can't overrule the European director's decision to move you out of her arena. This isn't a hill to die on. We'll expect you in the morning for debriefing, and you've got a 2:00 p.m. appointment with Dr. Reyes."

Alisha pulled her hand over her mouth, eyes closed as she deleted the message and listened to the next one. Greg, this time, sounding somewhere between concerned and angry. As the messages went on, the concern disappeared, leaving only anger. The last one was from Boyer again, his voice so calm it bespoke far more danger than Greg's increasingly infuriated tones. Alisha folded the phone shut for a few long moments, then lifted her chin and opened it again to place another call.

"You didn't call him, did you."

"They gave you the psychic powers to go with all the brain wrinkles?" Alisha asked. She'd stopped on a stretch of mostly deserted street, and now sank down against a cool building wall. Not the wisest action for a woman alone at two in the morning, she thought wearily, but if someone wanted to pick a fight, she wouldn't mind the release. Her head felt heavy, the headache returning just enough to be faintly bothersome, and she propped an elbow on her knees, forehead planted against the heel of her hand. "No. I didn't call him." A few strands of curling hair fell through her fingers, and she rubbed her scalp, trying to worry the headache away.

"And you want me to not tell that you called me."

Alisha snorted a faint laugh. "Don't I always?"

"Yeah, you're very consistent, you know?" The last words looped upward, trace Yooper accent returning.

"So are you," Alisha said. "You just blew off an *H-A-W-T* date for me."

"Don't remind me. Tell me about Reichart instead."

"You know how I used to bitch about his crosswords?"

"Yeah. Endlessly. I always thought if that was the worst thing you had to fight about, you guys would probably make it." Alisha could hear Erika's shrug. "'Course, then he shot you, so what do I know. What about them?"

Alisha thudded her head back against the wall, looking up at the autumn stars that glittered above the city. "I should've realized it wasn't just a quirk."

"Because *you* got the psychic powers to go along with the studly arms," Erika said. "Spit it out, Ali."

"It's where he gets his orders from. At least some of them. The code's a simple scramble, but it's cut across, I don't know, at least two papers at any given time. The one I broke was across six. The folds line up to make letter strings and then it's a replacement followed by taking the twelfth, fifth, fifth, nineteenth and eighth letters in repeating sequence until you've got the orders."

"And how the hell did you figure that out?" Erika sounded admiring, even envious. "What'd you get?"

"A weird phrase, *no fate.* I figure maybe run a cross-check on our surveillance files, see if anything comes of it."

"What else did you get?"

Alisha pulled a quick smile at the phone. "Nothing I'm telling you about." A name, she answered silently. A date, and a place.

"Alisha." Warning came into Erika's voice. "Why not?"

"Because you'd have to report it to Boyer," Alisha said with a shrug. "And this one's mine, E."

"You know you're insane," Erika said. Alisha let go another half-snorted laugh.

"Is that Dr. Reyes's professional opinion, or just your two cents?"

"Sweetheart, I don't need a shrink to tell me that you field agents are nuts. But when it comes to Reichart, you might just have a short circuit somewhere."

"I can live with that," Alisha said.

"Can you?"

"I'm going to have to." Because she'd promised herself that she would once and for all understand the secrets that Frank Reichart and the Sicarii shared. Alisha had let that promise go for too long, falling back into habit over the past fifteen months. Now she felt she was paying for her slack, caught up a second time in a layer of espionage that no one else wanted her to pursue. "Are you going to do this for me, E?"

"Dude, I just blew off a god among men because you said a couple magic words. Do you really think I'm gonna say no now?"

Alisha gave the phone a weak smile. "Thanks, Erika."

"Call me back in...what time is it? Ten. Six hours. Most of the crew's gone home, I've got all the processing power I need. I should have your boy's activities tied up with a red bow by four. And, hey, Alisha?"

"Yeah?"

"When I get fired, I'm coming to live in your apartment."

"That's okay." Alisha climbed to her feet, watching the street. "I'm never there anyway." She hung up the phone, wishing briefly that there was more activity in this small hour of the morning. Anything that would give her the opportunity to move instead of think. A gang fight would be nice, she thought wryly. As long as there weren't more than five or so of them, it'd be just the exercise she wanted.

And it would no doubt attract official attention, which she couldn't afford. Alisha turned the phone off and dropped it in a garbage can, then hailed a cab to take her away from the silent Roman streets.

Even in the small hours there were people filtering through the train station, heads ducked and shoulders lifted as they each focused on their own thoughts and destinations. Alisha paid for a ticket to Paris in cash, idly tucking a curl beneath the bandanna she'd folded over her head. A few hours and she would be—what? she wondered. Free? Untraced, at least, and in her world the two were as close to one another as they could be.

The man behind her in line was jostled forward by a tired-looking fat woman whose luggage seemed to have a mind of its own. The man caught Alisha's sleeve to regain his balance, then murmured, "Erika says sorry," in English.

Alisha heard her heartbeats counting off as she waited for the words to make sense. Then alarm contracted in her belly, shooting adrenaline through her system and sending a shard of pain through the cut.

The man gave her an apologetic smile. "There's no point in making a fuss," he said softly, still in English. Alisha's thighs clenched, preparation for a break, but there were other casual passengers standing around her. Casual to an untrained eye, at least: to Alisha's gaze there was a painfully recognizable readiness to their stances. They busied themselves with reading newspapers and searching train times, but they were all attuned to her presence and actions.

Six, no, *eight* of them, the closest five men, to counteract the superior upper-body strength she had. The outer three were women, taller and leaner than Alisha herself; runners, she thought distantly. In case she made it past the muscle. It was flattering, in a peculiar way, though she knew it wouldn't take eight agents to bring her down. It only took that many to assure she came quietly.

Alisha looked down at her train ticket and gave a tight smile. "I guess I wanted a vacation anyway."

"So what are you thinking about? I'm sure my diplomas can't have you that enthralled." Peggy Reyes spoke from the door, where she'd stood for over a minute, watching the unmoving Alisha. Ninety-three seconds, to be exact, Alisha's internal chronometer supplied silently. She'd heard the doctor come into the room and close the door, the latch clicking even though there'd been no sound of the door settling into its frame. Alisha hadn't intended to play a game of waiting it out, but wasn't eager to begin a conversation, either. She turned her head slightly when Reyes spoke, resenting the action even as she made it. She didn't want to give the psychoanalyst anything, not even so much as an acknowledgment.

Nor was she interested in drawing this out, though. The flight back to the States had been a quiet one, most of the agents dispersed once Alisha was safely on the plane. She might have disabled the pilot and stolen the plane, or simply gotten a parachute and jumped for her life, but the fire was gone from her belly. She didn't sleep, only sat at a window and watched the clouds or the flat gray ocean five miles below, thought nothing more than a distant companion. She'd played her hand and lost; it was how the game went. There was no call to be rude or violent with the agent sent to bring her back. Passive-aggressiveness was an ugly trait, and Alisha had no desire to indulge in it.

Planning, though, she whispered in the very core of her, and then put the thought away so she could respond to Reyes without distraction.

"Cristina Lamken." Alisha let her shoulders rise and fall as she spoke the name, and heard Reyes's sound of surprise as the doctor went to sit down.

"Your old partner. That's not what I expected you to say. What brings her to mind?"

"My best friend turning me in, I expect," Alisha said with another shrug. There was a high-gloss reflection of herself in the glass covering Reyes's diplomas. Too much light washed out her features, turning her into a faceless ghost that moved fluidly without giving anything of herself away.

"How do you feel about that?" Reyes's tone was perfunctory enough that it pulled a faint smile from Alisha's lips, and she turned to look at the doctor.

"Say it like you mean it, Doc."

"I'm sorry." Reyes sat forward, her hands clasped and her eyes widened in a mockery of conciliation. "How does that make you feel, Agent MacAleer?" she asked, infusing the question with syrupy tones and a lilt that was full of false interest. Alisha laughed aloud.

"That's much better." Her laughter faded and she turned back to the diplomas with a guttural, "Eh. I don't blame Erika. I mean, I'm going to kick her ass later, but I'll give her a running head start first, so she'll probably be able to MacGyver her way into kicking my ass instead. Either way, I might've done the same thing in her shoes."

"Would you have?"

Alisha watched her faceless reflection in the glass. "I have no idea. E's gone out on a limb for me before, but never when I was working directly against orders. You have to have hierarchy and rules for this kind of operation to work."

"But you decided to forgo those rules this time," Reyes said. Alisha deliberately stilled another shrug, then found herself holding her breath, as much a giveaway of her state of mind as the shrug. She let the breath go in noisy exasperation.

"I never got a chance to ask Cristina *why,*" she said after a moment of working to arrange her thoughts. "She was my best friend, and it was all a lie. I mean, the FSB—the KGB, then—recruited her when she was eleven. Everything she did in her whole life was toward the end of getting into the CIA so she could report back to her bosses in Russia. And when she was finally exposed, it seemed like there was about three minutes between her cover being blown and her dying."

"How long was it really?"

"I don't know. Days." Alisha closed her eyes momentarily. "Eight days, fourteen hours, twenty-seven minutes. And nine seconds. Between me finding out and Cris's suicide." *My life,* she thought, not for the first time, *is a series of countdowns.*

"Greg wanted to pull me from the chase," she added. "He thought I was too close to the situation. But I knew her better than anybody. Even if I didn't know her at all." Alisha huffed a laugh that had no humor in it. "I chased her over half the globe. I knew how she'd jump, where she'd twitch to, what she'd try next." Her shoulders rose and fell again, helpless shrug. "I actually got to Peru before she did. I kept hoping she'd surrender."

"And instead?"

Alisha looked over her shoulder at the doctor. "You've got to know the story."

"I'm familiar with your case history," Reyes agreed. "But I haven't heard it from you."

Alisha sighed. “And instead of surrendering or making me shoot her, she jumped off a mountain in the Andes and fell into a crevasse we couldn’t even retrieve her body from.” She closed her eyes again, remembering the tiny smile Cristina had offered her in the midst of the Peruvian night. There’d been a hundred emotions in that fragile expression, and the worst of them all had been the understanding in Cristina’s blue eyes. Regret and determination, fear and desperation, maybe even apology, but without question, there had been understanding. There were higher ideals to answer to than friendship and partnership, and when those ideals schismed as violently as the FSB’s and the CIA’s, the only way for it to end was down the barrel of a loaded gun.

The report of the Glock firing came an instant too late. Cristina had already fallen, a backward fatal dive into thin, icy air. “I had permission—orders—to terminate,” Alisha said thinly. “But I was aiming to disable. I wanted to understand why she’d done what she’d done. And instead she died, and I’ll never really get it. I’m not mad at Erika.” She lifted a hand to rub her eyes, then lowered her forehead against her fingers, as if a headache needed tending. Position of weakness, she thought wearily. Giving away too much with body language.

“I’m not mad at Erika, but I goddamn well want to understand for once and all what’s making Frank Reichart tick. You guys are probably right,” she said, lifting her head again with a sharp movement. “I probably don’t belong on any case dealing with him. I don’t have my head on straight. And the truth is that even when I was engaged to him I couldn’t get an answer out of the man to save my life. Maybe that’s why I don’t seem to be able to stop trying.”

“How many times have you let him go without getting the answers you wanted?”

"*Let* him go? Once." A blustery day in London, years ago. "Had him disappear when he'd promised he'd stay, or when I thought he couldn't escape? More than that. Does it matter?"

"It might. Why do you trust him to stay?"

"Hope springs eternal." The answer was flippant, but laced with more than a little truth. Alisha shook her head as she said it, adding, "I guess I want him to be better than he is." Just as she'd recognized; just as Brandon had recognized. "Maybe to justify my bad taste in men." She gave a thin smile to her own reflection, blocks of light making the expression ghoullike. Speaking of which, she thought, but didn't say aloud, and asked, "How's Brandon doing? Nobody on the flight could give me an update."

"Speaking of which?" the doctor asked drily. Alisha's shoulder blades pinched together as the woman echoed her own thoughts, and she didn't answer, no doubt as telling a response as words would be. "He'll be all right," Reyes said. "His father's concerned, so they're keeping him for observation for a few days. I'm sure Greg can tell you more."

"If he's still speaking to me," Alisha muttered. She heard Reyes's quiet chuckle.

"He's your handler, Alisha. I think he's under orders to be speaking to you, and even if he wasn't—" she paused significantly enough that Alisha imagined her eyebrows rising in warning "—I'm sure he's got a few choice things to say to you."

"Thanks," Alisha said. "That's very reassuring. Maybe I'll just stay hidden in here."

"I'm afraid I've got another patient in a few minutes," Reyes said with an audible grin. "I'm throwing you out to face the wolves on your own. I'll see you tomorrow, Alisha."

"Great." Alisha sighed and headed for the door. "Just great."

Chapter 13

Greg waited outside Reyes's office, leaning against the wall with his head lowered and his hands shoved into his pockets. Brandon stood like that, Alisha thought. She came up short and folded her arms over her ribs defensively, mouth thinning as she put pressure against the cut there. "I expected you to be at the airport."

"I was." Greg raised his head, tired wrinkles showing around his eyes. There was more silver in his curling hair than Alisha remembered; maybe Brandon's injuries had taken a toll on the father, as well. "They whisked you by me so you'd make your psychiatric appointment on time." He tilted his head down the hall and began walking without waiting to see if she joined him. Short of going out the third-story window, she had no choice, and that, Alisha thought, was a greater extreme than she was willing to go to just then.

Besides, she'd be going out the window onto CIA

ground anyway, and in broad daylight. That was no way to stage an escape, if escape was needed.

It only took a step or two to fall into rank next to Greg Parker. He was a small man, shorter than Alisha herself, and her stride was easily longer than his own. Today he was walking faster than usual, an outlet for anger and frustration, Alisha suspected. She let the silence ride out, sure Greg was choosing his words for greatest effect.

"You don't trust me anymore, do you?" The question was sufficiently unexpected that Alisha missed a step, looking at the dapper man by her side. "Not since China."

"Greg, I saw you there with Brandon. You lied to me about where you were and you lied to me about the Attengee program. You knew about it. You knew about the production facilities. You were even in contact with Brandon, the son you weren't supposed to have spoken to in years." Alisha caught herself as her voice rose, inhaling through her nostrils as she put her teeth together to stop the litany of accusations. "I know Director Simone provided all the paperwork for your undercover contacts with Brandon while he was working for the Sicarii, but you lied to me. How am I supposed to trust you again?"

"You lied to me, too, Alisha," Greg pointed out. "You went above my head for mission protocols and set yourself up as a free agent without telling me."

"Because by all appearances you were one of the bad guys," Alisha said through her teeth.

"And now I'm not." Greg stopped abruptly and stepped in front of her, halting her progress. "Alisha, it's our job to lie to people, but in our situation we have to be able to trust that we're telling each other the truth."

"Why is this coming up now, Greg? Why not fifteen months ago? Because Brandon got hurt? It's part of the job, and he wanted to be in on it. He wanted me in on it. I set up a situation that looked viable. It went bad. It happens."

"You didn't clear that situation with me first."

"You're too close to it." Alisha felt nasty triumph flash through her smile as she turned Greg's stance back on him. "Brandon's your son and yes, I did send him into a dangerous situation, and I don't have a problem with that. If you do, maybe you shouldn't be handling this case, either." She stepped around him and stalked down the hallway, ignoring the sound of her name being called after her. She knew it was petty to savor the tiny victory, and she should be above it.

Should, she thought, and shrugged. *Welcome to being human, Leesh.*

Boyer wanted to see her. Alisha closed the door to her Vienna apartment behind her and leaned on it, her head thumping back. He hadn't said when. Morning would be good enough, she thought. An evening at home, refamiliarizing herself with her own belongings, might even her temper out enough to make the meeting with Boyer less confrontational.

There was a lingering scent of chlorine and dust in the air, telling her that the maid service had visited while she was gone, but long enough ago that the dust had had time to resettle. The faint smell of cleaning fluids undisturbed by human habitation still rode the air. She would get used to it in a few minutes, and by morning her presence would have helped to dispel it. Alisha dropped her bag by the door, letting it fall and spill her gun, a phone, a handful of other materials, onto the polished hardwood. No scuffs, but then, there was no traffic in her house most days to mar the floors.

She left her shoes by the door and walked into the middle

of the living room, toes curled in the braided rug by a glass coffee table. She squeaked her finger over the glass, picking up a thin residue of dust, and rubbed it between her fingers as she turned around to study the room. The sofa and love seat were fashionable, big square cushions in dusty green with purple throw pillows for accents. There was an empty basket on the coffee table, meant to hold fruit. Alisha couldn't remember the last time she'd been home long enough to bother filling it. She padded to the window, pulling drapes a few hues darker than the couch open to flood the room with afternoon sunlight. Dust sparkled in the light, making her nose wrinkle.

Looking around the room left her cool and uncertain, as if she didn't entirely belong. As if she visited the apartment, rather than lived there. Even the art on the walls went with the furniture more than it had any of her personality attached to it. All except one piece, she thought as she pushed her bedroom door open. Next to the bed hung a poster of Sean Astin as Samwise Gamgee, and she gave it a silly, teeny-bopper grin the way she always did. Beyond that—

Beyond that, she didn't feel as if she knew the person who lived there at all. Alisha sat down on the edge of her bed, then turned and curled up in it, drawing a pillow over her head in hopes of blocking the world away. It was a lousy course of action, but the only one that took no thought, and she felt remote from even her own thoughts.

The feeling of displacement would pass; she knew that. There was even something of a familiarity to the distance her own thoughts seemed to be from herself. It felt not unlike moments of stillness in yoga, when everything came together and was for a brief instant clear. This was its antithesis, a holding place of silence where nothing seemed easy to understand. It could mean a dozen things, maybe nothing more profound than she was tired, or maybe that her mind was at work on a problem she wasn't ready to acknowledge yet. Alisha wrapped her arm over her pillow, and let sleep wash away the uncomfortable silence in her head.

"Alisha?"

Alisha came awake reaching for a weapon that wasn't at hand, then shoved her weight around, pivoting on her hip, to bring her leg in a broad sweep. Recognition settled in the instant before the kick connected, and she pointed her toe, slapping Erika's hamstring with the arch of her foot instead of driving her heel into the muscle hard enough to cause a charley horse. Even knowing who was there, the move finished with Alisha's fist drawn back as she came into a sitting position, a punch waiting to be thrown.

Erika skittered back toward the door, her hands lifted and her eyes wide. "Whoa, babe, it's just me, not the bad guys. Wow, what the hell was that about?"

Alisha drew in a breath through flared nostrils, her jaw set and tight: the fight impulse on waking hadn't taken into account the healing slice across her belly, and it shot needles of pain through her torso. It took a few long moments to breathe the pain away, and then to convince herself to lower her fist. She wet her lips twice before speaking, her voice rough and low from sleep. "Bad dreams, I guess. You okay?"

"Yeah. You pulled the punch." Erika looked down at her legs. "Kick. Whatever. You didn't answer when I knocked, so I let myself in. I think I'm glad you didn't have a gun." She squinted. "Why didn't you?"

"It's in my bag," Alisha muttered. She raked her hair back, pulling it into a ponytail that she had no holder for. She climbed off the bed, lips pressed together, and went into the bathroom to find one. Erika followed at a judicious distance, stopping a few steps outside the door.

"So does pulling the punch mean you're not gonna kick my Yooper ass?"

Alisha planted her hands on either side of the sink and lowered her head, watching a few curls escape the ponytail and dangle around her cheeks. "You were doing your job."

"Yeah," Erika said, "so are you gonna kick my ass, or what?"

"I don't know. You going to apologize?"

"For doing my job? No." Erika shrugged, a motion Alisha could see from the corner of her eye. "For busting my friend? Yeah. Look, I really am sorry, Alisha." She folded her arms under her breasts and shrugged again, uncomfortable. "The whole situation's a mess. Nothing was the right choice, you know?" Her vowels looped up in the last two words, accent coming through strong.

Alisha lifted her head enough to study her friend through the frame of the bathroom door. Erika wore a black leather biker's jacket that hung loose on her slender frame, theoretically adding some bulk to go with a height a couple of inches greater than Alisha's. To Alisha's eye, the oversize jacket gave Erika an aura of waifishness, making her seem a little delicate and vulnerable. Her skin was sunbrowned, freckles scattered across her cheeks, and long brown hair was lightened into paleness by summertime hiking. She wasn't as fragile as she looked, but neither would she stand a chance in an honest knock-down drag-out with Alisha.

"C'mon, Ali," Erika said in a low voice. "I'm sorry."

Alisha sighed explosively and pushed away from the sink. "Yeah, I know. How'd you find me?"

Erika twisted a smile. "I know you pretty well. You don't take planes when you're leaving a city. After you called I had a watch put on the train stations and car-rental agencies."

Alisha shook her head. "Knew I should've walked out. Damn it." The reproach was for herself, not Erika, whom she glanced at again. "I'm not pissed. I mean, I am, but it's cool. I don't blame you. Did you bring dinner?"

Relief brightened Erika's eyes. "It should be here in ten minutes. A pizza bigger than our torsos combined and enough pop to drown an elephant in."

"Elephants can breathe through their trunks," Alisha pointed out. "Haven't you ever seen pictures of them walking on the bottoms of lakes?"

"It's a lot of pop," Erika promised. "And I brought ice cream. It's melting all over your counter right now."

"What're you trying to do, weigh me down so they can't send me out again?"

"No." Erika puffed her cheeks out. "I figured you wouldn't have much food here, and we're going to need it."

"Why?"

Erika crooked a smile. "I might've turned you in, Ali, but I'm not a total jerk. I brought everything I could dig up on Reichart. I mean…" She lifted an eyebrow curiously. "You're not just gonna let him go, right?"

Alisha felt a grin start to spread over her face, like a black dog leaving her shoulders. "Shit no, I'm not. You're the light of my life, E. All is forgiven."

"Yeah?"

"No," Alisha said, grinning more widely, "but between pizza and soda and some good old-fashioned paper-shuffling, I'm willing to consider it. Show me what you found, Mighty Brain." She shooed Erika out of the bedroom and sprawled on the living-room couch as the tech geek went into the kitchen to put the ice cream in the freezer.

"Why am I doing this?" she asked as she went. "If I'm the Mighty Brain, that should make you the Mighty Brawn, and you should be doing the grunt work."

"Consider it penance," Alisha suggested.

"You're not going to let me live this down, are you?"

"Not until I've got all the answers I want," Alisha said.

"Dude, that could take years."

"Better get used to paying the piper, then." Alisha sat up and reached for Erika's laptop, which was propped in the fruit bowl. "Your keyboard's locked. What's the password?"

Erika gave her a look of such utter disbelief that Alisha laughed aloud. "What? You don't trust me?"

"I do system administration for fun, Ali. I don't trust anybody with my passwords."

"I spy on people and steal things for a living," Alisha said cheerfully. "Who else are you going to trust?"

"I've gotta get a new set of friends," Erika mumbled. "The kind who don't think obtaining my confidential information is fun."

Alisha held up one finger, then another. "First, you'd be bored with friends like that. Second, not until I've gotten all your confidential information on Reichart, anyway."

"All right, fine." Erika took the laptop away and typed in her password, then jumped up as the doorbell rang and went to pay for the pizza. Alisha grinned and shook her head no as Erika looked at her in hopes of getting cash.

"Pizza was your idea, babe. Besides…"

"Yeah, yeah, I owe you." Erika paid, grumbling without rancor, and Alisha relaxed into the couch with a sigh, feeling more comfortable with the good-natured banter and in her own apartment than she had earlier that day. There was an itch under her skin, like a promise that a course of action would be settled on, and soon.

The only thing left to see, Alisha whispered to herself, was whether her course of action would be in line with the CIA's.

Chapter 14

"I expected you yesterday afternoon, Agent MacAleer."

"I know, sir. I'm sorry." Alisha's apology was perfunctory and she made little effort to inject it with sincerity. Boyer flicked an eyebrow up.

"Most people at least try to sound cowed when they've been called on the carpet, Alisha." There was no trace of amusement in Boyer's smooth, deep voice or in his dark eyes, but Alisha thought she sensed a hint of humor in his overall demeanor. She chose not to play on it, in case she was wrong, and instead spread her hands slightly.

"Yes, sir." She'd gone to some trouble that morning to dress for battle, wearing black slacks and a burgundy shirt so dark it bordered on black itself. The colors of war, she thought: red and black. She even wore heels to help erase the height difference between herself and the man who was her superior. The result had been startling when she'd walked past Greg, finding herself all but towering above him rather than the usual two-inch advantage she had. He'd pulled his shoulders back, straightening, as if an additional three inches of height on his protégé was a personal challenge.

The few inches the heels lent her made less difference with Boyer, whose six feet of height was still well out of Alisha's range, even in heels. Still, half of any fight was in the mind, and Alisha at least felt prepared for one. "I was in no condition to talk with you yesterday afternoon, sir. I apologize if I inconvenienced you."

"Dr. Reyes didn't mention that you were distraught after your session."

Alisha lifted an eyebrow, settling into parade rest, her hands folded behind her back. "What did she say, sir?" There was no point, she thought, in giving away more than she had to. Anything she could learn that Reyes said would help her in playing out the situation with Director Boyer.

"That you internalize emotion very well," Boyer said, and a thread of amusement did come through that time. "That the Reichart situation stems partly from a lack of resolution with Cristina Lamken."

"Frankly, sir, I could've told you that without a shrink's intervention." Could she have? Alisha wondered. Maybe. It had certainly sounded plausible enough when she discussed it with Reyes.

"She further recommends you be removed from the case." Boyer went on as if Alisha hadn't spoken, but his words drew her into a more formal stance, her chin lifting as her shoulders tightened. "She suggests a vacation might be in order."

"When a psychoanalyst says vacation, she means involuntary relief from duty until further notice, sir." Alisha focused on the wall beyond Boyer and spoke crisply, as if doing so would force the idea out of his mind.

"I'm aware of that, Agent MacAleer. I'm also aware that last time you were sent on vacation like that, you ended up locating and nearly engaging Frank Reichart."

Alisha's gaze snapped back to Boyer, betraying the complete surprise that swept through her and raised cold goose bumps on her arms and neck. "Sir?"

"We *are* the CIA, Alisha," Boyer said a trifle wryly.

Alisha tightened her hands together behind her back and returned her focus to a point somewhere behind Boyer. "For what it's worth, sir, I was not looking for Reichart at that time. It was coincidence that I encountered him."

"Do you really expect me to believe that?"

Cold washed through Alisha again, this time carrying the icy burn of anger. She felt that burn rise in her cheeks, bringing color with it, and knew her mouth thinned as she said, "I don't give a shit whether you believe it or not, sir. It's true."

Boyer barked out a laugh that made Alisha flinch, though she tried to hide it. "You think you've got nothing to lose, don't you, Agent MacAleer?"

"Am I wrong, sir?"

"What would you do if you weren't an agent, Alisha?"

A pinpoint of nausea stung in Alisha's stomach and grew rapidly, taking her breath and, it felt like, her will to live away with it. The grip she held her hands in slipped, muscle turning watery at Boyer's unexpected question. Alisha abandoned all pretense of formality and stared at the director, trying to swallow away the sickness that lodged in her throat. "Sir?"

"What would you do if you weren't an agent for the Central Intelligence Agency?" Boyer repeated.

"Sir, I…" It felt as if someone had removed the top of her skull and replaced it with air, making her so light-headed that she might easily float away, like a child's escaped balloon. Alisha was afraid to look down, for fear that her feet would have left the floor and she would find herself adrift. The act of simply standing was difficult; she thought she must be swaying, like a tall building in the wind. The muscles in her neck felt stiff and creaky from holding still, an attempt to hide that rocking from Boyer. Her throat was too tight to make words properly. "I have no idea, sir" came out as a dry whisper.

"It's a question you should consider," Boyer said, "before you make any rash decisions about what to do during the next two weeks while you're suspended from active duty. You've had your second chance. I'm assigning someone else to the Firebird case. For what it's worth, I'll attempt to have Reichart brought in long enough for you to obtain some closure in that arena. You're too good an agent to lose, but this cannot go on."

"Reichart's not the sort you bring in, sir," Alisha whispered hoarsely. "He comes to us with information and a price, you know that." She could feel her chest and ribs expanding and deflating as she breathed, but no air seemed to be coming through. There was a knot of pain replacing her lungs, denying every breath its rightful place. What she said about Reichart didn't matter; it was only a way to fill up silence and try to break through the heady feeling of detachment from her own body. Her fingers were cold. She could feel that, distantly, but it seemed meaningless. Everything seemed meaningless. What *would* she do, if she wasn't an agent?

"I suppose I'd actually become a yoga teacher," she added numbly. Speaking the idea aloud sounded flat and lifeless, like the promise of a lifetime's imprisonment. Something regretful darted through Boyer's expression.

"I'll do my best with Reichart," he said. "You're dismissed, Agent MacAleer. You'll be assigned desk duties until further notice." Boyer gave her a brief nod and went around to the other side of his desk, settling into his chair as Alisha gathered herself and turned for the door. Her reflection caught in the door's glass window, red and black. A thin strain of music played in her mind, the matching words coming unbidden:

Red, the color of desire; black, the color of despair!

Alisha tapped on the door to Erika's fishbowl—a glass-encased office lined with so many computers that the actual fishbowl effect was greatly diminished—and went in without waiting for an invitation. Erika, bent over a tiny processing chip with a sparking soldering iron in hand, lifted one finger in acknowledgment and warning. Alisha sat down in a chair that wheeled a few inches back with her weight, and watched a fractal screen saver on one of the computer screens while she waited. There was a faint scent of burned ozone in the air, combined with the thrum of multiple computers running.

Air-conditioning in the fishbowl was always at full blast, and two oscillating fans swept back and forth, tired-out ribbons flapping from them. It was still hot in the room, probably explaining Erika's penchant for a working outfit that consisted of a sports bra and biking shorts. Hanging from the side of one computer monitor were three different professional outfits, all of them carefully pressed and ready for wear. They were Erika's compromise for situations when she had to give presentations and look reliable. The rest of the time, she said, she was paid for her brains, not her fashion sense, and the dress code could go hang itself. So far her gadgetry knack and computer skills had overcome the resistance to her style. Alisha imagined she would find another job, if she wasn't given her dress-code perks, and suspected that the CIA had come to the same conclusion.

A yoga teacher. Alisha tilted her head back far enough to stare at the fluorescent lights gridded into the ceiling. Erika's intellect might not be replaceable, but Alisha's superior upper-body strength certainly was. A yoga teacher, she thought again, and bit her lower lip.

"Arright." Erika pushed her soldering glasses up on her forehead, catching a floppy 1980s wave of too-long bangs in the plastic lenses. "What's up? You look—" She took in Alisha's posture, slumped in the chair, and turned the iron's heat off. "You look awful."

"They took me off the case." Alisha was surprised at how calm her voice sounded, the cool remote that still lingered inside her coming through in the words.

"Oh. Oh, shit, Ali. Are you okay? You knew it might happen."

"Mmm." Alisha slid her gaze from the lights to the top of the window frames without really seeing them. "I knew it might, but that's not all that much like having it really happen."

"Are you okay?" Erika repeated.

Alisha pressed her lips together and returned her regard to Erika, whose forehead was wrinkled in concern beneath the edges of her protective glasses. "I'm on desk duty. Until the Firebird case is resolved. Maybe longer. I stopped by my desk to look at my schedule. I've got a meeting with Reyes every day for the rest of the month. And more paperwork than I thought I'd ever generated."

"Yeah, whatever." Erika pushed away from the chip she'd been working on, chair wheels creaking as she rolled across the room. "Are you *okay?*"

"I'm…you know," Alisha said slowly, "I think that pretty soon here I'm going to be really pissed off."

Erika flashed a little grin. "Pissed off's better than sulking."

"I'm not sulking," Alisha said instantly. "I'm just… cold." She could feel the chill of shock starting to flake away, though, uncovering sparks of anger. "I either take desk duty or I'm out."

"Jesus, Ali. I'd say you always wanted a nice safe desk job, but I know better than that. You field agents have got a screw loose. All danger all the time. What *is* it with that?" she added rhetorically. Alisha pulled a faint smile.

"You get addicted to the adrenaline," she admitted, "but it's mostly that it's a job I'm good at, and somebody has to keep people safe. My sister's got three little boys."

"So you're doing it for the kids?" Erika teased. Alisha managed another smile.

"You could say that. I like the idea of making the world a better place to live in. I think that's what I'm doing."

"I just like making cool shit and getting paid for it," Erika said with a grin, but then her smile faded. "What're you gonna do, Ali?"

"I'm going to go to my desk, and I'm going to do my job, and I'm going to go see the doctor at two o'clock like a good girl." Alisha spread her hands and gave a helpless shrug. "What else can I do?"

"What about the stuff we—"

"It doesn't matter," Alisha said with brittle clarity, overriding Erika's question. Erika's eyebrows rose, shifting the safety glasses on her forehead. Then she pursed her lips, one corner curving up skeptically.

"Right. Arright. Good luck with that, then, eh?"

"Yeah. Look, if they'll unchain me from the desk you want to have coffee tomorrow morning?"

"I can't make our usual coffee break," Erika said with unusual precision. "I probably won't see you until at least lunch." Alisha's eyebrows wrinkled curiously as she met Erika's too-guileless gaze.

"Oh." The word came slowly, as did the lie that followed it a moment later: "Well, I've got a lunch date off-site. Maybe afternoon break?"

"Mmm." Erika dropped a nod that said she was in on a conspiracy. Alisha turned away with a quirky smile, not quite daring to follow her own thoughts to fruition.

"Hey, Ali."

"Yeah?" Alisha looked back and twitched her hand up into the air to catch a glittering silver pin from the air. She turned her palm up, studying its beveled edges and the red stone set in mesh at its center. Eyebrows raised quizzically, she looked at Erika, who shrugged a shoulder.

"Experimental communication system. I've got the other one. In case your car breaks down when you're out at lunch. You know. Just in case."

Alisha felt a crooked smile grow as she lifted the pin and murmured, "Thanks."

Ninety minutes later a breathless Karen Buckner, armed with a briefcase of paperwork, was the last person to board an early transatlantic flight to London.

Chapter 15

She changed planes and passports twice before coming into Paris, using an Agency-issued passport as ID to rent a sports car in Stockholm. She tossed the keys to a sleepy-looking youth in line behind her and made her way to the nearest bathroom without waiting to see his reaction.

The third passport was an illegal one, a thought that always made Alisha grin, even in the midst of jet lag. It wasn't Agency-issued, nor was the name on it—Mona Bryers—on Alisha's list of known aliases. She exited the Stockholm airport restroom a coppery redhead, a far more distinctive color than her own tawny locks, but the color was one her skin tones could pull off believably. Contacts altered the shade of her eyes to grayish blue, lighter and more striking than her usual color. Alisha MacAleer dressed well without being over the top; Mona Bryers flaunted what she had with push-up bras and plunging necklines. Her makeup was subtle, stressing her cheekbones and the strength of her jaw until she appeared far more angular than she really was. That, combined with the lyrical accent that went with Mona's Welsh homeland, would distract most people from lesser details like actual facial structure and height.

She flounced through customs on both ends with a wave of her passport, blessing the European Union's open-border policy. It made traveling through the Union countries easier; especially it meant avoiding any lingering inspection by the security cameras. As a spy, that was an inevitable bonus, but when it was her own government she was trying to avoid, Alisha was even more grateful for it. The thought made her shiver uncomfortably as she disappeared into the turmoil of the Charles de Gaulle airport. Being circumspect was a matter of course in her job, but she'd never gone so deliberately AWOL. Even fifteen months ago when she'd apparently turned mercenary, it had been with Director Boyer's blessing. This—

This would cost her her job. Alisha pushed the thought away with an imperceptible shrug. There was no point dwelling on it; she'd made her decision. *You made it days ago, Leesh,* she told herself as she stepped out into the October morning and raised her hand to hail a cab. *You've just been dancing around the inevitable since then.*

Six hours until Reichart's rendezvous. Six hours in which she could make certain she hadn't been tailed, before she faced her former fiancé and got all the answers she'd let slip through her hands. Until then it was simply a matter of going unnoticed.

Alisha ducked into a taxi, slipping on an oversize pair of sunglasses to help further disguise her from the vehicle's onboard camera. That form of surveillance always made her twitchy, though she appreciated the reasons behind it. Better for the cabbie—and the company—to be able to give a physical description of someone who injured their drivers than not, but for a woman looking to avoid contact with any authority figures, it was just another way of getting caught. At least the tapes weren't typically reviewed except in cases of emergency.

"Jardin du Luxembourg," she murmured to the cab-driver, and turned her attention out the window, letting body language say she wasn't interested in gossip. The park was a matter of blocks from Reichart's rendezvous point, a sixty-acre tourist attraction too full of people for any one woman to stand out. It would more than do as a place to disappear into the city, and would allow her to approach Reichart's meeting place as one visitor among many.

No fate. Alisha mouthed the words, tapping a finger against her briefcase. The late night over cold pizza and pop had been successful, though it had taken cross-references and Erika's punch-drunk suggestion of a thesaurus to begin pulling up hits on the phrase. *Fate* was often replaced by *destiny* in news references and files that touched time and time again on humanist philosophies. On man's ability to forge his own future, predestination a relic of the past. The idea, Alisha thought sourly, fit Reichart well. He'd certainly made a profit off chiseling a niche as a mercenary in the espionage world.

But there was a pattern to be found in the articles and stories. A pattern that very few people would be able to see, Alisha thought, without knowing Reichart's movements over an extended period of time. Even she had to go back years in order to establish it, back to their engagement, when she'd often known where he'd be going. With a glance at the rearview mirror to make certain the cabbie paid her little mind, Alisha opened up her briefcase and bent a folder wide enough to scan its contents.

One article had been the anchor for the pattern she'd found. Alisha remembered the mission specifically: a trip through war-torn West Africa into malaria-ridden Ghana. Reichart had grumbled bitterly about the variety and intensity of shots he'd been given in order to stave the disease off. Alisha recalled the instinct to ask him not to go, and even now, years later, it made her smile briefly at the pages she read. She'd quashed the impulse, of course: she would no more have asked Reichart to give up a mission than he'd have asked her to. Not that it mattered, because they both answered to higher powers, and their duty lay beyond the borders of safety. It had added an intensity to their lovemaking, not just that night, but many nights, knowing each time it might easily be the last.

Alisha lifted her eyebrows, glancing out the cab window with another brief smile. Erika had rightly called her an adrenaline junkie. Her relationship with Reichart had been built under pressure. It was a wonder it had lasted as long as it had.

It was a CIA job that he'd gone in on that time, illegally delivering weapons. Had the media not been firmly in the government's pocket, that might have been a story in itself. Instead, the story came weeks later, the World Health Organization reporting a drastic drop in the malaria outbreak. Inoculations that had been impossible to finance had arrived, barely in time to prevent an outbreak from becoming a plague. Barely, but just. It was the kind of massive gesture that governments promised but rarely came through with, and the WHO had no one to thank but anonymous benefactors.

Alisha glanced into the folder again, not really seeing

words that she'd already read half a dozen times on the airplane. A similar story had emerged in Colombia after an earthquake, villages and cities in ruins. Reichart hadn't been in the CIA's employ that time, his smile wicked and cheerful as he stole a kiss before loping to his helicopter. "The money's good," he'd said. That was early enough in the relationship that Alisha hadn't realized how regular an answer that would be to why he did the things he did. She believed—without basis, perhaps—that he wasn't running drugs or illegal weapons on those ventures, at least not unsanctioned illegal weapons. That mission had been a drug bust, in fact, bringing down an Argentine drug lord. Reichart had been hired for his familiarity with the countryside. American-born to an Argentine mother, he'd spent long stretches of his youth in the South American country. He'd never said so directly, but Alisha thought it was where he'd learned fighting and had decided on his mercenary career.

"I don't answer to ideals, Leesh." She remembered his statement clearly, partly because she'd never been able to determine what it was that his voice held. Not contempt or mockery; those were too cruel, and regret too soft. Alisha had wondered a time or two if it was envy she heard in the words, that she could put her faith in something that Reichart could not. "I answer to the money. That's all."

But there was a series of serums available after the Colombian earthquake, vaccines against typhoid and malaria, pills for purifying water, that the Red Cross couldn't account for. They were tested, proved safe and used gratefully.

In disaster after disaster, desperately needed goods, from food to medicine to rough tents for housing, arrived without warning or explanation. Erika had searched CIA files and the Internet alike, pulling up cross-references to unexpected, unaccounted-for goods and materials showing up when and where they were most needed. Very rarely were those stories newsworthy on a global or even national scale. Most of the time the recipients were grateful without wanting to ask questions.

The missions Alisha knew about more often than not didn't bring Reichart anywhere near the affected areas, but there were enough close calls to raise a flag. And none of those miraculous deliveries were claimed by any governmental body. Like terrorism in reverse, Alisha thought, not for the first time, and still without any answers. It took organization to provide that kind of support. Once or twice could be coincidence, but this was repeated all over the world.

No fate, Alisha mouthed again, and closed her briefcase, turning her gaze to watch the city slide by. The files brought a pattern to light, but that pattern only made more questions. She thanked the cabbie in French and tipped him, then made her way through the gardens, enjoying the admiring glances thrown her way. It felt absurdly free, tossing copper curls over her shoulders and putting a little extra swing in her step. She was playing a part again, of course, but it was a part wholly of her own choosing this time. There would be a price to pay for it, she thought, but not yet. Not yet.

Les Deux Magots. The café was another tourist point in Paris, an establishment peopled by Hemingway and Sartre, in their day. Not, Alisha thought, the sort of place she imagined Reichart to hang around at—which made it an excellent meeting place. Besides, like the Luxembourg gardens, tourists and students filled the area year-round, making anyone unobtrusive. The outdoor tables under the green-trimmed awnings were the most popular, allowing anyone to watch the city scurry by while enjoying a cup of coffee.

Two seven ten three. Twenty-seven October, 3:00 p.m. Alisha trusted the *p.m.* part of the message to be implicit—the Magots was open late, as was almost every Parisian café, but three in the morning struck her as unlikely. Her arrival at the Magots' rival across the street was just long enough before three that Alisha had time to settle in and order coffee. Fingers curled around an oversize mug, it occurred to her that Reichart and his contact might opt for the clean, well-lighted place within the Magots' walls, and put her troubles to no good end.

Did he stand out in a crowd, Alisha wondered a moment later, or was it just long familiarity with the man that made her eyes go to him when dozens of others thronged about him? The brief hitch in his step from the knife she'd put in his thigh was the only thing extraordinary about him. Certainly nothing in his clothing was unusual, especially in Paris: the soft black leather jacket, the jeans still black enough to be new. It was his usual costuming, an avant-garde James Dean, but as always, it drew her eye. Alisha was as familiar to Reichart as he was to her, and he would be sensitive to anyone's gaze resting on him too intently.

A sandy-haired man sitting by one of the Magots' windows raised a hand briefly, and Reichart worked his way through the tables with a nodded greeting, dropping into one of the cream-colored chairs.

Facing Alisha.

She lowered her head slowly over her coffee cup, hiding a smile in the mug, and glanced up again over the tops of her sunglasses, watching the men. They sat next to each another, though the adjoining chairs had a man's shoulder-width between them. It allowed them to both sit with their backs to the building, excusing the seating arrangement that was more feminine in nature than masculine. Alisha pushed her sunglasses up and watched from the corner of her eye, taking in their body language as she studied the quick phrases formed by their lips. Distance ate the sounds, but she'd expected that, preferring to risk errors in lipreading than coming close enough to Reichart's sphere of influence to be noticed.

I'm meeting her at the cathedral at six. Reichart, expression sly, as if he was planning a seduction. The other man—Tyler—lifted an eyebrow.

Is that wise? The gig's gone sideways.

I can pull it out, Reichart answered, easy confidence obvious even with the words unheard. *And if I can't, it's my own neck, no one else's.*

A faint, unamused smile graced Tyler's expression. *Don't forget there are other people counting on you. You're supposed to be in Korea in three days.*

Have I ever let you down?

The look Tyler shot at Reichart was sharp, making the dark-haired man's mouth thin in irritation. *Leave her out of it.*

As soon as you do.

Korea. Reichart spat the word with enough venom in it that Alisha imagined she could hear it. *Can you give me details?*

Tyler shook his head. *They're still murky. The cover is the usual. Weapons.* He tilted his chin down as he said the word, clearly lowering his voice. Reichart allowed himself a sigh.

Just what that part of the world needs. More guns.

Just what any part of the world needs, Tyler said. *You'll be there?*

I always am. Reichart got to his feet, tossing a few euros on the table despite not having ordered.

All right. Fas infitialis, Tyler replied. Reichart nodded once, short action, and left the table.

Fas infitialis. Alisha squinted at the words, repeating the shape of them behind the rim of her cup before she sipped. If she'd read the words correctly, they had to be Latin, but she didn't know their meaning.

I'm meeting her at the cathedral at six. There was only one cathedral in Paris. An interception after Reichart's meeting would afford the opportunity to have any number of questions answered. Alisha cocked an eyebrow at her drink, pleased with the reconnaissance, and settled back to watch traffic. Tyler left the Magots after another twenty minutes, and Alisha ordered a second cup of coffee before finally standing to leave the rendezvous point in search of a pay phone. They were becoming ever more scarce with the popularity of cell phones soaring, but she preferred that the call she placed to the Roman café she'd waited at two mornings earlier be unattached to any phone she might potentially be associated with.

"Tell Jon the little bird has left her cage," she murmured in Italian to the man who answered, and gave the pay phone's number before hanging up. Two days since Rome. It seemed longer.

It took less time than she'd expected for the enormous man to call back, his jovial voice filled with curiosity. "This is most unusual, little bird."

"I know." Alisha's words were an apology. "I need help, Jon. I need gear and I need it from someone with no inconvenient loyalties."

"When?"

"By tonight."

Jon's laughter was rich and surprised. "You ask for a great deal, little bird."

"I know," Alisha said again. "I'll owe you one, Jon."

"You already do," he reminded her. "You will owe me

a great deal. Be ready for me to call it in, little bird. Go to this address," he added smoothly, giving her a street name and number. "Tell them you are a friend of Marco's. If you are asked how he is, tell them he says the wine is sweet, the women warm and that the old man sleeps as yet."

Alisha repeated the phrase back, then took a deep breath. "I owe you, Jon."

"Yes," he said too mildly. "You do. Goodbye, little bird."

Chapter 16

The healing cut across her belly left no room for acrobatics unless her life depended on it. It was a shame, too: Notre Dame's vaulted ceilings loomed high and dark. The temptation to hide in the lofty rafters and scale one of the enormous stone pillars that supported the building's great weight was high, and not just for the concealment, Alisha freely admitted. There was an inordinate amount of sheer drama attached to the idea of slipping down one of the columns, spiderlike as she crept around the width of the pillars, using shadow to hide herself from prying eyes.

Realistically, it was a bad idea anyway. She, like most people, had cast her gaze upward upon entering the massive cathedral, looking into those shadows simply because they were there. There was no sense hiding in such plain sight.

And so she hid in even plainer sight, knelt at a pew near the back of the church. Even in the cathedral lighting she wore her oversize sunglasses, and she'd tied an expensive silk kerchief over her head, drawn forward enough to blur the line of her cheek and jaw. A fold of fabric dipped over her forehead, and a riot of copper curls spilled out the back of the kerchief. Even to Reichart's knowing gaze, she ought not be recognizable, and the tourist groups would likely keep her unnoticed regardless.

His off-gait pace caught her eye among the throngs, and *faker* popped into her head clearly enough she was afraid she'd said it aloud. Reichart's movements were stiff and slow, the limp in his left leg far more pronounced than it had been that afternoon. She could see it in the deliberation of his steps, as if he counted an extra breath while moving the lame leg. Most people wouldn't see it. Why the act, she wondered. Who would be impressed—or distressed—by his injury?

Another woman. Of course. Alisha's smile faded as she watched him settle stiffly into a pew halfway down the cathedral from her. A woman with precisely held shoulders and pale blond hair beneath a drinking-and-praying hat sat one row back and a good ten feet away from Reichart as he adjusted his hurt leg against the hard wood. The cathedral, meant for carrying sound, picked up nothing of what Reichart said, nor the woman's murmured answers, though Alisha could see the subtle movements of Reichart's lips as he spoke quietly to her.

The woman turned her head slightly, making Alisha catch her breath in hope, then let it out again in a soundless laugh of frustration. The hat—which was magnificent, brown felt and decorated by a long feather spotted with red at the quill end—was also veiled, more than one layer of mesh cupping the woman's face all the way past her chin, so her features were thoroughly obscured. As effective as Alisha's own sunglasses and scarf, but much more elegant, Alisha thought. She felt a brief flash of amused jealousy at the other woman's fashion sense, then turned her attention back to Reichart, watching to see if any emotion might flicker across his profile and betray him.

Instead he slipped something from the inside pocket of his soft leather jacket and set it on the pew beside him, slight and subtle movements meant to go unnoticed. Then he got to his feet, more awkwardly than Alisha had ever seen him move, and limped forward to the front of the cathedral, where he knelt and lowered his head in evident prayer.

The woman was on her feet a moment later, pausing very briefly to pick up the package Reichart had left and to slip it into her purse. The rest of her outfit was as smashing as the hat: a brown tweed fitted jacket and pencil skirt, with laced-up leather granny boots on her feet. She looked like a forties movie star, Veronica Lake or Ingrid Bergman, her face carefully obscured so that adoring fans wouldn't accost her in a holy place. As dramatic in its own way, Alisha thought ruefully, as playing spider from the ceilings would be.

She stood up from her own pew, walking toward the front of the church in hopes of passing the blonde and getting a better glimpse of her face through the veils, but the woman turned toward the altar, as well. There were small doors to other rectories on either side of the main hall, and the blonde stepped through one of those before Alisha, unwilling to hurry and draw attention to herself, came anywhere near catching up.

Reichart, though, didn't move, and Alisha grinned as she came to the front of the cathedral and knelt a few feet away from him. "Exchanging lovers' notes?" she asked, voice pitched to carry no farther than the man beside her.

There was no gratifying flinch this time, but Alisha saw

a ripple of tension flow through his shoulders before he glanced her way. His gaze darkened, candlelight from dozens of vigil candles suddenly narrowed away from his eyes. She could almost see him choosing what volley to open with, and when it was a neutral "The red suits you," she fought back laughter.

"How much did that cost?" she wondered aloud, and let herself smile at him. "Why don't we take a walk, darling? We've got a great deal to talk about."

The pronounced limp didn't fade from Reichart's steps as they exited the cathedral. Alisha took it as a warning that they were likely being watched, and stayed several feet behind the man, disassociating herself from him. He wouldn't run, she trusted that for two reasons. First, exaggerated limp or not, the stab wound in his thigh would guarantee she could outpace him. Second, and perhaps more importantly, she'd tilted her purse to show him the gun she'd obtained from Jon's friends. Reichart had smiled tightly and agreed to a walk.

His stride lengthened as he went around a corner two blocks farther on. Alisha chuckled beneath her breath and caught up with him in a few running steps, offering a bright sunny smile that made his jaw tighten. "My place or yours, Frank?"

He shot her another look that made Alisha's smile broaden. "Yours it is. Shall I hail a cab?"

"What the hell are you doing here, Alisha? I thought you got recalled to D.C." Even angry at her, he was cautious with his words, leaving *Langley* hanging in the air unspoken. Alisha shrugged easily and lifted a hand to flag down a taxi.

"I was, but I decided to take a walk." She turned back to

find Reichart staring down at her in open surprise. The naked emotion looked good on him, lightening the brown of his eyes and taking some of the lines from his face until he looked younger than his years. "I'll tell you about it at the hotel," Alisha said more quietly. "We've got a lot to talk about."

"I thought that was my line," Reichart said after a moment. Alisha twisted a quick smile.

"Maybe if I'm delivering it I'll be more willing to listen." A cab drew up and Alisha opened the door for her dark-haired companion, gesturing him in and climbing in after him. She'd be more willing to listen, she vowed, because this time she had enough information to get real answers out of the man.

Best intentions aside, they were silent in the cab beyond Reichart's gruff instructions as to where to drive. Alisha watched the cabbie slide curious glances at them in the rearview mirror, a spark of mischief in his eyes suggesting he believed them to be quarrelling lovers. Close enough, she decided, and gave the man a thin smile in the mirror. He brought his gaze back to the road, looking ever more secure in his knowledge about them.

The hotel was of a better quality than she'd expected, Alisha giving it a startled look as she climbed out of the cab. "Paying in euros, are they?" she murmured, and Reichart shot her a dark look.

"You can get the cab," he said shortly, and limped into the building while Alisha paid the fare.

A bellboy in the elevator prevented them from speaking still further, though they watched each other warily in the polished steel of the elevator walls. There was an absurdity to it, their silence so ritualized and full of weighty expectation that Alisha wanted to laugh, though she kept her features schooled. Not until Reichart keyed his door open and she followed him inside did either of them speak, and then it was at the same time.

"How's the thigh?"

"How's that cut?"

Alisha did laugh, the finger-thickening tension she felt disrupted by the questions. Laughter made the cut on her belly protest and she put a hand over it, still smiling. "Hurts. Could be worse. You?"

"I've spent the last two days wondering if you meant to hamstring me and missed or if you weren't trying to permanently cripple me."

Alisha's laughter fell away. "You got lucky. I wasn't trying to hamstring you, but that knife wasn't meant for throwing."

"You picked up any horrible blood diseases I should know about?" Reichart limped to the room's tiny refrigerator and pulled out a six-pack of glass-bottled beers, arching an eyebrow toward Alisha as he lifted one. She raised a hand and he tossed it to her in a smooth arc across the bed. Alisha tapped on the bottle top as she shook her head.

"I forgot my blood was on it. But no, bill of health came back all clear. What the hell were you doing there, Frank?"

"That's twice." Reichart sat down on the bed, still moving much more fluidly than he had in the cathedral, but stiffer and more awkward than Alisha was accustomed to seeing him. "You must really want something."

Alisha took a seat, as well, pulling a well-padded chair away from the round table in the room's corner. She kept the purse open and at hand, the gun easily available, knowing that Reichart would watch her for a slipup. "You know, I was never sure if you'd noticed that."

"It's my job to notice, Leesh. You only call me Frank when you're trying to butter me up, or when you're furious with me. I'm not getting lividity off you right now." He dug into his coat's pocket, coming up with a bottle-opening key chain. His beer let off a *fssht* of escaping carbon dioxide as he popped the lid, and condensation wafted from the bottle top. Alisha put her hand out and he tossed her the key chain. Two keys, one a safety-deposit box key, the other for a vehicle. Unmarked, but at a guess Alisha thought it probably belonged to an Audi. She cranked the top off her own beer, holding it away from her lap in case it spilled thanks to its journey through the air, then flicked the key chain back onto the bed.

"Pissed doesn't begin to cover it," she admitted then. "I'm so many things I don't have names for half of them anymore."

"How about you start with you deciding to take a walk?"

Alisha looked up sharply. "Don't fool yourself, Frank. This isn't your interrogation."

"Of course it is." Reichart shifted and winced, an action Alisha was all too familiar with in the past few days. "You want to interrogate me, so it's my interrogation."

"Christ, but you're a pain in the ass. What were you doing in Rome, Frank?"

"You'll tell me why you walked?"

"Reichart."

He closed his eyes and chuckled before draining his beer. "What'd Parker tell you?"

"I'm going to tear the stitches open on your thigh and pour beer into the hole, Reichart. I swear to God."

Reichart opened his eyes. "You're a mean woman, Alisha."

No, Alisha thought, though she stopped herself from saying the words aloud. Leesh is a mean woman. The one you used to like so much. "Brandon said you told him you'd allied yourself with the Sicarii."

"If you believed that you wouldn't have thrown the knife at my leg."

"Unless I wanted you to be able to answer my questions. How does it always end up like this?" Alisha tilted her attention up to the ceiling and shook her head. "You and me, sitting in a hotel room somewhere, dancing around each other's questions."

"We'll always have Paris," Reichart murmured. Alisha shook her head again.

"Don't count on it. I believed him, you know. You were there, you betrayed me to them, you nearly killed Brandon. I should still believe him."

Reichart refocused on her, taking a long drink of his beer. "But?"

"But you had a gun," Alisha said, "and instead of using it you were throttling Brandon. I can only think of two reasons why you'd do that."

Reichart lifted his eyebrows, invitation to speculation. Alisha breathed out a smile and took a sip of her own beer. "One—you wanted him disabled but not dead. Maybe to keep Phoenix happy, maybe to use him for your own ends."

"And two?"

"You figured I'd get there in time to save him if you didn't do anything as final as shooting him." Alisha wet her lips. "Which doesn't preclude theory number one."

"You know me too well," Reichart said into his beer.

Alisha shook her head. "I don't think I know you at all. What were you doing there, Reichart? Last chance."

"Or what?"

Alisha lifted one shoulder and let it fall again as she set her beer aside and tilted her purse over, reaching into it for the gun. "Or I'm going to shoot you and let Langley do the interrogation. All I want are answers, Frank."

"You wouldn't really shoot me."

"I thought that about you once," Alisha said. "The thing is…"

"Yeah?"

"I was wrong, too."

Reichart had enough time to widen his eyes in dismay before she pulled the trigger.

Chapter 17

Flechette feathers sprouted in Reichart's left shoulder as the dart hit home with a quiet but solid *thunk.* His arm spasmed, sending his beer to the side, foamy liquid spilling over the bedcovers. Alisha darted out of her chair to scoop the bottle up, clicking her tongue in mock dismay. "Don't you know there's a special hell reserved for people who spill good beer, Frank? You'll be upended in a barrel full of all the beer you ever wasted."

Reichart's movements were already slower and clumsier as he fumbled for the dart in his shoulder and managed to pull it out with a thick movement. It gleamed black in his fingers, a trace of blood on its tip. "You utter bitch," he said incredulously. Alisha flashed him a humorless smile.

"I went for a walk because I needed answers from you, Reichart," she said in a low voice. "At this point I don't really give a shit how I get them. If it takes putting you in a glass cell and feeding you psychotropic drugs for the next six months, I'm good with that. At least I'll know where the hell you are and what you're up to, and that'll make me sleep better at night."

"You don't really expect me to come quietly," Reichart asked, pronouncing the words as carefully as a drunk might. Alisha gave him another quick smile.

"Yes, I do. C'mon, sweetheart, upsy-daisy." She slid herself under his arm, grunting as levering him off the bed made her belly protest.

"You can't carry me!" he said in astonishment. Alisha huffed a laugh.

"Not easily, but it doesn't matter, I just need to support you. You don't feel like arguing with me anyway, do you? C'mon, let's take a few steps. I want you on my turf away from any visitors you might get."

Reichart's lip curled, a furious expression as he shuffled forward, leaning heavily on Alisha's shoulder. "What's in this?"

"Just a little cocktail," Alisha said cheerfully. "It won't knock you out. That'd be too much of a pain in my ass. You're just going to be really agreeable and prone to suggestion for the next several hours, and too damned groggy to do anything about it." She hitched around the end of the bed, grabbing her purse on the way, and guided Reichart toward the door.

"When I shake this off..." Reichart warned. Alisha grinned broadly.

"I know," she said cheerfully. "But in the meantime, why don't you tell me who Phoenix is?" Weight on one hip so she could support both herself and Reichart, Alisha reached for the door, pulling it open with her grin firmly in place.

The well-dressed blonde from the cathedral, still heavily veiled, stood outside the door, a pearl-handled derringer in her gloved hand.

Behind the veils the woman's eyes widened in surprise, clearly not expecting to be met at the door any more than Alisha was. Alisha, in a moment of pure irrational flippancy, said, "Nice gun," and then dropped Reichart to fling her weight against the door. It closed as rapidly as she could force it to, while she cursed the fact that hotel room doors were designed *not* to slam.

There was no sound of a bullet firing, no telltale *thunk* in the wood of the door that said the trigger had been pulled. Alisha slapped the locks closed and snatched at Reichart's arm, ignoring his yowl of protest as she shoved herself under the shoulder she'd shot only moments earlier. Reichart sagged against her and let loose a completely undignified giggle, slurring, "That'll show you."

Alisha snarled a wordless reply and backed away from the door, hauling most of Reichart's weight with her. His feet slipped and stumbled, tangling in hers, and he gave another mewling objection when she tromped on his toes.

The door shuddered, sound of a blow echoing through it. Not a gunshot, but a foot, Alisha thought: a well-directed kick. Certainly not given by the blond woman, whose shoes were impractical for kicking doors down. Alisha swore again and herded the increasingly loose Reichart onto the balcony. "Keep on your goddamned feet," she ordered, and he gave her a sloppy grin in response.

A giggle of misplaced outrage erupted from her throat. Alisha choked it down and left him leaning dizzily over the balcony railing. "Don't *fall,*" she muttered, but the room door shuddered again and she didn't dare return to steady him. The woman and at least one thug were outside the door. Alisha pulled her flechette gun out of her bag and put it in the small of her back, still swearing under her breath. Without knowing how many waited for them, escape was better than trying to bring her assailants down.

She yanked the table light out of the wall and pulled the alarm clock free of the bedside table as well, knotting their cords together. Not enough. "Damn it." She more vaulted the bed than went around it, jerking open the closet. Two extra pillows, an iron, ironing board and one of Reichart's very fine coats peopled the closet. Alisha closed her hand around the breast of the coat, feeling paper and stiffness within it, and pulled the soft leather jacket on before taking both the iron and ironing board out.

The iron had an extralong cord. Alisha moved her mouth in a prayer of thanks and pulled her entire haul back to the balcony. Reichart leaned so heavily on the railing he was nearly bent double. Alisha muttered, "Don't fall," at him again, and he gave her a cheery, upside-down smile.

A crack sounded: the door beginning to shatter. Alisha swore again and dropped the table lamp and the alarm clock on the balcony floor as she scrambled to untie their cords again. Once they were free, she popped the ironing board open. "Move," she snapped at Reichart, and he wobbled a few inches without moving the bulk of him. Alisha bared her teeth and worked around him, jamming the board legs-first through the balcony railing. The cords from the lamp and clock dangled over the balcony's edge, the appliances themselves captured behind the ironing board. Still cursing all but silently, she bent over the railing to scoop the cords up and stuff the plugs into her pocket so they couldn't escape, then eyed Reichart and made a loop of the iron's long cord. A little chorus sounded in her head, *right down Santa Claus Way,* and she cut it off with a muttered, "Fuck. Hold on to me, Reichart." She swept the looped cord around both him and herself, pulling him upright to do so, and stepped up to him, fitting her bottom against his hips.

He wrapped her in a clumsy embrace and Alisha made a loose knot of the cord, binding the mercenary spy to herself. "I want you to concentrate, Reichart," she said through her teeth. "We've got to coordinate to climb over the railing. Okay?"

Reichart nodded agreeably, an action that was too exaggerated for his usual economy of motion. Alisha pulled the cords from her pocket and wrapped as much of their length around her forearms as she could before guiding Reichart over the railing. His weight, clumsy with the drug, began pulling her backward, and Alisha cast one wary glance at the ground five stories below.

"What the hell," she said under her breath, "who wants to live forever, anyway?"

She pushed off from the balcony with all the strength in her thighs. Burdened by Reichart's weight, the jump wasn't as extreme as it might have been, but it was more than enough to fully clear the concrete balcony. The last thing she remembered hearing was the sound of the room door collapsing entirely beneath the assault, and a frustrated shout from above.

The cords unwound from her forearms with distressing speed, and Reichart bellowed in her ear, a sound of pure animal alarm. Drugged or not, his grip on her turned to a death hold, for which Alisha was grateful. Dropping him four stories after staging the unexpected escape would have been infuriating.

Even drugged, he had the sense—or self-preservation—to curl himself around her as tightly as he could. They swept over the balcony below theirs, Alisha thrusting her legs out to meet the glass door with all the momentum of their swing and the strength of a kick. Glass exploded inward and someone screamed. For an instant Alisha thought it might have been her, as the cords wrapped around her wrists met with the resistance of her clenched hands and cut deeply into her flesh. The stitched puncture in her upper arm ripped open with a series of pops that felt as if she could hear them. White agony washed over Alisha's vision, making her gag with pain and stress.

Then she managed to let go of the cords and they whipped free, leaving deep pale welts in her arms that would soon enough be purple and bruised. The screaming faded: it wasn't Alisha at all, but the woman whose room they'd crashed into, and she, in a fit of good sense, had run from the room. Alisha staggered forward, dragging most of Reichart's weight with her, then jabbed an elbow back into his gut.

He oofed in surprise as she yanked the cord that wound them together free. "Come on," she barked. "I need you to concentrate on running."

Reichart let go another nasty little cackle that told her he still had enough mental faculties left to appreciate just how bad Alisha's timing had been in drugging him. She grimaced and shoved herself under his arm again, supporting his weight. Later it might be funny, assuming they both survived. "Stairs," she hissed. They would send one to the stairs, one to the elevator, to cover all bases.

Unless they've got more, Leesh, she warned herself. "Who the fuck is she?" she demanded of Reichart, but he only chuckled again as they ran awkwardly for the stairwell.

Two dark-suited men came down the stairs three and four at a time. Alisha dropped Reichart again and snatched her gun out of her pants, bringing it up to squeeze off a series of near-silent shots. Two went entirely wild and one struck home, sending its recipient tumbling down the remaining stairs with a crash. Alisha heard herself chanting, "Thank God, thank God, thank God," under her breath, even as the second thug sprang over the stairway railing and appeared on the landing beside her.

The quarters were too close to use the gun, but having it in hand encouraged Alisha's instinct to try anyway. The shot was knocked askew by her assailant's meaty wrist smashing into hers with a quickness that startled her. He was over six feet tall, Reichart's height if not a little better, and barrel-chested. Men of his build usually relied on brute strength, not finesse. The misjudgment might prove fatal.

She heard the gun clatter against the wall, thrown far enough away by the hit that she couldn't risk going after it. There was insufficient room to circle her sparring partner, but they both dropped into combat stances, their centers low as they watched each other warily.

Her strength was nothing to match his. Alisha's wrist was still numb from the blow it had taken, for which she was oddly grateful: it reduced the throb from the cords that had been wrapped around her forearm. But it made her chances of winning the fight that much slimmer. She feinted in, a low hit that took advantage of her smaller size without opening herself up to the big man.

She literally didn't see his answering volley coming. It was one rapid move the instant she came forward to engage, his hand curling inside her defenses and catching her, with deliberation, in the long cut across her stomach. His fingers dug in as if he knew the wound was there. Pain exploded through her body as the bandages gave way under his grip, and blinding tears coursed down her cheeks. Spasms racked her abdomen and she gave a tiny cough, trying to force the shooting agony out that way, to no avail. There was no breathing past the pain: she couldn't even inhale, her stomach a knot of focused torment.

Breathless, blinded, Alisha stiffened her fingers and jabbed upward, driving them into her attacker's throat. Soft cartilage gave way and his hand convulsed tighter in her belly as he struggled to pull another breath.

A soft *bamf* sounded, the flechette gun firing. Alisha blinked away tears to see surprised dismay struggle with panic on the thug's face before his grip relaxed and he dropped to his knees with an echoing thud.

Reichart sprawled behind him, half propped against the stairway railings, the gun in hand. He stared at the fallen man, then rotated his head up in an exaggerated, wobbly movement to offer Alisha a messy, smug smile.

"I had him," she muttered, though it did nothing to wipe his helpful grin off his face. Then his eyebrows drew down as he took obvious effort to focus on her stomach.

"You're bleeding."

"Yeah," Alisha said through her teeth. "Trying not to think about that." She bent to examine the wheezing man at her feet, nabbing a gun from a holster under his jacket before dragging Reichart onto his feet again. "Upstairs, c'mon, big guy."

"Down's easier," Reichart opined as she slung his arm over her shoulders. Alisha let go a painful chuckle.

"Yeah, that's why we're going up. Two floors, c'mon, quick as we can, you sloppy bastard," she added under her breath.

"I heard that."

"Shut up and concentrate on walking." They made it four floors before neither of them had the wind to go farther, Reichart's steps splaying and going every direction but up.

"Now where?" Reichart asked cheerily as they staggered through the door and leaned on it, both panting. Alisha shot him a look that bordered on laughter.

"Hell if I know. My picklock tools are in my purse in your room."

"Mmm." Reichart squinted, leaning toward her heavily. "Hem," he said after several long seconds. Alisha scowled back at him, then closed her hand on the soft leather jacket she'd nicked from his closet.

"Oh, God bless you. I thought it might have papers in it, that's why I took it." She let him go, propping him against the wall, and lifted the coat's hem, running her fingers around it. Faint stiffness met her search at the kick pleat and she ripped the seam with no compunction, spilling slender wires and a strong stiffer piece into her palm. "Don't go anywhere," she ordered, and Reichart gave an evocative snort that made her grin in spite of everything.

It felt like an eternity before the locked door across the hall from the fire stairs clicked open. Alisha's shoulders dropped in a sudden release of adrenaline and she pushed the door open cautiously, holding her breath.

"It's empty." She toed a shoe off to wedge the door open before retreating across the hall to take Reichart's weight again. In a few seconds they were both inside, the shoe removed, and together they sank down against the inside of the door. Alisha leaned her head back against the wood, breathing deeply through her nose. With endorphins fading, the cut on her stomach throbbed, and dull warmth emanated from a numb upper arm. In a moment she would have to get to her feet again and deal with the injuries. "I'm bleeding all over your nice coat," she said absently. "Who the hell is that woman?"

Reichart stirred beside her. "Alisha…"

"No." Alisha giggled, a high, abrupt sound that she cut off. "I'm Alisha. I'm pretty certain that woman isn't me." She cut the words off, too, clenching her teeth together. Hysterics, while tempting, would do no good. Reichart shoved himself into more of a sitting position, the effort clearly costing him. Alisha turned her head toward him, as heavy and deliberate a movement as those he was making. "Why was she trying to kill you?"

Reichart, with all the concentration in the world, lifted a hand to Alisha's face and drew her in for a kiss.

Chapter 18

He had big hands, Alisha recalled distantly. She'd forgotten how his touch against her cheek always made her feel fragile, the brush of his thumb against her cheekbone playing up a delicacy of her own features that she rarely felt otherwise. Like a grip that would hold a bird, she thought, soft and gentle, not threatening or caging in any way.

The kiss lacked the edge of competition that so often marked Reichart's advances. Warm, hungry, uncertain: vulnerability, Alisha thought, was an unfair card to play. And yet she let herself linger in it, remembering the man's taste and scent more intimately than she'd allowed herself to for years.

Not until his fingers slid back into her hair did Alisha groan and push him away, opening her eyes again. "Knock it off, Reichart." She rolled her shoulders forward, making a barricade of her own body against him as she shook her head. "I'm bleeding and you're stoned. This is really not a good idea." Stiff not just with pain, but also discomfort at the situation, Alisha pushed away from the door, climbing to her feet. Reichart watched her with an intensity born from drugged thought, needing to focus everything in order to say or do anything.

"What if we weren't?"

Alisha looked down at him wearily. "What if we weren't what? Bleeding and stoned? It'd still be a bad idea." One she would almost certainly give in to. No need to mention that to the man at her feet. Alisha offered her left hand, and Reichart slapped his hand into hers, another too-exaggerated movement. She had to step back and brace herself through the thighs, using the hotel-room floor to ground herself and borrow its strength, to pull him to his feet. Partly her own physical weakness, partly his drug-induced stupor. Well, it was her own fault.

Reichart staggered as he came to his feet, then locked his knees to keep himself from tumbling over again. He let go of Alisha's hand to put his hands on her waist instead, and her stomach clenched, both in response to the touch and out of fear that the expanse of his hands against her waist would smack the reopened cut there.

"Leesh…" He ducked his head as if to steal another kiss, and misjudged the distance. Their foreheads collided, white spots exploding in Alisha's vision. She laughed, a startled sound of pain, and clapped a hand against her head.

"Ow! Christ, Reichart, you see? Go lie down. Come on." She wrangled him to the bed, realizing the last of her strength was draining as she did so. "Sit. Down. Give me a chance to…" She let the words trail away as she slipped his leather coat off. Blood stained the inside of her right arm, the bandages over torn stitches unable to absorb all the scarlet liquid. A smear of red told her the arm of the jacket was already stained, but it could be salvaged as long as she washed it before the blood dried. Alisha flared her nostrils and went into the bathroom to strip her shirt and pull the bandages from her arm.

Ripped stitches looked much worse than even the original injury had. Alisha breathed a curse and sat down on the edge of the counter, mouth pulled in a sick grimace as she pulled the threads out of her flesh. Every tug sent a wave of nausea through her, sweat beading on her forehead. She didn't dare look at her reflection, afraid of the paleness she'd see there. "Tell me what the hell is going on with you, Reichart," she said loudly enough for him to hear her. Anything to distract her from the job she was doing, and the questions had to be asked before the drugs wore off. "Tell me what you were doing at the Sicarii base."

"Infiltrating," Reichart said airily. "S'why I had to give you up. Sorry, Leesh."

"Brandon said you were one of his interrogators."

Reichart snorted again, a broad dismissive sound. She heard him mumble, "Pansy," before saying, more clearly, "Had to. It was a test."

"Keep talking." Alisha ground her teeth together as she dug for a thread deeper inside the wound.

"Went to 'em about a year ago," Reichart said agreeably. "All that Tudor shit you told me, apparently it's true. True enough to make 'em consider me, anyway. Think I'd be a good dictator, Leesh?"

"Yeah," Alisha muttered. "You like having all the secrets to yourself. So what happened?" she asked aloud. Her head hurt from concentrating on pulling stitches out.

"They didn't trust me. Go figure. Even when I brought the Attengee plans to them."

"They already had them." Alisha straightened, unable

to focus on the stitches any longer. The pain would recede, she told herself, and then she could finish the job.

"Sure, but I thought it was a nice show of faith. Anyway." A crash sounded in the main room, and the light went dimmer. There was a longish pause before Reichart said, "Oops," and went on with his story, leaving Alisha with a painful little grin directed at the mirrored closet door. She could see him lying on the bed, and could see the reflection of the lamp he'd knocked to the side, fallen down between the nightstand and the wall.

"I spent the last year tryin' to work m'way high enough to get some real data on 'em." Alisha watched him try to push up on an elbow and then flop back into the bed, giving it up as a bad job. "I was s'posed to meet the one they call Phoenix the night you came barging in. She's way up there in their echelon.

"Echelon," he added after a moment, sounding pleased with himself. "Pretty good for a stoned guy, huh?"

Alisha ducked her chin to her chest, grinning. "Very good."

"But you and Parker fucked it up," Reichart went on. "Of all the…"

"Gin joints to walk into?" Alisha asked. Reichart snorted again, indelicately.

"Yeah. Something like that. Of all the nights, Leesh. So I had to give you up, or they'd've figured it was all a setup. Didn't want 'em thinking I was with the Company."

"Who are you with, Frank?" Alisha looked up, watching his reflection in the mirror. He lifted an arm and dropped it over his eyes dramatically, going silent for long moments. She could see his jaw working, a struggle against the drug-induced impulse to answer blithely and without regard for consequence. When silence had gone on long enough, Alisha took a washcloth from the towel rack and stuffed it under her arm, stopping the bleeding as she walked back into the main room. "Who are you with, Frank?"

"Fas Infitialis," Reichart replied, voice low and full of frustration. "Leesh, don't do this."

Hairs stood up on Alisha's arm, a wave of delighted triumph. "What's Fas Infitialis? Latin, I know that, but what does it mean? Who are they? Are they the ones making medical drops worldwide without any apparent government support?"

Reichart flopped his arm away from his eyes, surprise washing through the drugs enough to give him a moment's clarity. "I caught a lucky break," Alisha said, choosing her words carefully. "I found a pattern to follow in the news stories. Who are they, Frank? Who are you?" She leaned against the wall, letting its pressure help stop the bleeding in her upper arm, and watched her ex-fiancé's lips thin with muted anger.

"This is unforgivable, Leesh." His response was a raw warning, the words spoken carefully and clearly. Alisha's heart twisted, a pang of regret lancing through her. Without thought, her left hand came up to brush the all-but-invisible scar just below her collarbone, and she lifted her chin. "I'll take my chances. Tell me what Fas Infitialis is."

Reichart closed his eyes. "No fate. It means no fate, no destiny. You might consider them the Sicarii's sworn enemy."

Alisha laughed, a short hard sound. "Thanks. That clears up a lot. What the hell does that mean?"

He opened his eyes again, focus gone soft and weary. "You're still bleeding," he said quietly. "Patch yourself up and I'll tell you."

Alisha pressed her lips together and retreated into the bathroom. "I'm listening." A thud and a muffled curse followed her, and she peered at the closet mirror. Reichart's reflection showed he'd fallen off the bed and was holding his forehead as he crawled awkwardly toward the bathroom door. "I told you to lie down," Alisha said.

"Didn't say stay there." Reichart hauled himself around to the bathroom door, where he slumped, boneless. "Stuff's making me agreeable, not spineless. I'm not a dog, Alisha." He watched her in the closet mirror, a knee cocked so he could prop his elbow against it and hold his head upright. "The red suits you," he said again.

Alisha twitched a tangle of curls over her shoulder to glance down at it and shrugged. "Thanks. Fas Infitialis, Frank."

"My mother was a member." Alisha heard the dull smack of sound as he let his head fall back against the wall. "I grew up thinking it was how the world worked." A little bark of derision followed, the dark shadow of his hair moving as he shook his head. "Mothers slipping around quietly leaving desperately needed drugs and medical care and food in remote locations. I was probably twelve, fourteen, when I realized it wasn't normal."

Alisha dug the last threads out of her arm and sat down on the toilet, holding her head against waves of dizziness. She took a deep breath as it passed and reached for one of the hotel towels, swallowing a whimper as she ripped a length of the fabric free to create a makeshift bandage with. "I'm not following, Reichart. Start at the beginning."

"I am. Where it began for me, anyway. The Sicarii date back to the Magna Carta, Leesh, at least formally. The Fas Infitialis goes back to Rome. Days of blood and roses."

"What *is* it? You're talking in circles." Alisha threw a painful smile at the bathroom tile as she wrested the bandage into place over her biceps. "Probably on purpose, but knock it off."

Reichart shoved himself into a more upright position, as if doing so would lend strength to his clarity of thought. "You know how the United Nations tries to help improve the world's status quo?"

"Yeah," Alisha said patiently. "And?"

"And they're stymied by lack of funding, by politics, by governmental changes within its member nations." Reichart's voice was clearing, threads of passion warming it. "The Fas Infitialis is a private organization that answers only to itself and is funded by its own members which shares the same, uh..." His focus split again and he rubbed his eyes. "Ideals," he said after a moment, wearily.

Alisha laughed, a disbelieving sound. "Are you telling me you work for a group that's trying to save the world?"

Reichart nodded heavily. "Yeah."

"Pull the other one, Frank, it tickles." Alisha stood up and turned to face the mirror again, wincing as she tugged bandage tape off the long slice over her belly. "I've known you ten years," she said through gritted teeth. "I've watched you drop the ball on things that really would help the world in order to collect on a bigger paycheck a dozen times." The wound on her stomach oozed thin red blood and the sticky clear material of forming scabs. Alisha curled her fingers, trying not to scratch, then reached for a washcloth to clean the injury again. She would need new tape, preferably from an out-of-the-way corner store, to rebind the cut properly.

Reichart lifted a shoulder and let it fall again. "Never said saving the world had to be totally altruistic. Nothing wrong with getting a little rich on the side." He shook his head. "I'm like a double agent, Leesh. You're right. I sell out all the time. But I'm doing it for the greater good."

"What exactly," Alisha asked, still through her teeth,

"was the greater good in shooting me? Or stealing the Attengee schematics? Is building an army of your own part of the Fas Infitialis game plan? Hostile takeover?"

"Infitialis. We just call it the Infitialis, usually. The Attengee's a great piece of work," Reichart said quietly. "But we didn't want it for an army of our own. We wanted to modify it, create a delivery system out of indestructible drones, send them in where it's hard to get people in and out safely. Civil-war zones, natural-disaster sites. Is that drug supposed to make me nauseous?"

"It's not *not* supposed to." Alisha looked over her shoulder at him. "You okay?"

"Would I have asked if it was supposed to make me sick if I didn't feel sick?" Reichart asked irritably. "Of course I'm not okay. My ex-girlfriend put a knife in my thigh and then set me up on a drug cocktail." He rolled away from the bracing wall and crawled past Alisha's knees toward the toilet. She watched him without sympathy.

"You shot me," she pointed out, "and I'm not going to get started on the rest of the list. What greater good did shooting me serve?"

Reichart's answer was a groan that did elicit a sympathetic wince, though Alisha frowned to cover it. "You're a lot more coherent on that stuff than most people," she muttered. Reichart put his forehead against the edge of the toilet bowl and gave her a one-eyed dirty look.

"It's like iocane powder. Work up resistance to will-bending substances. I'd think you'd be the same."

"I am," Alisha admitted. "Part of the training. The adrenaline burst probably didn't hurt your body's attempt to burn through it, either."

"Yeah. That was pretty good, by the way." Reichart rolled his head back over the toilet with another gut-wrenching groan. "Too bad you rescued me from the woman who was supposed to bring me back in to the Sicarii. That was the drop at the cathedral. The Sicarii shot down that glider, Leesh. They just couldn't get to the box. My whole mission was to retrieve it and bring it back to them. You screwed it up in Rome. This was my chance to make good." He fumbled for the toilet's handle, flushing before pushing himself into the space between the counter and the toilet, his bulk fitting surprisingly well. "A verification," he added. "How the holy living hell did you find me?"

"The woman had a derringer, Reichart. It takes a gun to bring you in?"

He lifted an eyebrow. "Didn't you just shoot me?"

Alisha pushed her lips and looked away. "Yeah, okay. How'd shooting me serve the greater good?"

"You're kind of hung up on that, aren't you?"

"Reichart, I swear to God—"

"It kept you alive." The answer came in a snap, much sharper than anything he'd said since the drug had entered his system. "It was a pure shit situation, Alisha. They knew the Cardinal had a CIA contact. They'd been watching for ten months. It was the fourth drop you'd made with him. They knew you were the contact, and you were both on the hit list. The only way I could think to keep you alive was to take you down before they had a chance to."

"You couldn't have told me not to make the drop?" Alisha asked incredulously. Reichart gave her a baleful look.

"Would you have listened?"

"Not without a goddamned good reason," Alisha retorted. "Which you wouldn't have provided."

He shrugged and turned a hand up in agreement, then

let it fall before saying, quite softly, "I just wanted to keep you safe."

"Funny damned way you've got of showing it." There was less rancor in her voice than she wanted there to be, more than six years of healing time, both physical and mental, giving her room to be calm. "Were you ever going to tell me about any of this, Reichart? The Sicarii? The Infitialis? Any of it?"

Reichart thinned his lips. "Does your prisoner-taking policy include getting a thirsty man a glass of water?"

"You're feeling better," Alisha muttered, but got him the water. "You should be loopy for another six hours, at least."

"I wouldn't want to trust me with my life just yet," Reichart offered as he drank the water. "My tongue's working better than my brain right now."

"Yeah, well," Alisha said before she could think to regret it, "you were always good with your tongue."

Reichart choked and spat a mouthful of water out, looking up with tears of surprised laughter in his eyes. Alisha crinkled her face. "Don't suppose you could forget I said that."

"Oh, hell no," Reichart said fervently. "Alisha...Leesh. Come down here." He made an impatient gesture and Alisha knelt cautiously, unwilling to crouch and scrape her stomach with her thighs. Reichart brushed his fingers across her cheek, slipping a curl of hair behind her ear. "You've fucked up my life, you know that?" he asked with good-natured weariness. "No, I wouldn't have told you, not when we were together, not for years. You were too wedded to king and country back then, sweetheart. You even saw me as a rescue project."

"You're stoned, Reichart. Stop talking. You'll embarrass both of us." Alisha started to stand again, but Reichart tightened his fingers against her face, a plea for her to stay.

"I'm stoned," he agreed, "so I'm past being embarrassed. I knew better than to fall for a girl like you, all wide-eyed idealism and in love with serving her country. You're better suited for me now." He gave her a crooked smile tinged with regret. "My Leesh never would've taken a walk, back in the day. A woman who's willing to is more the kind I need. Why'd you do it, Leesh?"

"Because I finally needed answers from you more than I needed the job," Alisha answered quietly.

"Does that mean we're in this together, kid?"

Irritation exploded through Alisha, making her pull back despite Reichart's protest. "*God,* I hated it when you called me that! You're five years older than me, Frank. That doesn't make me a kid, for Christ's sake. How many times have I told you that?"

Surprise filtered through Reichart's expression and he let his hand fall. "I didn't think you meant it."

"Yet another reason it's over between us. You never listened to me." Alisha set her jaw, glaring down at him. "You need a hand up?"

"…no," Reichart said. "No. I can make it on my own."

Chapter 19

Alisha kept her eyes turned away as Reichart pushed himself up, an uncomfortable sense of guilt lingering as he fought against the drug in his system. *You couldn't have known, Leesh,* she reminded herself. "Your Sicarii friends are going to keep looking for you."

"You should've thought of that before you shot me," Reichart muttered.

"You should've told me what was going on with you years ago," Alisha countered, then set her teeth together, struggling to not go down the too-familiar path of bantering and one-upmanship. "Can we set aside the coulda-shoulda-wouldas?" she asked, wanting to make it an order but knowing that doing so would end any possibility of further discourse between them. "Can we just…try working together? The Sicarii know who I am. This—" she twitched a lock of coppery hair "—won't throw them off for long, if at all, and if they put you together with the Agency you're screwed, Frank."

"Blued, and tattooed," he agreed. "Fifteen months, Leesh," he added in a frustrated growl. "You just blew fifteen months of work."

"Then I'd say we're even." Alisha heard coolness come into her voice and for once was grateful for the training that allowed her to switch from hot to cold inside a breath. "Since you pushed me out of a job." The accusation was as fair as the one Reichart made, and she watched irritation glimmer in his expression even through the haze of the drug.

"All right," he said after a few seconds. "We'll call it even."

Until one of us has the chance to pull the wool over the other's eyes again, Alisha thought, but she nodded. "They're going to be all over the building for a couple of hours, trying to find us. You should sleep some of that stuff off."

"And you?"

"I'll keep watch. Unless you wanted to just go turn yourself over to your blond friend to see what happens."

"She's not my friend, Alisha." Reichart edged around the bathroom door toward the bed, steadier on his feet than Alisha expected, but still far short of his usual grace. "How the hell'd you follow me to the drop? You were back in the States."

"Why do you even know that, Reichart? You have someone keeping tabs on me?"

He shot her a look that answered the question, the drugs in his system overriding his usual emotional remoteness. Cold surprise laced through Alisha's stomach, making the cut there hurt, and she pressed her hand over it without touching the injury. "Who? Not Greg."

Reichart curled a lip and sat down on the bed's edge. Sweat stood out along his hairline and on his upper lip, and he lowered his head into his hands, moving as if doing so increased his nausea. "Not Greg."

"Who, Reichart?" Alisha took a few long steps to crouch in front of him, trying to inhale away the protesting pain in her stomach. "Brandon said you'd gotten me into this whole mess. What was he talking about? Is he your guy?"

Reichart exhaled a dismissive snort. "Nah. I don't like blondes that much." He swallowed thickly, as if trying to wash away the answer to her questions, but the serum compelled him. "I tipped Boyer off to the research facility in Kazakhstan. I even recommended you for the job because I knew you wouldn't make any lethal choices regarding Brandon Parker. Not with Greg still being your handler after all this time."

"Boyer?" Alisha asked incredulously. "Director Boyer's your inside man in the Agency? Does he—is he—part of the Infitialis? Why was it important to keep Brandon alive?"

Reichart jerked his head in a short denial. "Just a sympathizer. He knew my mother. We go back a long way. The Parkers are part of the Sicarii, Leesh. Keeping him alive and putting you on him gave us access to their activities in a way we hadn't had the opportunity to explore before. It even flushed Greg and him into public together." He let a shoulder rise and fall in a small shrug. "Not very public," he admitted, "but you and I saw it."

"In China." Alisha straightened out of her crouch, taking a few steps away. "Director Simone provided the paperwork for that whole operation, Reichart. Everything was aboveboard."

Reichart crashed over on his back, arms spread wide across the bed, his feet still on the floor. "Unless Simone's dirty, too."

Alisha closed her eyes against the thought and murmured, "Go to sleep, Frank. I'll wake you up in a couple of hours." The only response was a grunt that faded into steady breathing. Alisha turned the solitary light off and stepped over to the windows, brushing the curtain aside just enough to watch the street five floors below.

Unless Simone's dirty, too. She hadn't quite put words to the idea in her own mind, more reluctant to do so than she wanted to admit. "We're supposed to be the good guys," she whispered to the nighttime reflections beyond her. It was possible, yes, possible, that there was a line of corruption running through the CIA into high-enough departments and levels that an entire mission could be fabricated with the support documents to prove it. Certainly if the Sicarii were possible, if Reichart's Fas Infitialis was possible, then deadly factions within the Agency itself were possible.

A smile creased the corner of Alisha's mouth. Even to her own mind, she sounded naive. As in any company, there were rival factions inside the CIA. Connections to interests outside of the United States' were almost certainly much more regular than Alisha wanted to believe. *You're not so far gone from that girl Reichart was talking about, Leesh.* The bright-eyed idealist, whose faith in her country overrode any doubts she might have.

Alisha sank down against the curtains, keeping the crack in them open just wide enough to continue watching. There were no balconies on this side of the street, only a fire escape several rooms down marring the building's line as it rose up from the earth. The business of the road below told her that it was only seven-thirty or eight at night, though she felt it must be close to midnight. It was raining again, streetlights reflecting in the sheen on the sidewalks, and umbrellas were cropping up, hiding the people below from her vision.

What did she become, Alisha wondered, if she lost that idealism? *A yoga teacher,* she thought wryly, and then with more honesty, *a cynic. Like Reichart.* She shook her head against the curtain, minute movement. Reichart's cynicism seemed to mask a man she'd never even known existed. The Fas Infitialis he claimed to work for only existed in the shadows, but so too did the Sicarii, and she had ample experience with the latter to believe in their existence.

It was bitter dredges, she thought, that the best way for an organization to help others was to remain so secretive that no one could foul up their missions with external politics. Still, if that was the Infitialis philosophy, then by its nature Alisha liked it better than the Sicarii.

Unless she happened to be that grab-bag princess that Brandon had suggested. Alisha flashed a quick smile toward the street below, shaking her head again. Even if, the idea of predestination was ludicrous.

Brandon, despite Reichart's beliefs, couldn't be a part of it. Alisha thinned her lips, trying to hold on to that confidence but feeling it waver. If Simone was dirty—

If Simone was dirty, Alisha was going to have to take action and make choices that might put her even further off the path she'd once thought was her own. She'd already taken a walk, the euphemism meaning she'd left the CIA's fold, but if Director Simone was part of the Sicarii network, then neither Alisha nor anyone with any true Company loyalty could afford to ignore it. Simone had too much access to too much information. Her deception could be the undoing of everything Alisha held dear.

"In for a lamb," she murmured softly enough to not disturb Reichart's sleep, and pushed the curtain a little further open to watch the street below.

* * *

"Wake up." Alisha knew better than to shake Reichart awake, and spoke quietly from the door, where she cast quick glances through the peephole, making sure the hall remained clear. "Wake up, Frank. We've got to go."

"What time is it?" Reichart's voice was muzzy from sleep, but no longer held the thickness lent it by the drug.

"Almost one. We've got to go," Alisha repeated. "There's trouble."

"With you and me, babe, there always was." Reichart came to his feet, moving more easily, though he scrubbed a hand over his eyes. "One. I thought you were going to let me sleep for two hours."

"I wanted to make sure the drug had worn off." Alisha tossed him the leather jacket she'd taken from his closet in the other room. "You weigh too much for me to haul around."

"Not last I checked." Reichart slid the jacket on, checking the breast pocket.

"Last you checked I was in full fighting condition." Alisha lifted her arms, forearms bound with what had been extra pillowcases in the closet, now ripped into strips and wrapped around the welts and bruises. "I'm not right now. Your papers are there," she added, quiet and impatient. "Rodney Evans. You don't look like a Rodney."

"What does a Rodney look like?"

"Thinner. Balding. Are you ready?"

"What's the rush?" Reichart finally focused on her more clearly, sleep burning away to leave intensity in his dark eyes. "We made?"

Alisha tilted her head at the curtained window. "Leave the lights off."

Frowning, Reichart strode across the room and flicked the curtains back enough to look down. A moment's observation was all that was required before his shoulders tensed and Reichart scowled over his shoulder at her. "We're fucked."

"I know. Let's go." Alisha cast one more look out the peephole, then eased the door open. The hall beyond was empty, but she shook her head even as she moved. "There's no way to get to the next buildings over via the roofs," she murmured. "We're going to have to risk the ground floor."

"Elevator," Reichart answered. "How're your hot-wiring skills these days?"

"Fantastic. How are you at ripping steel plates off walls?" Alisha ran down the hall on her toes, light long strides, and without discussion took up the opposite side of the elevator door from Reichart, both of them standing with their backs pressed to the walls. "You ever wonder what Joe Average would think if he saw us doing this?"

The elevator doors dinged and a young couple reeking of wine staggered out, giggling at each other. The woman stopped with a delighted gasp as Reichart made a swift turn toward the elevator, his presence abruptly commanding. "Clear," he said to Alisha, and the woman goggled at them as Alisha took a few quick steps that put her inside the elevator car.

"Shh." She lifted a finger to her lips, making a shushing motion at the wide-eyed young woman. "National security, miss. Nothing to see here. Move along."

The doors slid shut on the couple's startled expressions, and Reichart gave Alisha a smile mixed with amusement and chagrin. "I don't have to, with you around. I forgot you did things like that."

"Only around you." Alisha knelt in front of the control panel, examining it for screws or a loose weld. It was true: it didn't take rereading her chronicles to know that the moments of lightest heart were ones spent in Reichart's presence. "You bring it out in me. Remember the hotel in Prague?"

Reichart laughed, so loud and unexpected that Alisha's grin turned into a laugh itself. "I hadn't," he said. "Until now. Did you ever go back to explain?"

"What could I say?" Alisha demanded. "'I'm sorry for playing Lady Godiva through your lobby, but it was that or risk a civil uprising that would have preceded World War Three?' Of course I didn't go back. This thing's locked up like a vestal virgin, Reichart." She slid the picklocks out of the suit jacket, shaking her head. "As long as nobody calls the elevator I should—"

The car jerked, then hummed. Alisha looked up and Reichart snorted out a laugh. "At least we're going up."

"Mmm. Let's hope it's not our friends looking for us." Alisha slid the smaller pick into the control panel's keyhole, eyes closed and head tilted to the side as she listened for the telltale click that would announce the panel's opening.

"Up," Reichart said the instant before the elevator stopped. Alisha came to her feet in a graceful motion that belied the stiff pain lancing across her stomach, and Reichart swept her into his arms, murmuring "Sorry" as she grunted against his chest. The apology was all that kept Alisha from biting his lip as he lowered his head to steal a no-nonsense kiss.

"Oops," a flustered American said as the doors opened. "Er, sorry. Uh. Ah. I'll, uh…"

Reichart lifted his head and suggested, "You could join us, no?" in an outrageous French accent. The American stumbled backward, waving his hands in distressed surprise, and the doors slid shut again as Alisha fought back laughter.

"What would you have done if he'd said yes?" She pushed him away and knelt again, ignoring the elevator's downward journey.

"Punched him," Reichart said cheerfully. Alisha grinned and tapped the straight wire inside the lock. It clicked satisfyingly and the panel popped open. "Basement," Reichart said, as Alisha twisted the wires to push the keyhole far enough to allow basement access.

"I'm going to be very disappointed in you if there's no way out of the basement, Reichart."

"I thought disappointment in me was a perennial state."

"It is," Alisha said, knowing the words would cut, but meaning them less harshly than they sounded. "You're never what I hope you'll be."

"You still believe that?"

"I need to talk to Boyer before I'm sure I'm willing to accept your story," Alisha answered. "And damn it, Frank, handing over that black box would be a good show of faith on your part. What in God's name does your Infitialis need with it? I know why I need it."

"Do you?" The doors dinged and slid open again, harsh fluorescent lights glaring down on the maintenance areas of the hotel. Everywhere else the lighting was gentler, the guests' comfort at obvious odds with the employees' comfort. Alisha squinted against the brightness, stepping out in tandem with Reichart as they both scoped the hall.

"Laundry's to the left," Reichart murmured, conversation set aside in favor of stealth. "Kitchen's to the right."

"Stand up, sit down, fight fight fight," Alisha said under her breath. "Where's the exit?"

"Laundry's more likely to be quiet, even at this hour." Reichart nodded down the hall, and took point, Alisha trailing a step or two back and watching the hall behind them.

The laundry room was deserted, enormous dryers silent, washing machines not producing a hum of activity. White flooded Alisha's gaze, neatly folded towels and sheets all of one color, waiting to be brought upstairs during the new day. "This way," Reichart said, still quietly, though Alisha could read the exit sign as easily as he could. She held back the retort, hoping she'd remember to use it later, and followed Reichart out into the suddenly dark night.

An Attengee drone, silver dome reflecting amber streetlights, rose up on ratcheted legs in front of them, lasers already primed for attack.

Chapter 20

"You know," Reichart said into the respite between observation and action, "I don't remember dating you being this dangerous."

Explosive red blasts of heat seared the darkness, leaving smoking scores in the building walls. Alisha and Reichart leaped in opposite directions, racing against laser fire. Even if only one of them got away, Alisha thought. She could see, across the alley, the way the glowing striations followed Reichart's path as he ran, and didn't dare look back to see the same deadly evidence splashed over the walls behind her.

The drone froze for a moment, quiet whir seeming loud in the rain as it assessed its two targets. Choosing one, Alisha thought: who was more important to the Attengee's controllers? The artificial intelligence mastering the drone would almost certainly recognize them both. She had fought the machines twice before, though remembering those battles left her heart missing beats and making sickness in her stomach. The electricity she'd used to fry one of the drones had drained her gray. She'd been in therapy for days and watched for weeks: even with the energy-absorbent armor she'd worn, the human body simply wasn't intended to be a conduit for that much power. Her heart had come out unscarred, except for this lingering effect of recall.

And now she had neither raw electricity nor any other weapon effective against the Attengee's glittering silver dome. A hitch formed in her breath as she ran, lancing down into the cut across her belly. She stumbled, tears of startled pain blinding her for a moment. Laser fire crackled above her head, a shot that seemed more warning than deadly, though only her clumsiness had kept it from splitting her skull. A thread of gratitude for her injuries slithered through her mind: the AI could predict zigzag evasive maneuvers she might take, but the trips and spills brought on by a damaged body were far more random, and might well keep her alive.

Especially with the silver machine turning away from her now. A flash of offense sizzled through her, as if the drone choosing Reichart as its primary target was a personal insult. Alisha gathered herself and sprang forward, reaching for one of the drone's three ratcheting legs. It snaked out of her grasp just before her fingers closed on it, the trifold foot whipping up to snap over her face. It wasn't large enough to wrap around her entire head, but the pressure it exerted was more than sufficient: it clamped down, squeezing bruises that were precursors to shattering bone into her skin. Too late, Alisha wondered if the machine had feinted, choosing Reichart in order to draw her closer. *Stupid,* she thought, but there was no more time for recriminations as she curled her fingers around the droid's foot, focusing all her strength on the task at hand.

Strength that was already greatly weakened. Her fingers cramped and loosened as she tried to pull the clamped foot free. The welts in her arms throbbed, warnings of her own weakness, and black spots began to swim in her vision. Breathing in deeply hurt, reducing her ability to focus through her breath. Even the preternatural hearing that she was so accustomed to counting on in the midst of battle seemed faded with the force bent on crushing her skull.

It was a stupid way to die, she thought dizzily, and the worst of it was she still didn't have all the answers about Reichart, Brandon and the Sicarii. Dying in the line of duty was something she'd always been prepared to do, but dying without answers seemed a particularly bitter pill.

She was yanked forward with such strength that for an instant Alisha thought her head might actually separate from her shoulders. Then the clamp around her head released so suddenly that it seemed outraged. Alisha, full of forward momentum, skidded across wet cobblestones on her stomach, half expecting to hear the Attengee let out an angry whine like R2-D2 might. Clarity of vision returned in a painful burst and she rolled onto her back, searching for an answer to what had released her.

The drone's foot slapped down onto the stones beside her, clutching the time-worn rock for balance. Reichart stood a few feet away, an arm wrapped up in one of the drone's sinuous legs. Alisha reacted before conscious understanding could form in her mind, knotting her hands around the machine's leg. Her stomach muscles sang with pain as she tightened them, using the ground beneath her to draw strength from as she lifted and pulled the Attengee off balance, just as Reichart had done. With two of its three legs down it was stable, but with two captured, its capability was severely limited.

The silver dome that topped the drone's tripod spun around, firing blasts that came dangerously near its own imprisoned limbs. Alisha rolled, deliberately tangling herself in the drone's leg. Thought was dangerous now, as dangerous as it was in a knife fight. Avoiding the fire was going to be impossible. The best she might do was entangle the drone enough to allow Reichart time to escape.

The thunderous silence of battle finally descended on her, her hearing so focused she thought she could count individual raindrops splashing to the cobblestone. There was no way both she and Reichart were going to come out of the fight alive, and she was already on the ground. Even gathering herself to shout "Run!" was beyond her, all her attention on knotting up the drone's legs sufficiently that any fire it lay down would damage itself as surely as it would destroy her.

Greater love hath no man than this, that a man lay down his life for his friends. Alisha twisted a smile. Maybe Jon had been right after all. She reached for the drone's silver body, forcing strength into her tired hands as she curled her fingers around its laser-blasting gun. A wordless scream erupted from her throat, the sound meant to focus everything she had left into tearing the gun away from its couplings.

It loosened with a shriek of metal, not coming free. Not coming nearly free enough, Alisha realized with dismay. Her strength was even more badly diminished than she'd realized. She could twist the blaster in several inches, enough to threaten the Attengee's body, but its own artificial intelligence warned of danger and the blaster ceased firing. It was something. Maybe not enough, but it was something.

Her own harsh breathing sounded in her ears, the only sound in the world. Alisha's fingers felt thick as she pulled at the metallic leg she'd wrapped herself in, fumbling the drone's foot upward to jam it into the coupling that held the blaster. A wave of exhaustion swept over her and she slumped in the bindings she'd created for herself, but even her weight relaxing didn't release the foot from where she'd stuffed it. Gears ground, almost against her ear, and she let out a high, startled laugh. The Attengee dome's ability to spin and fire was compromised by the damage done to it, a bonus Alisha simply hadn't expected.

Above her, an arc of silver cut away from the sky, falling with deliberate precision that was accompanied moments later by the sound of engines whining. An out-of-place thrill stabbed through Alisha, childish glee at seeing the Doppler effect in action.

Then fire rained down from the screaming arc, laser heat as deadly and rapid as the Attengee's. Delight turned to dread and Alisha curled herself into as small a ball as she could while still tangled in the drone's leg, waiting for the end to come in fiery bursts. With any luck, at least Reichart might have made it out. It was enough. It would have to be.

Metal boiled and spilled in rivulets beside her, the heat so overwhelming she could smell the bitter stink of her hair singeing. A blast shattered part of the leg she lay snarled in, concussive force rather than heat. Pain lanced through her abdomen, ribs bruised if not broken, but the next breath was unexpectedly easier to take, the drone's leg no longer crushing her. Another volley of fire and metal clanged around her, followed by an instant's reprieve. Alisha lurched from the Attengee's fallen body, scrambling as far as she could on hands and knees.

The alley wall stopped her before she had moved more than a few yards, and weariness kept her from moving farther. She used the wall to push herself up against, no farther than a sit, and wrapped an arm over her ribs and stomach, trying to crush the pain there away. Reichart was gone, nowhere in her line of vision, and faulty memory refused to tell her what might have happened to him. Only a vague mix of exhaustion and amused offense spilled through her, carrying the memory of his last words to her.

"That's because we're not dating," she whispered to the empty air, and then, for a moment, gratefully allowed herself to slip into painless unconsciousness.

A scent worse than her scorching hair woke her. Alisha coughed, batting at the smelling salts as her forehead wrinkled hard enough to ache. "I'm awake, I'm awake. Get that stuff away from me." She pressed a hand to her forehead, trying to push away the pain forming beneath her skin, and squinted her eyes open. Brandon Parker smiled down at her, lopsided and apologetic.

"Sorry. I didn't think we had time to let you come out of it on your own. You're pretty banged up."

"We?" Alisha let her eyes close again, holding on to the idea that Brandon was there without yet being ready to question it. "Reichart?"

"Sorry." She could hear him shaking his head, the brush of his hair against his collar. "Just me and the Firebird."

"You call that a we?" Alisha's voice croaked and she swallowed, wondering if she had the energy to prop herself on an elbow. Rather than try, she squinted her eyes open again. "You look better."

He did. Blond hair was darkened by rain, but the bruises on his throat were faded and the scrapes he'd taken from the blast force were almost healed. One, along his cheekbone, gave him a bit of a rakish air, though not the James Bond debonair that Reichart could pull off. More like Prince William after a polo match, Alisha thought, then folded her hand over her eyes to try to hide a tired chuckle. It didn't work, and she heard the smile in Brandon's voice, as well. "Whatever happened, it looks like you came through with your sense of humor intact. You all right?"

"No." Alisha inhaled slowly, feeling her ribs shift and pinch with the breath. Not broken, just bruised, judging from the comparative lack of pain. "But I will be." She dropped her hand again, focusing beyond Brandon at the inside roof of a van. "What are you doing here?"

"Rescuing you, it looks like."

"How? I'm AWOL."

"The Firebird." Brandon's smile remained apologetic. "I've had her hunting for you since the sun went down."

"How'd you even know I left Washington? I thought you were still in the hospital."

"I got a tip. Anyway, the Bird's recognition software works from the bones out, so cosmetic changes won't fool her." He picked up a curl and let it fall again. "The red's nice, but you're going to need a haircut."

Alisha moved her hand to her hair with a wince. "How bad? A tip from who?"

"That'd be telling. You could do a mullet," Brandon added, grinning widely as Alisha's lip curled. "Yeah, I didn't think so. I came to Paris," he said, "because you seem to have a thing about it."

Inwardly directed irritation slid through Alisha, accompanying the memory of a clear summer night and a marriage proposal by the Seine. "I should know better."

Brandon spread his hand dismissively. "We've all got

our tells. So I've been casing the hotels all night, looking for you, anyway."

"Nice nick-of-time arrival," Alisha said. Brandon shook his head.

"Not really. When the Attengees came online the Firebird picked up their frequency. I was on the wrong damned side of town, but she got here fast enough."

"She got here." Alisha pushed up carefully, feeling stiffness in all her muscles. The van was gutted, a sawed-off pallet covered with a narrow mattress on the left side, and a cabinet she imagined might carry the Firebird set against the right. "You weren't behind her?"

"That rescue was one hundred percent my girl," Brandon said, proud as a new father. "All her own brain power. I was watching it on my handheld, but she pulled your bacon out all by herself."

"And Reichart?" Alisha elbowed Brandon out of the way so she could fold herself over into a puppy dog pose, arms stretched in front of her to pull the ache from her muscles.

"I was hoping you could tell me." Brandon kept the words carefully neutral. Alisha sat back on her heels, twisting and stretching, then centered herself, chin up as she straightened her spine.

The van's dark interior faded away to the memory of rain spattering on the cobblestones and the mechanical whir of the Attengee drone jamming. Alisha focused on the sounds she'd heard when her hearing had finally kicked in so clearly, and let her eyes drift shut.

It was part of the training, to observe unconsciously even when the mind and body were too busy to pay close attention. In the seconds between the Attengee being yanked off balance and being jammed, what had happened?

Footsteps. Not human: the harsh clatter of another Attengee drone, but not on the cobblestones. She knew that sound intimately. This was different, digging in and clenching, rubble falling to hit the paved street below. The pattern was wrong, as well. Too many feet clinking against concrete and wood. At least six, moving spiderlike, so their sound was an almost constant rattle. No new weapons were fired, but beneath the memory of her own struggle Alisha heard a muffled, startled outburst. Reichart.

She opened her eyes, staring sightlessly through the van's side at the Parisian walls beyond. Then, with a blink, she refocused on Brandon. "Someone's altered your design. They've got a climber. They took him. Over the buildings." Despite the trembling ache in her muscles, Alisha pushed to her feet, ducking to avoid hitting her head on the van roof. "I've got to get him back."

Chapter 21

Even as she spoke, Alisha swayed on her feet, the momentary rest in asana doing too little to rejuvenate her. Brandon slid a hand under her elbow, light touch that supported her without being invasive. "Alisha," he said gently. "Even if you were in the condition to go after him, are you sure it's a good idea? He's—"

Alisha lifted her hand sharply, taking her elbow out of Brandon's grip. "Don't," she said. "Don't tell me he's Sicarii. I'm sick to death of the two of you pointing fingers at one another. I swear I'm going to just shoot you both in the back of the head and be done with it." She sat back down on the low bed, her body in agreement with Brandon's assessment of her condition even if her mind was not.

Brandon's answering silence was so charged she spoke through her teeth, feeling drawn into an explanation she didn't want to give. "It's all he-said/he-said with you two," she muttered. "The truth is I don't have any hard outside proof who either of you is working for. You were right. He got me into this whole Sicarii mess." Alisha closed her eyes, then shook her head. "And as soon as I can talk to Boyer I can verify whether the rest of his story is true."

"Boyer," Brandon said mildly. "The director whose orders you're blatantly disobeying right now?"

"At this point I think he's at the bottom of a long list of people I'm ignoring." Alisha looked up. "I need to know, Brandon. I need to know who you're really working for, and I can't trust you to tell me. The Sicarii treat you as one of their own." She rubbed her fingers together, sudden tactile memory coming back to her. "You even carry things with their emblem on it, don't you? That lighter you lent me in Rome."

Brandon put a hand in his pocket and came out with the lighter, rotating it between his fingertips to offer to her. "This?"

Alisha closed her eyes again as she took it, brushing her thumb over its smooth surface. Nearly smooth: a crown marred the silver, so faint it was difficult to discern with the eyes alone. "Yeah."

"That was a gift from my father, Alisha. He gave it to me when he quit smoking. The Sicarii symbol is the circle of daggers. I've never seen them use any other emblem."

The lighter felt abruptly heavy in Alisha's hand, the warmth from Brandon's pocket fleeing it. "From Greg?"

"He gave it to me when I was seventeen." Brandon sighed. "Don't tell me you've been holding it against me all this time."

"I didn't know he'd ever smoked." Alisha stared at the lighter, light-headed with surprise and tiredness. It made her feel fragile, as though her preconceptions had been placed on edge and all it would take was one solid thump to shatter them irrevocably.

Compartmentalization, Leesh, she whispered, silently mocking herself. *This is why they preach it.* Because emotional investment was too complicated and too dangerous. It led to bad assumptions and often to worse choices.

It led, Alisha thought wearily, to safety-deposit boxes scattered around the world, each containing a journal that her heart was poured out into. Her way of marking passage through a world that went largely unknown to people outside the espionage business. It led to shots fired by lovers, in hopes of saving lives, and it led to betrayals by partners, all in the name of a greater ideology. Alisha lowered her head into the spread fingers of one hand. Emotional investment would very likely be the death of her, but she had experienced the cold isolation of the alternative, and it was unthinkable.

Brandon sat down beside her, dropping his chin to his chest. "He had a real thing about that particular lighter. Never used any other one to light a cigarette. So giving it to me was a big commitment to quitting smoking. You really thought I was hiding something with it."

"One of a hundred little things that made me think I shouldn't trust you," Alisha said, speaking into her hand. "An innocuous thing like a lighter." She lifted her head again, feeling its weight, and turned her focus on Brandon. "Simone's cleared you. God, I am so tired of not trusting people. Of feeling like I'm always looking over my shoulder."

Brandon pulled a brief smile. "You *are* a spy, Alisha."

She shook her head. "This is different. The last year, fifteen months, it's been different. Not being sure that the people I'm surrounded with really are the good guys. Not knowing if Greg's got some kind of agenda I don't know about or whether you're a double agent or—"

"Or if Frank Reichart really is as mercenary as he's proved himself to be over and over again?" Brandon asked a little wryly. Alisha exhaled and looked away, shaking her head.

"I don't want to talk about Reichart. I've got to get out of here and rescue his sorry ass, but you're right." She heard the aggrieved edge come into her voice and lost the brief struggle to modulate it away. She could, if she had to, retain perfect control over her tone and delivery, but for the moment it was a blessing not to have to. To feel as though she was safe, and with someone she could trust. It was a relief to let the facade go for a few minutes. "I'm too beat-up and too damned tired to be more than a danger to myself and anybody else right now. The last thing that's going to do any good is going on a wild-goose chase with no idea where I'm going or what I'll be up against when I get there. Can the Firebird track the Attengee drones without being detected?" The question came abruptly, a moment of clarity interrupting her tiredness. Brandon glanced at the cabinet, eyebrows lifted.

"Sure. Her fuel source ought to keep her going all night."

"Send her after them." Alisha pulled her feet up on the tiny bed. "That way we won't go in blind."

"We?"

Alisha turned to Brandon, managing a quick smile. "You're not going to confess to being a double agent *now,* are you?"

"I am a double agent." Brandon touched Alisha's cheek, so briefly and gently she might have imagined the contact. "But I'm working for the good guys, Ali. The only reason I'm part of the Sicarii is to do what I can to bring them down."

Alisha sighed and lay down on her side on the hard mattress. "Then send the Firebird after Reichart, and let me get some sleep before we go save the world."

She didn't hear his answer.

* * *

The air was stifling, too warm and too still for too long, and tainted with the scent of heated metal. There was weight over her ribs, enough that taking a breath could be felt in the pressure against bruises. Discomfort, nothing more. Alisha came fully awake without letting her breathing pattern change, examining her memory and the unseen surroundings for danger.

Her ear, resting against her biceps, ached in a way that told her she hadn't moved for hours. The rest of her body felt similar, muscles settled into a curled-up position on the bed. It would take a good hour of stretching to loosen herself up properly, but aside from that she felt surprisingly good. *Content,* she thought, then wondered at the word.

"Go back to sleep," Brandon mumbled behind her ear. Alisha drew in a slow, careful breath, then moved his arm from her ribs. A chill swept through her despite the overwarm air in the van, and she fought back both a shiver and the impulse to cuddle closer to Brandon and do as he suggested.

"Can't. Got a guy to save." She peeled her cheek from the arm of the leather jacket she still wore and sat up gingerly. "Time is it?"

"Late enough to be hot in here." Brandon interrupted his own answer with a yawn and rolled onto his back, putting his fingers to the floor to keep from falling off the narrow bed. "Don't worry. The Firebird won't disappoint us."

"Never dreamed she would." Alisha twisted to crawl over Brandon as professionally as she could, wincing as she braced her weight on her swollen wrist. Brandon slid his hand against her right hip, fingers in her belt loop to hold her above him. Alisha's heart lurched as she looked down at him, and he gave her a brief, sleepy smile.

"Now this is nice."

Alisha pushed up on her knee, taking her weight off her arm, and put her other foot down on the van floor to keep her balance. "Knock the cute sleepy act off, Parker. You're as awake as I am." There was less censure in her voice than there should have been, and Brandon heard it as clearly as she did. He tugged on her belt loop and Alisha tightened her core, not letting him pull her down. The cut across her stomach twinged, but less painfully than she'd expected: the sleep had done more good than she'd hoped it could.

"Knock it off, Brandon," she repeated, and while the tone was edged with regret this time, Alisha filled it with steel. "This isn't the time and even if I weren't a walking bruise, it sure isn't the place. I haven't had sex in a car since I was—" She broke off with a sudden grin. "None of your business."

Despite the disappointment that flashed through Brandon's expression, he laughed and let her go. "It's been that long, or you started that early?"

"None of your business," Alisha said again, still grinning. She got off the bed, groaning as she doubled over and let the big muscles of her thighs and back stretch. "I need a massage and a hot tub. And breakfast."

"And a haircut," Brandon said ruefully. Alisha looked at the cascade of auburn curls that brushed the floor and sighed.

"Guess it's your job to get breakfast and some clipping shears, then."

"And then?"

Alisha closed her eyes, drawing her forehead against her ankles. "Then we go find Reichart and the other Firebird's black box."

* * *

"I'm not a hairstylist."

"It doesn't matter." Alisha had sat cross-legged in the middle of the gutted van's metal floor, opting for easy cleanup over the relative comfort of the bed. "Anything's better than this." She'd looked at herself in the rearview mirror and had been caught between laughter and tears at the disaster her hair had become. The laser blasts fired as the Firebird freed her from the Attengee drone had melted chunks of her hair into mats, and destroyed strips wholesale. The damage was almost exclusively around the top of her head, but Brandon's suggestion of a mullet still didn't appeal. "Even if you have to take it all the way down to a buzz, it'll be better than this."

"I might have to," Brandon said helplessly. "There's enough left for somebody to do something with, but that somebody's not me."

"Just cut away the damaged stuff first," Alisha answered grimly. "We'll see what we can do from there."

She turned her head now, watching her own reflection in the side-view mirror. The back and sides of her head were almost shorn, the hair so short that its natural tawny shade had reasserted itself even though it had only been dyed two days earlier. The short gelled curls that stood up every which way were still copper-red, and just long enough to miss being a man's military cut. There were places where the curls were too short, the damage very close to her skin, but the result wasn't too bad. Alisha thought she looked like a boy. A very pretty boy, but a boy. The haircut made her want to wear distinctly feminine earrings, in part because she was unaccustomed to having her ears so exposed. "I need makeup," she mumbled. Brandon, driving, glanced at her.

"Not really. You look good."

"I feel naked."

Brandon gave her a quick, hopeful grin that made her laugh as she shook her head. "You're used to wearing your hair short. I feel exposed."

"And makeup would help cover you up?"

"Yeah." Alisha rubbed her hand over the back of her head, feeling the soft bristles shift with the pressure. Brandon had been delicate in cutting her hair, exploring her skin for burns—there were none, and she knew how lucky she was—before taking the scissors and razor to it. Despite his protestations, his hands had been steady and warm, confident as he cut away the damaged hair. Alisha had allowed herself to revel in the tactile sensation for a few precious minutes, though she had closed down her thoughts as they wandered further afield with what those warm hands might accomplish elsewhere on her body. It was neither the time nor the place.

When will it be, Leesh?

Alisha shook her head, despite knowing that Brandon would see the gesture. He did, glancing her way curiously, and she shook her head again. "Just thinking." She put the thought away resolutely, adding, "About makeup and masks, I guess. Funny old world we live in."

"Usually when people say that they don't mean it's funny at all. Are you going to unmask?"

Alisha waved her fingers at her unmade-up face and shorter hair. "I already have." She gave him a sideways look, then turned her attention out the window again. Paris was left behind, the countryside smoothing out into hills and hamlets. *Peaceful,* Alisha thought, and then, more cynically, *or hiding something.* "Have you?"

"God, we're a suspicious lot, aren't we?" Brandon asked under his breath.

"Sorry. Habit." Habit developed with Reichart, who never gave a straight answer to a question, if he could avoid it. Alisha flexed her fingers against the van's window frame. "Have you ever heard of the Fas Infitialis?"

"Sure," Brandon said instantly. "They're always in the Sicarii's hair. Diametrical opposites, from what I've gathered. If the Sicarii are about the divine right of a few, then the Fas Infitialis is about man creating his own destiny." He shot Alisha a smile mixed with despair, then frowned as he took in her expression. "Ali?"

Alisha shook herself, trying to clear the surprise from her face. Independent verification, she thought. Maybe she wouldn't need to talk to Boyer.

Which, under the circumstances, was probably a good thing. Alisha flared her nostrils at the thought then pushed it away, too, paying attention to Brandon again. "Sorry, I…wasn't sure they really existed. I didn't know I was opening myself up for a lecture."

Brandon huffed out a sound of mild offense. "That wasn't a lecture. I was sharing my knowledge."

Alisha laughed aloud. "I stand corrected. Jesus, Brandon, how many shadow organizations are there out there?"

"The CIA agent wants to know this?" Brandon asked, amused. "If you didn't know they existed, how'd you know to ask?"

"I found a code," Alisha said. Brandon shot her another look that dissolved into laughter of his own.

"Not the Da Vinci Code, I hope."

Alisha snorted, but found herself grinning. "No. Besides, they'd have to be the Illuminati then, wouldn't they. What else do you know about them?"

"If I answer that, am I going to get harassed about lecturing again?"

"Probably."

Brandon grinned again. "I can live with that. I get the impression the Fas Infitialis are a lot less hierarchal than the Sicarii. More like terrorist cells, with three or four to a cell, nobody knowing who else belongs. Except instead of terror they're trying to spread education and health. You wouldn't think that kind of thing needed to be done in secret."

"I don't know." Alisha frowned out the window. "It's to the advantage of any government that doesn't intend to give up power to keep the people undereducated and scrabbling to make ends meet. There's not a dictatorship in the world that doesn't hold on to power through show of force and intimidation. I could see them regarding a group like Fas Infitialis as being horribly dangerous to the status quo."

"You're a cynic, Alisha."

"I know." Alisha's smile, reflected in the side-view mirror, turned sad. "It's what happens when your ideals start to show tarnish. The surprising thing is how long I lasted before losing my faith."

"Happens to the best of us." Brandon pulled the van to the side of the road, eyebrows drawn down. "Firebird lost her tag on the Attengees here."

"There's nothing here, Brandon." Alisha opened the van door and stood up in it, leaning on the frame as she looked over the vehicle's top. "Trees and fields. Not even a decrepit old manor house to draw us in."

"You've been reading too many spy novels." Brandon opened his own door and stood in it as well, studying the landscape. "Even going underground shouldn't have blocked the signal."

"Turning the drones off would, though, wouldn't it? Or could your bird be fooled somehow?"

"Don't impugn my masterpiece," Brandon said, only half kidding.

"I'm not," Alisha said. "But at least one of her prototypes got shot down, so she's not infallible. Can you call her back?"

Brandon's shoulders tightened. "I've been trying," he admitted. "Since we got up this morning. There's no response."

"Brandon." Alisha felt herself straightening up, turning her focus from the field to her erstwhile partner. Despite the growing knot of dismay in her belly, a wash of humor came over her, more bleak than laughter-filled. "Don't tell me you've lost *another* submarine."

Chapter 22

"What?" Brandon stared at her, shaking his head. "I'm talking about the Firebird, Alisha. What in hell are you talking about? Submarines?"

Another pang swept over Alisha, this time of regret. Greg, her handler and Brandon's father, would have caught the film reference. Would have expressed his amusement and wondered how it was he and his youthful protégé ever managed to communicate. Alisha pressed her lips together and shook her head in turn. "Nothing." She could hear the touch of sorrow in her voice, and saw that Brandon heard it, too, though his drawn-down eyebrows told her that he didn't recognize its source. "Are you telling me that people who have the ability to create more Attengee drones have gotten their hands on your aerial AI system?"

Pain tightened Brandon's expression. Emotional, not physical distress, though Alisha suspected the second Firebird's loss came close to causing him actual body suffering. "I didn't want to tell you until I was certain it wasn't just a malfunction."

"Brandon." Alisha felt cords stand out in her throat as she spoke through her teeth. "What happened?" It wasn't the question she wanted to ask. She wanted to rant and rail, castigating him for keeping secrets. Not that she was one to point fingers for secrets kept; it was part of the world they both belonged to. Brandon flinched as surely as if she'd yelled, and for a nasty moment it made her feel better. Moving as if he'd had the heart taken out of him, Brandon sat back down in the driver's seat, reaching for a flat control pad. Alisha took it from him, her jaw set.

"This is like the Attengee command pad," she half asked. Brandon nodded, voice subdued.

"A little more sophisticated, but the same basic principle."

Alisha gave a short, sharp nod and thumbed the pad on, dancing her fingers across its touchpad to activate the last images sent from the missing prototype. "Does this thing control the Attengees, too?"

"No."

"Isn't that going to be a problem if we've got to get through them to get to Reichart?"

Brandon shook his head. "I've got it taken care of."

Alisha arched an eyebrow curiously, then frowned down at the touchpad, studying the night-vision video. Green and black shapes, easy to see as abstract art in motion, popped onto the screen. Three trucks followed the road, then came to a complete stop. Everything, even the glow of the taillights, blacked out, and a burst of static grayed the screen. Nothing more. Alisha shook the pad, as if doing so might loosen answers, then looked at Brandon.

He thumped the steering wheel, vision fixed straight

ahead. There was color in his cheeks, high and angry. "That kind of burst was the last thing we got back from the Firebird that went down in the mountains, too. That's why it's critical to get the box back. If there's some kind of malfunction in the system that's causing them to go down, the recordings might help me pinpoint it."

"This one was broadcasting back to you." Alisha lifted the control pad. "Wasn't the one in the Pyrenees?"

"I reconfigured it to after I lost the first prototype," Brandon muttered. "The continuous feedback wasn't enabled on the one you went after. It was supposed to send back its data every twelve hours. The static burst we got was on an emergency wavelength."

"You think the broadcast signal might've tipped the Sicarii off to somebody following them?"

Brandon cast her a withering look. "The Firebird operates on an unusual frequency to help prevent exactly that sort of thing from happening."

"And yet," Alisha said stiffly. Brandon's glare faltered and he nodded slowly.

"Yeah. And yet. Sorry."

"So we've got two choices." Alisha folded herself over, stretching her back muscles and speaking into her knees. "One—we can assume they didn't catch the signal until they'd stopped, and that they're close by."

"And two?" Brandon sounded skeptical. Alisha lifted her head, feeling the muscles in her neck pinch.

"We can assume they noticed before they reached their destination and that we've completely lost them. They didn't give me any kind of tracking device to pinpoint the Firebird I went after with. There's nothing on yours, either?"

Brandon smiled faintly. "Even if there was, they'd have

disabled its signal by now. All right. You're the field agent. You tell me what to do next."

"Get maps," Alisha said. "Talk to the locals. That truck had to have gone somewhere."

"Join the CIA, they said. Make the world a safer place, they said." Alisha crawled through a culvert, pulling herself along with her forearms. Bruised tissue had long since given up its complaints, numbness setting in when Alisha clenched her teeth and continued through the pain.

"Join the CIA," she repeated. "Be the sucker who takes a walk and hands advanced technologies to power-hungry shadow organizations. Good job, Leesh. Really well done. Proud of you, girl." The litany of self-recrimination made her feel oddly better.

Rock, meet hard spot. For a moment Alisha paused, lowering her forehead against her sore arms. Two items of—she breathed a laugh, closing her eyes. Reichart and the Firebird were not, by anyone else's standards, of equal value. Only her own, and she was reluctant to confess that even to herself. The job required her to go after the Firebird, despite her walking away from Langley with her own agenda.

Just like everyone else, she thought with bitter humor. The very thing that had driven a wedge between herself and the CIA was the same thing that made her continue onward now: personal motivations that no one else would understand, because she wanted to keep them close to her chest, not sharing her plans with anyone.

Just what is your plan, Leesh? The question whispered at the back of her mind, making Alisha shake her head in the darkness. That question had the sense of being larger than the immediate, too much for her to consider in the here and now. Walking away from Langley might have been an irrevocable move, but it was one she was willing to stand by in order to gain answers she didn't think she could find inside the Agency. What it would mean in the days and years in front of her wasn't something she was ready to tackle.

She began inching forward again, grateful for the leather that protected her arms from the culvert's muck. Over Brandon's protestations Alisha had insisted on stopping at her own hotel and collecting the equipment she'd purchased from Jon's people, as well as the gizmos Erika had provided, but she still wore the jacket she'd taken from Reichart's closet. She would owe him a new one when this was over. The thought made her smile, heat coloring her cheeks. It had been years since the idea of owing Frank Reichart anything had held appeal.

They all had to get out of Sicarii hands alive, though, for her to owe him anything. Alisha's smile faded and she moved forward with more determination.

It was a bad plan. Neither she nor Brandon had any doubt on that matter, but neither could they see a better way through the mess that was partly of Alisha's own creating.

Mostly, she amended. Mostly of her own creating. Alone in the dark, there wasn't much point in lying to herself about it. Had she not interfered with Reichart's drop, had she not drugged him—

Had he told her the truth early in their relationship, she reminded herself forcefully. Had he not stolen the corrupted Attengee plans or the Firebird's black box. There was blame to lay all around, and taking it all for herself was as arrogant as accepting none of it. Whose fault it was no longer mattered, if it ever had. A fatalistic streak whispered that all paths led to where she was now: that a life built on deception inevitably came to making the best of nothing more than bad choices.

Had Brandon not betrayed her in Rome. The list of what-might-have-beens insisted on playing itself out. Hairs stood up on the back of Alisha's neck, making her shiver in the clammy darkness. That, above all, made this a bad plan. *Trust takes time,* she thought a little wryly, and even still her trust in Brandon Parker was…limited. Wanting to trust and actually investing herself in the emotion were very different things. If they came out of this whole—with or without Reichart, with or without the Firebird—her confidence in him would be well restored. But for now, she had no other partner to choose from. It was Brandon or going it alone, and she liked her odds by herself even less than with a partner of uncertain loyalties.

Cave systems littered the land beneath the fields they'd lost the trucks by. Haunted caves, a schoolboy had told them matter-of-factly. Haunted by the spirits of men and women forty thousand years dead, whose contemporaries had painted the walls of other French caves. It was a matter of youthful masculine pride to explore those caves, although, the boy added with an annoyed sneer, now the girls wanted to explore them, too. Alisha had fought laughter, thanked the boy, and left willing to bet that *les filles* had been exploring the caves as long as the boys had.

Once upon a time she'd have thought it was romantic, the idea of a secret society hiding beneath the earth, in naturally carved caverns. Once, Alisha thought, a long time before there was mud in her hair and smeared over her nose from scratching itches that wouldn't go away. The girl who would have found romance in the idea had faded years ago, though not quite enough that Alisha couldn't remember her.

It wasn't just years ago. She could remember precisely the moment that anything under the ground had become less appealing. There was a stiffly written journal entry about it: even writing reminded her of how her breath had been taken from her, quite literally, and Alisha had held her breath through much of the chronicling. A missile had been lost underwater in a cave system riddled by coral. Alisha and Cristina had been assigned to retrieve it; weapons were their specialty. It had been a race against the clock, the FSB closing in as quickly as the Agency.

Biting humor lanced through Alisha. Back then she hadn't known how the FSB had gotten there so quickly. Hindsight told her that Cristina had tipped her people off, though Alisha still thought her pale blond partner was as surprised to find competition as Alisha had been. She'd expected them to be long gone with the missile, but it was more badly entangled in coral and rough rock than anyone had anticipated.

There'd been no warning that her air line was being cut, nothing more than a pull behind her head, and by then it was too late. Sixty feet underwater in a cave half that depth in length. Not an easy distance to swim in the best of circumstances, but it became insurmountable with no chance to hyperventilate and fill lungs and blood with extra oxygen. Even now Alisha felt the tightness in her chest, constricting the airways as frighteningly as it had then.

It was the cave itself that saved her. Rushing air from her cut line had nowhere to go and became trapped at the cave's roof, making bubbles that Alisha broke into. It took all her conscious effort to breathe slowly and deeply, to not panic and gulp what precious air she had.

And then Cristina came, blue eyes reassuring as she broke into Alisha's tiny air bubble and popped the breather from her mouth. "To hell with the missile. We've got to get you out of here. We can share my oxygen." Talking used the last of the bubble, but Cristina's smile was confident. She took Alisha's hand so they couldn't lose each other, and together they swam for the surface.

It was only much, much later that Alisha had reason to wonder if it had been Cristina herself who had cut her air line. By the time she wondered, she could no longer ask.

Alisha shuddered in a breath, flexing her shoulders as if doing so would expand her lung capacity. Going into basements and foundations, even underground bunkers, didn't set off the claustrophobia like caves did. Even being underwater didn't do it, but caves. Caves she did not like.

Speaking of keeping secrets, she mocked herself. But there was no point in confessing that particular one to Brandon: her claustrophobia was a controlled fear, and, unlike the missing Firebird, was unlikely to put more than herself in danger.

Though if it put anyone else in danger, it would be her partner. Cristina had known, not from Alisha's words, but from her body language, that caves disturbed her. Having someone else share the secret somehow made it easier to be brave.

But there was no one else who knew, now, and Brandon was squirming through another tunnel down into the cave system, so lingering over self-pity and job-induced trauma would have to wait. The schoolkid had been more than forthcoming with the secret passages used by generations of children to sneak into the higher levels of the caves, though he'd extracted a promise from Alisha that she wouldn't tell any other adults. She'd promised solemnly, hiding her expression as she wondered just how the boy thought the location of the exploratory tunnels had been passed down to him. Maybe he thought the knowledge had spontaneously erupted in the mind of someone just a year or two older than he was, or, more likely, he'd never thought about it at all. It wasn't the kind of thing that would have crossed Alisha's mind as a preteen. Nonetheless, she'd given her promise, and she even intended to keep it. All except a note in her journal.

There *had* to be a better way into the caves than the grimy tunnels the kid had told them about. Alisha could see a faint brightness now—the light at the end of the tunnel, she thought, amused—but certainly the trucks had come in another way, if she and Brandon were correct about their location. Not that she'd have wanted to follow them in through their front door. There'd be nothing sneaky about that, and ideally they would slip in and out without the Sicarii being any the wiser.

Feeling the strain in her arms, she pulled herself forward the last several yards, coming out on a ledge that was higher up than she expected. There were other small holes littering the rim where she lay, though she saw no sign of Brandon. He would be there, she promised herself.

Craggy walls narrowed and shrank to her left, the ridge she lay on melding with the stone as it became a tunnel. The cavern below was large enough to hold vehicles: the two trucks the Firebird had tracked sat there, their engines long since cooled, though a faint scent of gasoline lingered in the air. The path leading out was well-enough traveled that tire marks were visible in broken rock, but Alisha had no sense of how long the road might be before it broke to the surface. Children exploring this far could find themselves in terrible danger. She hoped the stories of ghosts kept them far enough away to maintain their safety.

Waiting for Brandon only increased her own chances of

being discovered. Alisha wriggled along her ledge, careful not to disturb fragments of stone enough to knock them to the floor below. There was a slight downward slope to the rim before it became one with the rest of the cave wall. Enough to make the drop to the ground a little less alarming, though it wasn't far enough to damage her badly except in the worst circumstances. Alisha held her breath, listening to the sound of her heartbeat and to the silence of the cave before slithering down the wall to land in a crouch beside the next tunnel entrance.

"There you are." Brandon's voice, coming from the vehicles behind her. Alisha's stomach cramped with warning and she turned to watch him step out of one of the trucks. He was impeccably clean, with no sign of having crawled through hundreds of feet of muddy earth. His smile was brief and unapologetic as he turned his focus to someone beyond Alisha.

"I told you I'd deliver them both."

Chapter 23

"Brandon." Alisha whispered his name as if it would stop the cold wash of fury and fear that cascaded through her. "Brandon."

"You make it easy," he said shortly. "If you'd stayed at Langley where you belonged, I wouldn't have been able to get to you. You're a fool, Alisha."

"Yeah." Alisha nodded, eyes closed. She didn't want to look behind her to see who was there. It didn't really matter. Cold spiraled around her stomach, making a knot of nausea there. *You knew,* she chided herself, but the castigation was without heat. *You knew you shouldn't trust him, Leesh.* And from the chill inside her, she hadn't. Anger, yes, and dismay, but no surprise. She'd gone in having weighed the risks, and the odds had turned bad on her.

At least now she unquestionably knew where Brandon Parker stood, in the fight between freedom and dictatorship.

"Hands behind your head," a woman said. Alisha was already lifting them, but the voice made her turn her head incredulously.

"Helen?"

"You remembered. I'm flattered. Hands behind your head."

"I thought you were with Frank." Even as she laced her fingers behind her head, Alisha winced at the use of the man's first name. He knew it as a tell. Whether Helen did or not depended on how much they'd discussed her.

Alisha, perversely, found herself hoping they'd discussed her quite a lot. Helen's irritated huff of breath told her nothing. "I got a better offer," the delicate Asian woman said. "It happens."

"Jesus." Alisha cast her eyes upward, absurdity overtaking her for a moment. "Is *anybody* besides me working for who they say they are?"

"You took a walk, Alisha," Brandon reminded her. "Don't exclude yourself from the party."

Alisha set her teeth together. "Right. I forgot." She kept her head turned, trying to get a look at Helen and anyone who might be with her. "How long? It had to be after Zurich, or you wouldn't have let me set that virus."

"After Zurich," Helen confirmed, but finished with, "now shut up and move. Better yet, give me an excuse to shoot you."

"Helen." Brandon's voice was low, but the warning in it carried. Alisha wished she could see the woman's expression, sensing that she was snarling. Regardless, she put a hand on Alisha's shoulder to turn her around, then prodded her in the spine with a gun, repeating, "Move."

Alisha moved, catching glimpses of other armed men and women in the shadows. "How do you keep the kids from finding you?"

"We're not here much. And we won't be back."

Startled hope sparked in Alisha's throat, tightening it. "That sounds like you might not be planning on killing us."

"You'd be dead if I was going to," Helen said sharply. "But go ahead. Give me an excuse."

"Someday," Alisha said under her breath, "we're going to have a come-to-Jesus meeting, you and I."

"I look forward to it." Helen shoved Alisha forward with the barrel of the gun, sending her stumbling into a smaller cavern. Reichart, as bruised and furious looking as Alisha felt, if considerably less muddy, knelt on the hard stone against the farthest wall. His mouth tightened almost imperceptibly as Alisha entered the room.

"Nice hair."

Alisha managed a faint smile as Helen knocked her into place beside him. "You noticed. I'm so pleased."

"I try."

"Shut up," Helen said. Alisha glanced at her, then back at Reichart.

"I blew the rescue card. Sorry about that."

"Trusted the wrong guy, didn't you."

Anger flared, making Alisha flex her hands against her shorn hair in a futile gesture. "I have a knack for that." Her attention slid back to Helen and she added, "Maybe you shouldn't talk."

Reichart growled, deep and low in his throat. Alisha settled back on her heels, straightening her spine into a comfortable position, satisfied with his response. "So why don't we have bullets in our brains yet? What do you want?" She could see six mercs, not including Brandon, who leaned against the stone doorway, hands loose and casual in his pockets. His expression was pleasantly neutral, neither smug nor distressed. There should be *some-*

thing there, Alisha thought in frustration. Betrayal ought to carry some kind of mark that could be easily read.

Then again, she could feel her own expression lying to Helen: offhand gaze only mildly interested, her voice carrying cocky arrogance. There was no room to show fear or even anger when she was a prisoner, injured and outnumbered.

"Ransom," Helen said with a shrug. Alisha laughed, startled out of watching the room.

"The CIA doesn't negotiate with terrorists, Helen. What do you think you're going to achieve by trying to ransom us?" She felt Reichart's eyes on her, though he didn't make the comment she could all but hear: *I'm not CIA, Leesh. Why are you making this an "us"?*

Because I'm not leaving here without you, she thought in response to the unasked question.

"That's none of your concern," Helen snapped. Alisha slumped her shoulders, then kept a wicked grin from flashing across her face as she looked up again.

"Is this about him?" She tilted her head toward Reichart, still not looking his way. "I mean, since you've got me at a disadvantage anyway, can we at least get that cleared up? What is it you've got against me? Did he say my name when he was in bed with you, or something? Oh, shit," she said with another surprised laugh, as fury blanked Helen's expression. "Christ, Reichart, you really know how to screw up with a woman, don't you? Maybe you should just shoot him," she added, speaking to Helen again. The woman's mouth turned into a thin line and she lifted her gun, butt first.

"Shut up," she said again. "They said alive. Nobody said anything about being able to talk."

"Thanks for the vote of confidence," Reichart muttered. Alisha gave him a genial smile that she then turned on Helen.

"Look, I'm sure he didn't mean anything by it. You know how men are. They get a piece of ass and it's all over but the googly eyes. Most of the time I'm surprised they remember their own names, much less ours. After a while you decide, who cares, especially if he does that thing with his tongue wh...oh." She squinted up apologetically at the Asian woman. "He never did that to you, huh. My bad." Beyond Helen she could see Brandon's expression changing, slow incredulity creeping over it. Helen's cheeks were white with rage. "Well, Jesus, Frank," Alisha stage-whispered at him, "how was I supposed to know that was reserved for me?"

"It's not," Reichart drawled, "but some girls aren't worth the bother."

"You son of a *bitch*." Helen took two long steps forward, gun raised to bring the butt down across Reichart's cheek.

Alisha shoved forward, pushing all the way through her toes, and T-boned her shoulder into Helen's knee. Cartilage and ligaments tore with audible pops, the woman collapsing sideways as Alisha's weight drove her over. Alisha scrambled up her body to wrap a hand around her neck and lift her far enough to crack her skull back down against the rock, teeth bared in a predatory grin. "Shoulda tied our hands, bitch. Reichart?"

"Got it."

Alisha looked up from the woman she crouched over. The sound of weapons cocking rang loud in her ears, though she hadn't consciously heard the preparations. Only Brandon was unarmed, the surprise on his face replaced with approval. "I think we have an impasse," Alisha announced. "Yes? Somebody doesn't want you to kill us, and between Helen here being down and Reichart having a gun, I think the odds have evened out a bit. Brandon?"

"Why do you think I'm in charge now?"

"Because in a room full of guys with guns, the person in charge is the guy who doesn't need to carry one. Besides." Alisha felt her smile grow even more vicious. "You're the one I'm looking forward to beating to death. They never rescinded my termination orders."

"I'm sure that was an oversight, Alisha."

"One I'll be glad to take advantage of. Reichart and I are going to walk out of here now, and you're going to let us. I'll drop Helen somewhere safe. Like federal prison."

Brandon sighed. "I wish I could tell you how much I regret this."

Alisha sneered, not liking the feeling of the expression on her face. "But you don't regret it. Yeah. I know the story." She fisted her hand in Helen's shirt and hauled the woman upright, twisting her to wrap her arm around Helen's throat. Helen groaned and made a retching noise that Alisha ignored. "We walk out of here, everything's copacetic."

Brandon turned his head toward the nearest armed merc. "Shoot her."

Gunfire rang without hesitation.

"Helen!" Reichart's voice roared over the sound of the shot. The woman Alisha held jerked, a terrible full-body spasm that knocked Alisha backward. The sickness that had made Helen retch seemed to leap from her body into Alisha's as they collapsed to the ground together, Helen's weight dead in Alisha's arms.

Not dead, Alisha thought, cold panic around the illness in her belly. She rolled over, putting Helen on the ground, and felt for a pulse. *Oh, Christ, please, not dead.*

There were shots being fired above her, around her, the sounds playing out slow and whining in suddenly distorted hearing. Helen's chest heaved under Alisha's hand, a desperate drag of air, and the woman's eyes flew open. "You're going to be okay." Alisha's voice cracked as she made the promise, icy fingers searching for the bullet hole beneath the blood blossoming across Helen's shirt.

There. Above the heart, shattering the collarbone. Alisha felt her own white smile. "It's not a killing shot," she whispered. "I know. I lived through the same one. You're going to be okay. Breathe. Just breathe. I need you to breathe through the shock, Helen. You hear me?" System shock was what killed, with many gunshot wounds. Enormous violent trauma to the body too frequently shut everything down, the will to live overridden by pain and confusion. Bleeding out was a comparatively slow death. "Helen, listen to me. Breathe." The Asian woman's hands were waxy and cold, pained disbelief fading with the light in her eyes. "Helen, *no,* Jesus *Christ!*"

"Alisha." Reichart's voice was too cold, too controlled. It betrayed pain and fury, emotions that he would never normally allow himself to show. "We have a problem."

Helen's grip on Alisha's hand relaxed as Alisha lifted her head. There was sufficient chaos in the cavern, men lying dead only a few yards away, bullet patterns splashed in the rock behind them. Brandon had neither moved from the door nor taken his hands from his pockets, looking the picture of casualness amidst the remnants of a firefight. Two others were alive and uninjured, their weapons dropped. Giving up the guns had saved their lives, Alisha judged, though she didn't dare risk a look at Reichart to confirm it.

Behind Brandon, picking up the lighting in the cavern and throwing it back in soft gleaming silver, waited an Attengee drone and its six-legged counterpart. Alisha instantly thought of it as the Spider, regardless of the number of legs, and felt a shiver run down her spine.

You're not even afraid of spiders, Leesh. What gives?

"I'm going to give you a two-minute head start." Brandon finally took his hand from his pocket, examining his fingernails before glancing up, disinterested.

"And then?" Alisha wanted to force life back into the body at her feet, but instead slowly shoved her way upright, sickness pounding in her heart.

"Then they come after you."

"Why bother with the chase?" Reichart's voice was still raw, grating at Alisha's skin. He was the rock in her existence, the one man whose emotional state couldn't be discerned or rattled. To have his words sound like bleeding wounds made Alisha want to scream simply to break the tension of it. Instead she flexed and loosened the muscles of her thighs, preparing to drop into a dead run the moment Brandon gave the nod. She didn't care *why.* It was too late for explanations. Only action could drive away the feeling of Helen's hand growing cooler in hers, and the memory of ragged breathing that warned of death.

Brandon's gaze flickered to hers, and for an instant Alisha thought she saw things there. Apology. Guilt. Despair. A plea for understanding.

All the things she hadn't seen in Cristina's eyes, in the moment before her partner took her own life. For the thousandth time, Alisha wondered if Cristina's dramatic gesture had been to spare Alisha the need to pull the trigger and terminate her best friend's existence.

The certainty of firing the killing shot might have been easier to live with, she thought distantly, than years of questioning Cristina's motivations.

"Just to see what happens," Brandon said, and Alisha knew the words for a lie.

But she couldn't discern the underlying truth.

"Two minutes," Brandon said, and Alisha ran.

Chapter 24

Reichart was hard on her heels, his longer legs hampered by the knife wound still healing in his thigh. Neither spoke as they burst through the cavern entrance, not needing to discuss their tactics. Alisha, still a few steps in the lead, hit the hood of the closest truck and rolled over it, landing on the far side in a crouch that allowed her to spring into the driver's seat in the moment after she yanked the door open.

Blessedly, unbelievably, there were keys in the ignition. She heard her own laugh skirl upward, a sharp sound of violence and rage, but the vehicle was a clutch and she forced herself to take a steadying breath as she turned it on. Flooding the engine would be their death sentence.

Reichart was nowhere to be seen. She didn't wait, throwing the truck in reverse and whipping around the second vehicle in the larger outer cavern. Objects in the truck's covered bed thudded and crashed, one with the soft sound of a body. She would apologize later, if Reichart expected it. He slammed the window between the bed and the cab open and she reached for the gun he handed her without looking. Trusting, she thought. Trusting he would do his part. In the worst of it, she trusted him in a way she'd never trusted anyone else.

Except Cristina. Alisha swore silently and pushed the thought away, firing two rounds out the window as she careened up the rocky path leading out of the caves. A better shot would have guaranteed flat tires on the second truck, but it wasn't the mundane vehicles that were the danger. It was the drones, waiting their two minutes before remorselessly hunting down their quarry.

One minute, twenty-eight seconds. The corrected number came into Alisha's mind with the ease of long practice, a countdown that bordered on obsessive behavior. They might escape the Attengees. It was the Firebird that Alisha feared, its hunt unconstrained by having to keep to the earth. The only thing that might save them was that it was daylight, and Brandon might not want to risk his new prototype being seen by untrained eyes.

Brandon. You fool, you fool, you fool, Leesh. Alisha pounded the heel of her hand on the steering wheel, squinting as the vehicle burst out of the cave mouth into a damp stream bed. Trees scraped the windshield and roof, high squeals that made chills rise on her arms. Alisha cast a glance in the side-view mirror as they ripped out of the tree cover, watching branches settle back into place, effectively hiding the cavern entrance.

Beyond the trees was a brilliant gray sky. Damn it. Cloud cover, no matter how bright, would give Brandon confidence in sending his drones out. Smeary photographs of the silver machines would only feed stories of UFO sightings, and bring tourists through the area for a while.

You fool, she thought again, though the heat of it was already dissipated. She'd known going in he wasn't to be trusted, and her anger was directed more at Greg Parker's son than at herself.

"We need to get back to Paris." Reichart shouldered his way through the cab window, voice still tightly wound. The window was too small for a man of his shoulder breadth to fit through easily, and Alisha heard bone cracking against metal as he was too rough with himself. Hiding one kind of pain with another, she thought.

"I know," she said. Reichart's expression, reflected in the rearview mirror, tightened.

"We're too exposed out here. Not enough cover, too few witnesses. Too few unrelated casualties."

"I know." Alisha shifted herself to the side, giving Reichart the room he needed to work his way into the cab. One minute, two seconds.

"We can get lost more easily in Paris. You'll need to contact Boyer, tell him the situation."

"I know, Frank," Alisha said as gently as she could. "Frank, I—"

"Don't!" His voice cracked out, sharp and angry as he slid into the passenger-side seat. Graceful, even in pain and fury, Alisha thought. "Don't," he grated a second time. "Don't."

Alisha pressed her lips together, forcing herself to silence for a few seconds, until the urge to apologize had passed. Forty-three seconds. "What kind of equipment do we have back there?"

"We've got the guns. The rest of it, I don't know. Electronics. Means nothing to me." Reichart's voice was brittle.

Alisha glanced at him, then pressed her toe against the accelerator as she folded her other leg up under herself.

"You drive."

"What?"

"Drive, Reichart. I need to assess our materials. You're not in any condition."

Reichart snarled, "I'm *fine,*" but slid across the cab, slipping his foot under hers so the vehicle would never lose power. His hand on her hip guided her away from the driver's seat, Alisha twisting to face the open cab window as she climbed over his lap. For an instant she found herself studying his profile, a purely selfish thought intruding: had he been this upset when he'd shot *her,* his fiancée, six years ago?

Reichart gave her a sharp look. "What?"

Twenty-five seconds, the countdown in Alisha's head said, and she murmured, "Nothing," as she climbed into the back of the truck.

Electronics. Reichart was more—Alisha didn't know what word to choose. Distressed. Infuriated—than he'd let on, and she'd known from the barely controlled rage in his voice that he was more badly hurt than she'd ever seen him before. He'd seen the control pads that could be used to program the Attengee drones. Classifying them as merely *electronics* now suggested he was closer to the edge of despair than Alisha had imagined.

She crouched in the back of the truck, sightlessly stroking her fingers over a handful of the pads. They would operate on modulating frequencies, no one drone exactly attuned to more than one pad. They were intended to work as a unit, with a leader drone downloading orders and rebroadcasting them to its team. Once the objective was stated, the Attengees themselves were capable of deciding the best way to accomplish that objective. Alisha had watched them both follow a preset plan and think for themselves, sometimes reacting faster than even she could have.

The truck hit a bump and she rounded her shoulders, irrationally afraid she would fly up and hit the bed's roof. "Reichart."

"It's the goddamned road," he snapped. Alisha's chin came up in surprise and she looked over her shoulder toward the cab.

"Reichart, these aren't just electronics. They're drone control pads. Brandon might've given us the way to get out of this alive."

"How thoughtful of him," Reichart sneered. Alisha pressed her lips together and turned her attention back to the pads.

It might have been, Frank, she answered, but only silently. It was impossible that Brandon could cavalierly order a woman's death and with the same breath offer them their only chance at survival. Wasn't it? The keys could have been left in the ignition deliberately, the vehicles left where they could easily be stolen.

Except Brandon had been with her when the trucks were parked, and if the drone's masters had been confident of their triumph, they would have had no reason to take precautions against either the trucks or the control pads being stolen.

You're still *looking for ways to trust him, Leesh.* Alisha spoke over her shoulder again, for once in accordance with Reichart's sarcasm regarding Brandon. "It doesn't matter. The good news is we've got the means to control a dozen of their Attengees."

"What's the bad news?" Once, the question would have been infused with humor. Now Reichart only sounded as if he was waiting for the next blow to fall. Alisha dropped her chin to her chest, a wave of defeat sweeping her.

"They operate on different frequencies and there's no guarantee the ones that'll be coming after us will respond to any of these pads."

"Do something about it," Reichart said shortly. Alisha stared at his shoulder—the only part of him easily visible—then turned back to the pads, spreading them across the truck bed.

"Keep an eye on the sky," she muttered, just loud enough for Reichart to hear over the truck's rumbles. "The Firebird will be the first to reach us, and I don't have a control pad for it. It must be in the other truck."

"Too bad you didn't look before you decided which one to steal," Reichart snapped back.

"I'll try to be more careful next time." Alisha put no rancor in the response, knowing he lashed out to release pain and frustration. She shared the impulse, but kept it quenched. Bad enough that Reichart was distraught. Should she give in to her own anger and fear, they'd lose whatever edge they might have. "You have somewhere in Paris we can go? A safe house?"

Silence answered her, and then a growled curse. "I know a hotel."

Alisha nodded, breathing, "Please be awake," as she dug into her filthy jeans pocket and came out with the little silver communicator Erika had given her. Her first impulse—tapping its surface—got no telltale chirp of activation. Despite the past harrowing minutes, Alisha found a crooked smile to give the piece as she turned it over, looking for the way to turn it on.

A button too subtle to be accidentally depressed marred the device's back. Alisha pushed her fingernail against it, feeling it give a subtle click, and turned the communicator over again. "Erika? Hello?"

"Who the hell are you talking to?"

"Just drive, Reichart." Alisha gnawed her lower lip, palming the triangle and bringing it closer to her mouth. "E? You there?" She mumbled a curse when there was no response, then tapped the gleaming surface impatiently. "E?"

The comm unit gave an entirely familiar chirrup that made Alisha lose her balance with surprised laughter. "Oh my God, she's going to get in so much trouble. That's got to be copyrighted, or something."

This time, "What the hell?" came from two voices: Reichart in the front seat, and Erika's sleep-heavy grumble over the comm. The latter cleared slightly, though the next question was broken with a yawn. "Alisha? Is that you?"

"Hi, E. Sorry to wake you up."

"Liar. What do you need? And I got the sound off a cell phone ring, anyway. It's legal. What do you think I am, some kind of pirate? Arr," she added, somewhat compulsively.

"Arr," Alisha agreed. "How would I get an Attengee control panel to broadcast on all the Attengee frequencies at once?"

"You'd need the master board," Erika said with another yawn. "Or a resident genius."

"That's why I'm calling you, Erika. You're sure this thing can't be traced?"

"Of course it can be traced. Everything can be traced. But it uses a low-level subharmonic frequency that nobody except whales listens to."

"Whales?"

"Does it really matter right now? Look, you have a control pad? Not a master one, but at least one?"

"I've got nine," Alisha said, feeling an out-of-place burst of triumph at the admission.

"I'm sure I don't want to know how you got nine, eh?" Erika said. "You have anything to record the frequencies with?"

"Even if I did, I don't think I'd recognize it."

"Well, shit, Ali, you've got to give me something to work with. I'm going to have to..." Her voice trailed off, leaving Alisha deliberately twitching muscle groups as an exercise to keep herself from blurting out demands to her distant friend. "All right, look," Erika muttered a minute later.

"We've got company," Reichart said from the front seat. Alisha closed her eyes and swore.

"This really needs to work the first time, Erika."

"You *Mission: Impossible* types," Erika said. "Always with the emergencies. All right, look. Turn on all the pads. I'll give you the command line to type in and with any luck it'll overload the system and everything will respond on one frequency for about thirty seconds."

"With any luck?"

"You want flawless genius, you call me with the frequency codes. I'm working from memory here, so I can't guarantee it'll be right."

"Your memory is better than most people's solid facts."

"That's *your best guess,*" Erika corrected sotto voce. Alisha frowned at the comm, and as if Erika could see it, the other woman said, "Never mind. Ready?"

"God, I hope so."

The string of letters and backslashes that Erika rattled off meant absolutely nothing to Alisha, who found herself shaking her head as she typed them in. "I thought the Attengee's strength was that it could be programmed in plain English, E."

Erika snorted. "Its objectives can be, but you really want somebody to be able to rewrite all your source code in plain English? They'd be able to turn the drones around and send them back at you. What's happening?"

"All my handhelds blipped," Alisha reported. She heard Erika's hands clap together.

"Rock on, dude. Try your shutdown procedure now. If it works, the shutdown should be on a different frequency, so they're going to have to look for the right one to start 'em up again. You'll have some more time, at least."

"Shutdown sequence initiated," Alisha said beneath her breath, then lifted her voice. "Reichart?"

"You're with Reichart?" Erika's voice brightened with interest. "What's going on, Ali?"

"Firebird's still coming, Alisha." Reichart's voice rose with strain.

"Fuck," Alisha said. "Wrong code, E."

"You didn't say anything about a *Firebird!* Shit, Alisha, I haven't even gotten to play with one of those yet! God-damn it. Look, I'll call you back." Erika's vowels went long, a sure sign of her frustration as her Upper Peninsula accent came out. The comm blooped again and Alisha was left staring at it helplessly.

"Alisha," Reichart repeated.

Alisha twisted around to watch the Firebird soar in front of their truck, thrusters firing blue-white flame as it paced them, a few dozen yards ahead.

Chapter 25

"Why isn't it firing on us?" Reichart's voice was low and full of tension. Alisha's shoulders shared that tension, so tight they felt like steel bands around her neck.

"I don't know. Unless they still don't want us dead."

"Then what *do* they want!"

"I don't know, Reichart," Alisha said, keeping her tone deliberately quiet. She shoved a gun through the window between the cab and the truck bed, lodging it in the passenger footwell before climbing through the window herself, Glock in hand. "I do know I don't want Brandon's baby following us home." She rolled the window down, pressing the lock closed with her hip as she swung herself into the window, weight balanced on the frame. Wind, kicked up by the speed they traveled at, tried to whip her hair around her face, but could find no purchase. For a startled moment,

Alisha felt a surge of pleasure at the new haircut, as if it thwarted nature's master plan.

"Be careful," Reichart said, so quietly she almost missed it. Alisha cast a lopsided smile at the Firebird's rear thrusters, bringing her gun up to sight her shot. A .45 seemed like such a pathetic weapon against the sleek piece of technology soaring in front of them.

Any keep is only as strong as its weakest point, Leesh. The road wasn't as smooth as she'd like, making the chance of her shots going wild that much greater, but an Attengee drone would already have assessed her as a threat. There was no time to hope for smoother paths. Alisha fired, three rapid shots that drowned out the wind howling by her ears. A pause, barely longer than a heartbeat, to determine if she'd done any damage, and she squeezed off three more shots, her target the rear thrusters.

The fifth shot hit, an explosion of sparks and smoke. The Firebird lurched and Reichart yanked the wheel to the side, getting out of its path. Alisha squealed, grabbing on to the truck's roof as it skidded beneath the aerial combat unit. The Firebird turned on a wingtip, following the vehicle's path, and sleek cutaways opened beneath the drone's wingspan. "Good," Alisha said through her teeth. "We just moved up to *clear and present danger.*" She dug her fingers into the truck's roof, firing off more shots. One shattered a wingtip laser preparing to fire, the shot so unlikely that for an instant Alisha's jaw dropped. She knew she could make it in a controlled environment, but having it hit in the middle of combat seemed like a godsend.

The Firebird winged higher into the air, as if retreating long enough to better assess the situation. "Come around!" Alisha bellowed. "I need to get the other thruster!" She slid into the truck, banging against the dashboard as Reichart threw the vehicle into reverse and yanked the wheel around. "Four shots left, if you need them." She dropped the .45 on the seat beside her and dove for the second weapon she'd prepped. Reichart gave her a tight smile as she straightened up again.

"I do so love a woman with a machine gun," he said beneath the shriek of tires. Alisha returned the smile and bent herself backward out the window, bringing the gun out above her chest. Laser fire rained down, smashing steaming holes into the earth and asphalt around the truck.

"Hurry," Reichart said, too quietly to be heard. Alisha picked the word out anyway, battle-trained senses searching for every advantage or threat they might find. Reichart was right: it would only take one direct hit from molten light to end their chance of escape for good. She squeezed the trigger, sending up a spray of bullets that clanged and bounced off the Firebird's gleaming surface, barely scarring it.

"I swear to God I'm going to kick his ass," she breathed, not expecting to be heard. Reichart's laughter startled her, sharp and angry.

"Not if I get to him first, sweetheart. Hold on." The truck leaped forward with such violence Alisha slid along the window frame, cracking her arm against the edge. "That's gonna leave a mark," Reichart said without apology.

"And it was my good arm, too." Alisha pulled the trigger again, hearing bullets scream through the air and shatter against the Firebird above. Several smashed back down, bouncing off it to penetrate the bed of the truck as Reichart's driving left the flying machine a few yards behind. Alisha rolled, still firing a wide arc of noise.

Metal screeched and erupted, smoke billowing in thick white waves as the Firebird took another critical hit to its thrusters and slammed into the ground at full speed. Alisha let herself relax for half a breath, collapsing forward over the door, then shoved herself upright and back into the cab. "We should stop and pick it up."

"You're strong, Alisha, but you're not fireproof." Reichart spoke through compressed lips, inhaling sharply as he pulled the truck back onto the road.

"Reich—Jesus Christ, Reichart, you're hit." Daylight streamed in through holes punctured in the cab roof, bullets sizzling in the truck's front seat.

"Just a scratch," Reichart muttered. Alisha dropped the M16 and pulled her legs up on the bench seat, turning to face Reichart. A long score ran down his biceps, skin blistered and red, oozing blood. "I told you," he said. "Just a scratch."

"It still needs taking care of." Alisha leaned in to set her teeth against the shoulder seam of his shirt, ready to tear the material. Reichart jerked away.

"Leesh, let it be."

Alisha sat back on her heels, rolling her tongue inside her mouth, then nodded. "Yell if you see anything else coming after us," she said flatly. "I'm going to see if I can get Erika back." She crawled into the bed of the truck without waiting for an answer.

Weight smacked her hip bone as she wriggled through the narrow opening. Alisha sat down on a wheel hub, reaching for the comm unit as she dipped her hand into the jacket pocket to see what had knocked against her hip. Her fingers brushed body-warm metal and a missed heartbeat hit her in the throat, a deep thud that made swallowing uncomfortable. She traced the box with her fingertips, staring sightlessly at the truck's far wall.

Curiosity impelled the cat. Alisha had no discernible

reason for having slipped the box out of Helen's pocket and into her own, only a lingering sense of misplaced possession. She knew she'd taken it, but could only just remember having done it, as if the reasoning that had prompted her to disappeared when looked at head-on. She glanced toward the cab of the truck: Reichart's gaze, reflected in the rearview mirror, was on the road, intense with concentration. Alisha knew that intensity, having felt it within herself. It was the look of a man with a single goal in mind, that one purpose allowing him to push away any other thoughts that might intrude. He wouldn't notice much of anything Alisha did, short of beginning to fire her weapon again. She slid the box from her pocket, palming it.

Black, heavy stainless steel, the surface unscarred, too dense to be marked. Barely larger than a portable disk drive, but considerably weightier. Alisha had only held it for a moment, before Reichart and Helen made off with it.

She'd assumed Reichart had had it all along. Alisha rubbed her thumb over the smooth material. *You know what they say about* assume, *Leesh. It makes an ass out of* u *and* me. She folded the box into the sleeve of Reichart's jacket, hiding it before asking, "Who were you supposed to deliver the box to, anyway?" Her voice was hoarse and rough, much worse than it had been only moments earlier. Reichart shot a look at her via the rearview mirror.

"That was the drop at the cathedral. It was my final trading card to prove I was with the Sicarii. I don't know why the hell they wanted it. I just know delivering it was what gave them the all-clear on me. If I'd turned over the wrong thing they wouldn't have shown up at the hotel. Or they'd have shown up with guns."

"They did show up with guns, Frank. I don't think they were going to welcome you into the fold. I think you got used." The box's weight against her arm felt deadly, like it would drag her down into hell if she wasn't eternally vigilant. "Did Helen know where you were staying?"

Reichart's silence gave her all the answers she needed. Alisha traced the box beneath the leather and studied the floor, feeling cold. Worse than cold. Remote. Distanced. Exhausted. Despite the bumps in the road that jostled her body, she felt unattached from her own flesh as thought scattered randomly through her mind.

There had been three trucks in the Firebird's playback. Three vehicles that had stopped near the French countryside field, before the static blitz that had brought the glider down. Alisha could see them in her mind's eye, blocks of darkness that went suddenly black as the electric lights in the night-vision recordings were shut down.

And, as clearly, she could see the two trucks parked in the cavern, kitty-corner to one another. Two, just two. The third had gone on.

But not before the veiled blond woman had passed the black box to Helen. Alisha closed her eyes, almost able to see it for all that she hadn't been there. Helen, who was waiting for Brandon to deliver Alisha. Brandon, who had developed the Firebirds, and who would be best suited to unraveling any secrets held in the downed glider's black box. The scenario fit together with a click that sent a shudder of unhappiness up Alisha's spine.

Played. Used. Whatever the word was, she'd been taken in, and so had Reichart. The only thing that didn't fit was why Brandon had given them a chance to escape.

Alisha lifted her gaze, turning it to the blank wall across from her. *Ransom,* Helen had said. *Bait,* Alisha now translated that. The Sicarii were counting on Alisha and Reichart to be able to draw someone out.

"Don't let…" Alisha's voice was rough again, and she shook her head as she reactivated Erika's communicator. "Erika?"

"You're still alive?"

"Yeah." Alisha cleared her throat. "For the moment, anyway. E, you can't let anybody come after us. No agents, no backup, nothing. Nobody. Don't let them send anybody. I don't know what's going on, but I think we're being used to flush somebody out."

"Ali, you're totally AWOL. If anybody comes after you, it's not going to be backup, it's going to be a retrieval team."

"Right." Alisha put her head against the truck wall, feeling the short curls bristle against metal. "Don't let them do it."

"Yeah," Erika drawled. "Me and my army, we'll stop the Agency from taking you down, eh?"

"I mean it, Erika. I'll get back to you…" Alisha turned her head to look beyond Reichart's shoulder, out the windshield. "When I can, E. When I can." She blipped the comm off and turned it over, depressing the shallow button that deactivated it entirely.

The hotel was seedy and on the wrong side of Paris from where they'd dumped the truck, but no one would ask questions or even remember they'd been there, come morning. Alisha felt the key card in her hip pocket that would have let them into Mona's much nicer room in a far posher part of the city, and gave a groaning sigh. The accommodations might be lacking, but at least she could sit still and feel hidden for a while. Hidden, but filthy. She thought she might never be clean or unbruised again.

Reichart was already in the shower. Had been for more than forty minutes, in fact, long enough for Alisha to leave and return with rudimentary first-aid equipment. Paranoia had prompted her to crack the bathroom door open when she came back, making sure Reichart was actually still in the shower, and hadn't disappeared in the minutes she'd been gone. He'd felt the wave of cold air and pushed the shower curtain back, staring at her without curiosity or challenge, all the emotion and expression bleached from his face. Alisha had said nothing over the sound of falling water, only closed the door again before retreating to the bed.

The black box was a dead weight in her pocket, dragging her down with its undisclosed answers. Alisha folded a leg under herself and took the box out, running her fingers over it. Such a small thing, she thought, to carry the burden it did. It could be her keys to the kingdom, allowing her back into the CIA fold without much more than a reprimand and some counseling.

She breathed a laugh, shaking her head as she considered the idea. No: she'd gone too far this time. She'd deliver the box to Boyer, but she didn't see it as her redemption. Redemption required regret, and she had none for walking away.

The shower shut off and Alisha doubled over the edge of the bed, sliding the box under the mattress's box spring. A lousy hiding place, but Reichart didn't have any reason to go looking for it, so she trusted it would go unnoticed.

Reichart. She could hear him banging around in the bathroom, using ferocious motions where an economy would do. She clenched her stomach muscles, then her teeth as she heard a crash and a curse. Her feet acted without her command, taking her off the bed and into the steamy bathroom. Reichart was already half dressed, grubby jeans still unbuttoned. Alisha stepped into the room behind him and put her arms around his waist, feeling his muscles go rigid. "Beating yourself up isn't going to bring her back."

Reichart yanked away, both at the words and the touch.

Alisha lurched back a step, her lips pressed together as Reichart scowled down at her. "It's none of your god-damned business, Leesh."

"Yeah, it is. I'm sorry, Frank." *Guilt* was an emotion she thought she should feel, but in its place was regret.

"She made her choices. So did we. So," he said in a lower growl, "did Parker. Leave me alone."

"No." Alisha watched the man's hands knot and unknot, cords and veins flexing into relief in his forearms. "You want to hit something, Reichart?" She could hear the thread of sad humor in her voice as she spread her hands. "Come and get me."

Another growl erupted from his throat and he spun away, throwing a bunched fist at the mirror. Alisha was faster, stepping into him and knocking the blow askew. His knuckles scraped the wall and fury exploded across his face. Alisha ground her fingers around his wrist, staring up at him. "I know she made her choices. I'm still sorry. That wasn't how I hoped it would go."

"We'd both do the same thing again in a heartbeat, Alisha." Reichart pulled his arm back, but Alisha wouldn't let go of the grip on his wrist.

"I know." Regret, but no guilt, she thought. Compassion, but no regrets. Funny how one emotion could blur into another so easily, and be left behind even more easily. Thousands of hours of training and habit had left more mark than she wanted to admit, sometimes. "That doesn't mean you shouldn't mourn her."

"Did you?" Reichart's voice was harsh, and he pulled away more solidly, breaking Alisha's grip. "After Rome, did you mourn what you thought I'd become?"

Alisha let him go, rubbing her hand over the bruising on her forearm as she leaned against the bathroom counter.

"Why does it always come down to hotel rooms and dark secrets with us?" She put the question more to herself than Reichart, and closed her eyes, tilting her head back as memories skidded through her mind. The black blossom of pain in her shoulder from a gunshot wound. A glimpse more than four years ago of Frank Reichart on a London street, playing the part of a family man. Engagement rings and high-drama rescues: all the parts that made up her relationship with Frank Reichart. Dr. Peggy Reyes, asking intense questions, watching Alisha's every move and listening carefully to her choice of words as she discussed her former fiancé. Everything, every step, every play and every ploy, leading to where she stood now, facing a question she barely knew the answer to.

Alisha opened her eyes and looked up at the anger and pain hiding behind Reichart's expression. "No," she said quietly. "I never did. I was too angry and too hurt, and I've never gotten over it. I thought I had, but here I am." She spread her hands, encompassing herself and Reichart with the gesture. "Still struggling to understand my place in your world. Your place in mine. I walked out of a job I loved because after all these years I couldn't keep going without having those answers." She sighed and turned away, putting her hands on the counter as she dropped her chin to her chest. "Don't let Helen do the same thing to you, Frank. Mourning and moving on is better than hanging in an emotional limbo."

"Alisha." There was hesitation in Reichart's voice, weary and uncertain. Alisha lifted her head, meeting his eyes in the mirror. "Alisha, you know I never stopped—"

"Don't." Alisha interrupted harshly, shaking her head. "Don't. Don't say that, Reichart. Not right now." Her stomach muscles contracted with denial, as if she could cut off the confession through pure physical desire to do so. Tightening the skin made her suddenly aware of how badly the cut across her belly itched and she straightened convulsively, flexing her fingers wide-open to keep from scratching. "Grrgh."

"You all right?" Reichart turned her around before she could protest, tugging her shirt up to examine the cut. Action, Alisha thought distantly. Better for both of them than awkward words, or worse, silences.

"I'm fine. It's healing."

"You should take a shower," Reichart said abruptly. "Put some lotion on it to soften it up some. It'll help the itching." He stepped back, the distance between them suddenly seeming far greater than just a step or two. Alisha put her hand out, semiconsciously wanting to bridge that space. Her fingers brushed his stomach and he inhaled a sharp, deep breath before grating out, "Don't," as he caught her fingers. "I'm not in the mood for playing, Leesh. I'm not—"

"I'm not playing." Alisha's body ached without warning, so intense she felt like her head was floating. Reichart stood frozen for an instant, then stepped closer. Close enough to ghost his hand across the cut on her belly, sending a dizzying wave of itchy pain and want trumpeting through her. She dragged in air, savoring the hard pulse of desire that thumped in her groin and shot upward. Reichart knelt, unexpectedly submissive, and put his hands on her hips. Not possessive: Alisha was familiar with possession in his touch, and there was none of it now. It was more as if he sought to draw strength from her, and it made a new swell of want run through her, tingling in her breasts and making her cheeks hot with color. Alisha put her hand out to steady herself and found nowhere to put it but into Reichart's hair.

His shoulders slumped at the touch, his eyes closing as he leaned in to put his forehead against her stomach. "Alisha." His breath was warm, spilling over her skin like a promise. She curled her other hand into his hair, bending over his head to kiss the dark strands.

"This is a terrible idea," she whispered. Reichart laughed, rough against her belly.

"Do you care?"

"No." Alisha dropped down to her knees, slowly folding herself into Frank Reichart's arms to make the biggest mistake she would never regret.

Chapter 26

The subtle sound of the clock flipping its numbers over awakened Alisha. It read 6:05, though whether that was morning or evening she had no idea. Reichart was still asleep behind her, sprawled over two-thirds of the bed. Alisha smiled tiredly, letting her eyes drift shut again for a few moments. She was still on the edge of sleep herself, her breathing unchanged, or Reichart would have woken already. There was going to be all kinds of hell to pay later, but for the moment she felt absurdly content, warm and safe.

And she had a package to deliver to Boyer. Alisha's eyes opened again, though her smile didn't fade. It was just as well, she thought, that she'd slipped the black box under the bed *before* Reichart had the opportunity to undress her. Its presence was something she had no interest in explaining.

And you get annoyed at lies of omission when other people tell them, Leesh, she thought with an audible snort.

Reichart woke with a flinch, sitting halfway up. Alisha looked over her shoulder at him, still smiling, and rolled to trace her fingers over the bunched muscles in his stomach. "Sorry. Didn't mean to wake you up."

Reichart relaxed back into the mattress, then yawned through his nostrils until the breath became too big to contain. "'S all right." He rolled over, tucking Alisha up against him. She chuckled and unwound his arm from around her waist, then got up and went in search of her jeans. "Where're you going?" followed her, muzzy voice suggesting Reichart was barely awake. It wasn't a bet she'd place money on: he was fully capable of wreaking havoc when awakened from a dead sleep.

"I have to talk to Erika." Alisha's clothes—Reichart's, too—were piled one on top of another in the bathroom. She rooted through them, upending her jeans and sending the communicator falling to the floor with a clink.

"Eh?" Reichart sat halfway up again as Alisha came out of the bathroom, one hand raised to assure him nothing was amiss. She crawled back onto the bed, yawning, and thumbed the comm on.

"God, there you are," Erika said instantly. "I was starting to think you were dead, eh? It's been hours. Where are you?"

"Sorry." Alisha moved her hand to push hair back from her face and came up short, fingers startled to discover the length gone. Reichart crunched up on an elbow, giving her a crooked grin before kissing her shoulder.

It looks good, he mouthed. Alisha smiled back, then fought the smile's desire to turn into a grin as she looked at the comm again.

"I'm here now," she said. "It was kind of a rough…what time is it?"

"There? It's about six in the morning."

"Rough night," Alisha completed as her eyebrows shot up. "That late? I really was tired."

Reichart squinted at the bruises on her forearm as he got out of bed, making Alisha study them, as well. Purple and black streaks wrapped them, but the outer edges were turning to healthier green and yellow. The ridges she'd initially felt were faded, though still visible around her wrists. Reichart said, "They look better," and went into the bathroom himself, collecting the rest of their clothes.

"Is that Reichart?" Erika's voice rose with curiosity.

"Yeah," Alisha said, the word echoed in Reichart's deeper voice. A longish silence followed, in which Alisha could all but hear Erika pursing her lips.

"I so want the details," the other woman said eventually. "Look, Boyer's in Paris. He's just waiting for the word to meet you, Ali."

"Boyer? What? Why? I told you not to let anybody come after us." Alisha got to her feet as Reichart tossed her her panties. He watched with an appreciation as she slid them on, and she thought again about the price that would be paid for the night's antics. For the moment, though, she realized she simply didn't care, and watched him as avidly while he dressed.

"Right," Erika said, "because telling my boss he can't do what he wants is a great way to ensure job security. I called him to let him know you'd contacted me," she went on, oblivious to the strip show she was missing. Or whatever it was called when the participants were dressing instead of undressing, Alisha thought. She grinned again, this time at the comm. "Told him everything," Erika went on. "About the code and about you being with Reichart in Paris. He started swearing and got on the next plane out."

"We'll meet him—" Alisha shot a look at Reichart. "For coffee?"

He nodded. "Sure. The French make good coffee, and I could use some."

"Is that where you got your thing for French coffee, Ali?" Erika asked, clearly delighted. Alisha put her hand over her face, fighting back another grin. Reichart gave her a sly, curious smile and she laughed.

"You're blushing, aren't you?" Erika demanded. "Remind me to put a visual in this thing when I upgrade it. Is he naked?"

"Erika! No," Alisha added. Reichart tugged the top button of his jeans, clearly offering to remedy his lack of nudity. Alisha widened her eyes in amused exasperation and he subsided, pulling his T-shirt on. "Have Boyer meet us at—"

"Les Deux Magots?" Alisha asked. Reichart began a nod, then gave her a sharp look that Alisha fended off with a brief smile.

"Les Deux Magots," he agreed shortly. "At seven, okay?"

"All right, Ali. Be careful out there."

"Aren't I always?" Alisha blipped the comm off and reached for her bra and shirt.

"Thought you were AWOL."

"I was. Am." Alisha shook her head. "I don't know what the hell's going on." If nothing else, she thought, she could offer the black box as an apology for taking a walk. "He's going to read me the riot act."

"I'll talk to him," Reichart said. Alisha quirked an eyebrow and he shrugged. "We go back."

"I can handle myself, Frank."

"Yeah. I know." He gave her another lopsided smile. "We're still pretty good together, huh?" he asked. "After all these years apart."

Alisha looked at the shoes and socks still left on the bathroom floor, and back at Reichart. He pursed his lips and ducked his head, smiling again. "Believe it or not, that wasn't what I meant. I was thinking about getting out of there yesterday."

"In that case, yeah, you're right." Alisha straightened up fully, dropping her shoulders and lifting her chin high to create the proper flow for breathing. It took a few seconds before Reichart said, "Hey," in a mildly affronted tone, and despite her intentions of centering herself, Alisha opened her eyes.

"Men and their fragile egos. Look, Reichart—"

"Don't say it was a mistake, Alisha." Some of the warmth fled Reichart's voice, leaving it defensive and prepared for hurt. Alisha shook her head, slow motion.

"It wasn't. I'm not naive enough to pretend I wasn't making a conscious choice. We both needed it. But it's not picking up where we left off, Reichart. I'm not sure I want it to be picking up at all."

"You don't have a scar." Reichart's gaze fell to her left shoulder, the words betraying a question and a little draining of tension. Alisha folded her arm up to rub her thumb beneath the collarbone.

"Not on the outside."

"Leesh—"

"Don't," Alisha said. She delivered the ultimatum to stop a conversation she wasn't ready, might not ever be ready, to have. Whether she believed that he'd acted to save her life. Whether the shadows of their shared past might forever darken a future together. Whether *together* could encompass mere friendship, or whether history tainted that possibility, too. A weariness that had nothing to do with her recovering injuries washed through Alisha, leaving a knot of pain beating around her heart. Too many questions waited in the words that lay ahead, and she had no stomach for it. "Don't, Frank. Just don't."

Reichart drew in a breath through his nostrils, then nodded, looking away. Submissive body language, again. Another rare show from the man across from her. Helen's death had hit him hard. Or maybe, Alisha thought, she'd finally learned enough of his secrets that he could stop hiding behind his masks. She sighed and pushed her hand through her newly short hair. "I don't care what time we're meeting him. I'm taking a shower before we see Boyer."

It was hours before Paris—or any European city—got started. There were no shops or boutiques open to buy new clothes at. Despite having managed showers, they made a more than grimy pair, Alisha thought as she caught their reflection in the café window. They were filthy, clothes wrinkled and bodies stiff, but it seemed like there was more than just dirt staining them. She thought the marks went all the way through to their cores: shadows that seemed to come from inside tainting every action either of them made. They moved like wary predators, creatures that knew even the mightiest animal in the kingdom might be hunted. There was desperation in the bruised reflections, all the more dangerous for being controlled and contained. When had the woman in the mirror changed? Alisha wondered. She'd been tired and injured the last time she'd seen herself, but now she looked like someone who carried knives, and who wouldn't hesitate to use them.

Boyer was a studied contrast to their battered state, his suit impeccably pressed and shoes shined to a gleam. His bulk made a pleasant shadow of the corner he sat in, the slightest hint of a smile playing around his mouth keeping him from looking foreboding. That smile tinted with dismay as Alisha approached and dropped into one of the chairs at his table. "You two look like gypsies."

"I think gypsies are cleaner than I am right now." Alisha angled her body so it was between the director and Reichart, who stood at the counter, ordering coffee for himself and, Alisha hoped, her. She gave a brief nod that acknowledged his station as her supervisor without saying his title aloud, then leaned forward. "I have something for you, sir." She fished the black box from beneath her shirt—she'd returned the leather jacket to Reichart that morning—and slid it across the table to Boyer.

He took it without hesitation, dipping a hand into his inner breast pocket to hide the box, but his eyebrows elevated a little. "You never fail to astonish me, Agent MacAleer. This is what I think it is?"

"Yes, sir." A surge of pride lanced through Alisha, making her straighten her spine. There seemed to be a certain weight to Boyer pronouncing her title in public, as if it was the reprieve she'd hoped she might earn. "I have a question for you, sir."

Boyer's eyebrows rose again. "I thought you were here to answer my questions, Alisha." He spread his hand, though, an invitation, and picked up his coffee cup to sip while he waited. Alisha stole a glance over her shoulder at Reichart, making certain he was out of hearing distance.

"Did Reichart recommend me for the job in Kazakhstan, sir?"

Surprise filtered through Boyer's dark eyes, almost answer enough. "He told you that?"

"I came across some interesting material regarding his..." Alisha wet her lips, choosing her words carefully. "Loyalties," she finally said. "Organizational memos, you might say."

Another smile filtered across Boyer's face. "I told him you'd be like a dog with a bone if you got any hint of the matters underlying the Kazakhstan situation. He insisted."

"The matters underlying..." Alisha nearly laughed, but instead passed her hand over her eyes. The Sicarii. The Fas Infitialis. Relegating them to such innocuous terms as *the matters underlying* caught her somewhere between glee and despair, the wildness of the conflicting emotions testament to how on edge she felt. "And he insisted. Bastard," she added in a mutter. Reichart, on cue, appeared with two enormous mugs of coffee.

"You called?" He gave her a rakish grin that made her give in to laughter after all. It was too easy, she thought, to let him make her happy. Too easy to forget what had brought them together and there in the first place. Alisha shook her head, accepting the coffee cup. Smiles fell away again, though, as she explained in as few words as possible about Brandon's betrayal and the chase afterward. Boyer's lips thinned as she outlined what had happened, his demeanor darkening until Alisha felt a chill sweep over her.

"I'll talk to Susan Simone," he growled when Alisha finished. "This has gone too far."

"We still don't know why they didn't just eliminate us immediately," Alisha added. "They wanted something."

"And Simone ought to know what that is, if Parker's still on one of her ops."

"What about Greg?"

"You haven't seen—no, you wouldn't have. He's in Paris, looking for you." Boyer's expression changed again, becoming more neutral. "You're inspiring a whole rash of walkers, Alisha. I don't appreciate it."

"Greg walked?" Alisha asked, disbelieving. Boyer lifted one shoulder and let it fall again.

"He went looking for you, against explicit orders."

"My oh my," Reichart breathed. "Dissention in the ranks."

Boyer shared a look with Alisha that they both turned on Reichart. "As the ultimate instigator of this near-disaster," Boyer said mildly, "you might want to think about the wisdom of silent discretion."

"That was a lot more eloquent than my *shut up, Frank* was going to be," Alisha said with admiration. Boyer gave her a faint smile.

"Years of political experience. I'd say you'll get there, but your sudden tendency toward haring off on your own agenda might jeopardize that."

"You'd rather not know that the dagger people have access to higher-level technology than the U.S. would have seen for another ten years without this operation being busted open?" Reichart gave the Sicarii their literal translation rather than say the word, even in a conversation held in English in a French café. "You're an idealist, Rick, but I don't think you're a fool."

"Your mother would blister your hide to hear you talk to me that way."

"My mother," Reichart said, "is dead. As you well know."

Hairs lifted on Alisha's arms, rushing cold over the back of her neck. She curled her fingers around her coffee mug more solidly and risked quick glances at both the men over the mug's rim. Reichart held his jaw thrust out and tight, challenge inherent in the expression, while Boyer's expression remained so mild it seemed threatening. "And she died doing what she believed was right," he replied. There were undercurrents to the statement that Alisha couldn't read, curiosity driving her so hard she took a too-large sip of hot coffee to keep herself from blurting questions. The coffee scalded her tongue, making her hiss in air, and the tension was disrupted, both men looking at her.

"Sorry. Coffee. Ow." She opened her mouth, inhaling cool air over her tongue. Reichart looked away first, both from her and Boyer, and Boyer's shoulders relaxed fractionally.

"I don't want either of you to do anything rash," he said in his deep voice. "Alisha, you have my number. I want you to pick up a phone and call me in four hours. I'll have spoken with Simone by then, and we can arrange a time to meet and discuss what she has to say."

"She threw me out of Europe," Alisha reminded him. Boyer's mouth pulled down sourly.

"A dismissal which appears not to have taken. I want to get to the bottom of this, Alisha. That doesn't mean you're out of hot water when it's over."

Alisha dropped her eyes, pulling her lower lip between her teeth. "Yes, sir." She heard Boyer's skeptical snort and found herself caught between amusement and offense. The show of recalcitrance had been a real one, not put on for her boss's benefit. *Maybe a job where genuine emotion is automatically assumed to be a ploy is one you ought to reconsider, Leesh.*

Assuming she had any choice, when this was over. "I'll call in four hours."

Boyer nodded and stood, giving Reichart a brief nod as well. "Frank."

"Rick." Reichart didn't exhale until Boyer had left the café. Alisha got up and went to the window, watching the director walk down the street toward his car. She could feel Reichart watching her in turn, and kept herself from looking his way in order to stop the impulse to ask questions.

"She died on a joint endeavor in Ecuador," Reichart said abruptly. "Boyer was leading it."

Alisha's shoulders dropped and she put her temple against the window. "I'm sorry."

"So am I. It was twelve years ago this month. He focused on political rise after that. Less dangerous."

"Less emotional risk," Alisha said. Boyer, down the street, climbed into his vehicle, and Alisha turned her back on the window, leaning on it. "He seemed sorry, too."

"I think they were in love."

The glass Alisha leaned on shattered, an explosion of such power she couldn't hear it. She tumbled backward onto the sidewalk, flinging her arms up to protect her face as she rolled over glass shards. Heat bloomed from down the street, singeing the air and making it taste of burnt ozone. Pieces of debris rained down around her, clattering silently in the detonation's aftermath. Alisha shoved up on an elbow, one arm still lifted to protect her face, to squint against waves of rolling hotness.

Black smoke plumed up, stinking and thick, from the skeletal, fiery remains of Boyer's vehicle.

Chapter 27

The spray pattern from the blast pointed toward her, black scars blemishing the street. Alisha put her hand down against shattered glass and hot metal, and pushed up in the too-loud silence of destruction. The sidewalk slid beneath her hand and she curled her fingers around the broken piece, taking it up with her without looking at it. She put her other hand out and Reichart took it, as stalwart as he'd ever been disappointing. Together they slipped through the growing crowd, until sound suddenly erupted again, the *wee-ooh* of sirens so loud they seemed like they must be more explosions.

As if the sirens were a signal for panic, Alisha's ears began ringing with the babble of horrified, frightened voices lifting in fear all around her. She stumbled more than once as panicked early-morning Parisians pushed by, some running away from, and some running toward, the scene of violence. She felt Reichart's hand tighten on hers, a warning not to run. Unnecessary warning, at least in theory, but she thought it was as much a reminder to himself as to her.

Thirty steps down the street they rounded the corner, Reichart drawing her closer. "They'll be looking for us together," he murmured at the same time that Alisha said, "We need to split up." They shared a smile that had nothing to do with pleasure.

"The Louvre," Alisha said. "At ten. Otherwise—"

Reichart nodded and crossed the street. Alisha shoved her hands in her jeans pockets, discovering she still clutched the loose piece she'd picked up from the sidewalk. Rather than let it go, she knotted her fingers around it as if it were a talisman, then lifted her chin and hurried down the street, leaving Reichart behind.

"Boyer's dead." Alisha sat by the Louvre's reflecting pool, her head lowered as if she was speaking into a cell phone. Erika's comm unit was in her palm, too conspicuous to use publicly without masking it.

"What?" Shock made the question staticky as Erika's voice rose.

"A car bomb. Who else knew where he was?"

"Jesus, Ali, I—I don't know. Me, but I don't know who else he told. You're sure he's dead?"

Alisha closed her eyes, the imprint of the burning vehicle too clear in her memory. "Yeah. It was a setup. Somehow somebody knew." It couldn't have been Reichart, she told herself fiercely. She'd been with him constantly for more than twelve hours, since long before the meeting with Boyer had been arranged.

But another memory invaded, the casual invitation to dinner in Rome that had ended with a Catholic cardinal dead and Alisha's collarbone shattered by a bullet her fiancé had fired. Only three people had known where she would be that night, too, and one had betrayed her. Frank Reichart had betrayed her.

"Brandon?" Erika asked. Alisha shook her head against her cupped palm.

"I don't know. I don't see how, unless the drones were a distraction so someone or something else could follow us. It had to be someone who knew Boyer was coming. Erika, you've got to find out who he talked to before he left."

The tech geek at Langley sighed. "I'll see if I can get his phone records and I'll check the security tapes to see if anybody went through his office. It shouldn't take long. I'll comm you back when I'm done. Ali?"

"What?" Alisha felt all the gentleness had been stripped from her, leaving nothing more than raw bones and a need for forward motion.

"You should try to contact Greg. He's in Europe and he's next in line for Boyer's job. Somebody needs to tell him what's happened."

"Greg?" Alisha lifted her head, focusing on the pool's water, watching the surface pock with occasional raindrop. "Is up for Boyer's job?"

"Boyer'd been talking about retiring, Ali. There's been a lot of political shuffling around here. Greg's been primed to move into the directorship on Boyer's retirement for months." Alisha could hear the disapproval in Erika's voice. "You haven't been paying attention."

"I haven't been in the office much." Alisha thinned her lips. "I'll call him. Get back to me as soon as you can, E."

"He hasn't been answering his phone. Like some other people I know." Erika let out a sigh that said she was pushing away exasperation, and added, "Yeah. I'll comm you when I know something. Bye." The comm blooped off and Alisha closed her hand around it, still staring at without seeing the surrounding city. There was no way Boyer could have survived the blast. What little, desperate hope she'd held had dissipated when she finally looked at the heavy piece she'd slipped on on the sidewalk. It wasn't concrete at all, or a torn piece of metal from the vehicle.

It was the black box, battered and scarred but still whole. Alisha had watched Boyer slip it into his left breast pocket. Its material assured it was nearly indestructible, but the man who'd carried it was far more fragile. Any explosion strong enough to throw the box free would unquestionably have torn the man in the driver's seat apart.

Alisha knotted her hand around the box, her shoulders hunched as she stared down at it. Regardless of what else she did, she would find whoever was responsible for Boyer's death and see them come to justice.

"I didn't recognize you." Reichart spoke from a few yards away, voice pitched to carry only as far as Alisha's ears. She turned her head, then followed suit with her whole body, studying the man standing beyond the nearest corner of the pool.

He seemed to have somehow lost thirty pounds in the past two hours, gaunt angles to cheekbones that had always been sharp. His hair was white-blond and gelled into short curls, and the usual darkness of his eyes was now startlingly blue. His clothing had been changed, less in style than in color: a white leather trench coat, soft and supple, hung over a silk shirt so pale blue it was almost colorless, and over sharply pressed white pants. Alisha wagered on more weapons than she could count being hidden beneath the bright costume.

"That was the idea," she said after a moment. "Although

you should have. We're a matched pair." She slid the box into her jacket, then flicked her fingers at her own outfit, as new as Reichart's. Bronzing lotion had darkened her skin to the deepest shade she could believably carry off, and her eyes were still light from the Mona personality's contacts. Her own hair had been bleached blond, as well, surpassing its usual tawny shade and contrasting sharply with her newly dark skin.

The trench coat she wore was thigh-length and daringly sleeveless, showing off her biceps, but as blazingly white as Reichart's. Her forearms were wrapped in fingerless leather gloves, offering both protection and disguise for bruising, and the puncture in her biceps was tied off with a red bandana. The snug-fitting tank top she wore was scoop-necked and crimson instead of Reichart's blue. She wore jeans, not slacks, and flexible, heavy boots that she'd already slipped knife sheaths into.

Alisha rarely felt so much like *Leesh,* the combat-trained fighting machine, as she did in the white leather and red. She could feel the impulse to flex her fingers and find something to hit itching in her palms, waiting for action. She quashed it, promising herself that she'd have the opportunity to unleash soon. "I know we didn't go shopping at the same store, but damn, Reichart. We are not inconspicuous."

"Sometimes being glaringly obvious is as good as being invisible."

"We'd better hope so, because God himself couldn't miss us in these outfits."

Reichart gave her a thin smile. "At least we look like we belong together. If we get through this with the gear intact we should go out clubbing."

"I thought you didn't dance."

"I've gotten over myself since then."

So have I, Alisha didn't say, in part because it was needlessly mean and in part because she wasn't sure it was true. "I just talked to Erika," she said instead. "She's looking into who else knew Boyer was going to be here, and wants me to get in touch with Greg."

Reichart's jaw worked, sure sign of him swallowing words and choosing different ones. "You sure that's wise, under the circumstances?"

"Reichart, I haven't been sure of anything since you got me into this whole mess." Alisha pushed through her thighs, standing up from the pool's edge. "But Greg's more likely to get us to Simone than anybody else, at this point, and since that's where Boyer was going before he died, that's where I want to be going." She heard flint in her voice, a categorical denial of emotion. Giving in to grief and anger had to be constructive. Later she could mourn.

The memory of Reichart's hands on her hips, eyes dark as he watched her above him, came on abruptly, making Alisha glad of the bronzing lotion that could hide blushes. There were worse ways to mourn the fallen. The previous night had been as much about Alisha's acceptance of Brandon's betrayal as Reichart's sorrow over Helen. If there was more to it than mutual need tied together with familiarity and a degree of convenience, it could be explored later. Alisha wasn't yet ready to consider the possibility of *more.*

"You've changed, Leesh." Reichart spoke quietly, making Alisha's shoulders stiffen. "You always used to wear your heart on your sleeve. You could turn it on and off, but I used to be able to see you make the switch."

"I'm a lot older than I was when we were together, Frank."

"It's more than that."

"Blame the job." Blame the moment she'd clobbered

Reichart in the head and had not even a twinge of remorse. She closed her eyes and breathed, "'Cause I felt nothing," almost tunelessly.

Reichart rumbled deep in his throat. "That's what I'm afraid of."

"Not as afraid as I am. Come on." Alisha pushed the line of thought away. "I need to find a phone."

"Do you still wish to tell me this is not a love story?"

Alisha breathed a laugh and put her forehead against the side of the pay phone, closing her eyes. She could almost feel Reichart standing a few yards away, watching her with the insolent, possessive concern of a wealthy man who could afford to let the beauty on his arm go for a little while. She would come back, his arrogant expression said, because there was no one else worthy of her time.

Under other circumstances there might have been a certain heady joy in wearing the dramatic matching costumes. Even in Paris, heads turned, smiles directed at the small dark woman matching strides with the tall slender man. Despite the approving attention, Alisha kept her hands relaxed only through conscious effort. As soon as her focus strayed, she found them balling into fists. Even now she felt the leather cutting into her palms, and deliberately opened her hand to put it against the phone's box. "I'm not sure what to call it right now, Jon. Besides, how do you know I'm with Reichart?"

A laugh rumbled over the phone line. "It is my occupation to know, no? And this is why you call me. My little bird has flown her cage, and now the cage itself is shattering. This is three favors, *mia cara.* Someday I will need something and you will not be able to tell me no."

Alisha pressed her eyelids harder shut. "I haven't even asked for anything, Jon."

"But you never write, you never call," the big man teased gently. "Until you want something. And I will tell you what you want, but someday, little bird."

"I know." Alisha wet her lips and lifted her head, turning her focus down the street. "I know, Jon."

"No." Jon's smooth voice filled with cold steel, making Alisha straighten in wary anticipation. "You do not know, little bird. What I will tell you is very dangerous, dangerous to me. You will not contact me again after this phone call, and you will not hear from me until this debt is to be repaid. You will not hear from my people, and they will not see you. My little bird is on a wire, and it is not strong enough for a man like me to balance on, *capisce?*"

"I understand." Alisha's head felt light, her voice hollow, and she deliberately flexed her feet against the insides of her boots, making sure she was grounded.

"I wish to be certain you do," Jon said, warning rumble coming through the line. "I do not wish to threaten you, little bird—"

"Then don't," Alisha said harshly. Jon went on as if she hadn't spoken.

"—but you must know that there is nothing that cannot be had by the right men with the right persuasions. Even strongboxes locked away in banks."

Ice sluiced down Alisha's throat as she tilted her head back, staring at the sky. The idea of having her journals discovered was one she liked to cling to, but in her imagination they were only found after her own death. To have someone—an information broker, no less—aware of them in her lifetime was a thought she hadn't let herself fully consider.

"I've already left the cage, Jon," she said in a raw, light voice. "Those can't ruin me at this point."

"No," he agreed, "but how many names in them might ruin others? Do we truly understand each other now, little bird?"

"Yes," Alisha whispered. "Yes, I think we do."

"Good," Jon said. "Then this is what you need to know."

Chapter 28

I make it my business to know. Jon's words lingered in Alisha's memory, their simplicity giving lie to the power that they indicated. Spies, couriers, assets and agents, all manner of men and women trucking with the underworld and espionage: to know where any individual piece was on the board at any given time required a network and loyalties beyond anything the CIA inspired. Personal charisma, old favors and the heavy hand of blackmail all fed Jon's information stream.

And for the first time, Alisha was on the wrong side of it. *I should have worn black,* she thought incongruously. Not that it would have hidden her from Jon's latticework of accomplices any better; not that it would make slipping around the back side of a warehouse in broad daylight any less conspicuous. Gleaming leather outfits, whether black or white, were not subtle. Regardless, in black, Alisha would have felt slightly less like she was glowing whenever sunlight brushed over her.

Not that she was sneaking. There was no reason to, except the habit of thought. Reichart had circled the building from the other direction, both of them noting enormous double doors at one end of the warehouse and, without discussion, opting to find a less ostentatious entrance. An itchy thrill along Alisha's spine warned her that it was dangerous to split their forces, but for the tenth time she reminded herself there was no expectation of enemy action inside the warehouse.

Expectation of enemy action. She shook her head and smiled without humor as she strode toward an ordinary door at the warehouse's far end. It was the sort of cool, rational phrase the Agency preferred: no emotional content to it. Now, as ever, she didn't like finding herself using those unsentimental idioms, even—or especially—in the privacy of her own mind. *What you really mean, Leesh, is that you don't think anybody's going to try to blow you up.*

Boyer had also not expected anyone to try to blow him up. Alisha hesitated with her hand on the knob, chin lowered as she took a deep breath, searching for her center. Later, she promised herself fiercely. Later there would be time to mourn. Now she had bad news and a black box to deliver to Greg, and a rendezvous to arrange with Susan Simone. The European director wouldn't be happy to see her, but Alisha pulled another faint smile. She was far past caring what the authorities in her line of work were happy about.

She turned her wrist up, regardless of knowing there was no watch there. The action seemed to trigger the mental countdown she'd begun: two minutes from leaving Reichart; they were both supposed to enter the warehouse from different directions. Twelve seconds left. Alisha over-rode the impulse to go in with a drawn gun. There was a meeting going on beyond the warehouse doors, and a warning from Jon's intelligence lingered in her mind: *He will be meeting with others. I am not certain of their loyalties.*

There had been something in Jon's voice that had triggered alarm, but there was no time to ask questions. The conversation had been over, Alisha left holding a dead line. Greg was incommunicado from Langley, not armed and dangerous, she reminded herself. The reason he'd walked was to go after his badly behaved protégé.

And she no longer trusted him, much less anyone he was meeting with. Still, going in with guns blazing would assure a bad situation, and there was too much to be said to risk it.

Zero seconds. Alisha turned the handle, hearing the click, and pushed the door open.

Rectangles of light spilled across the warehouse floor from two angles, her door and Reichart's, their shadows cast long. The air rang with the silence of voices cutting off, and before her eyes had completely adjusted to the change in light, Alisha heard her name barked out in utter surprise.

Greg broke away from the trio of silhouettes in the middle of the warehouse, taking a few long running strides before falling back into a more cautious pace. "Alisha?" he repeated. "What—how—*Reichart?*"

Alisha managed a brief smile as she matched Reichart's gait, the two of them flanking and converging on Greg as he stood alone, apart from his compatriots. "It's a long story, Greg." Her vision settled in the light-and-dark of the warehouse and she glanced beyond him, betraying surprise with an upward dart of her eyebrows. "Director Simone," she said carefully. "I didn't expect to see you here."

Below her words, Reichart growled, "Parker," but his gaze was fixed on the third man in the warehouse, not on

Greg. Brandon Parker inclined his head, such a stiff motion Alisha thought it must hurt to make.

I am not certain of their loyalties, Jon whispered at the back of Alisha's mind. No wonder, she thought now. Not with the Parkers making up two-thirds of the meeting. No wonder he'd considered the information dangerous. Alisha knew very clearly what happened when the Sicarii no longer regarded an asset as useful.

"Agent MacAleer," Simone said sharply. "Gregory was just explaining how it was that you'd seen fit to give yourself fresh orders and blatantly ignore mine."

"With all due respect, Director," Alisha said, not bothering to hide the insolence in her voice, "we've got bigger problems than that right now. Boyer is dead."

Something indescribable and nasty contorted Greg's features for an instant after Alisha spoke. Not grief. Not even surprise, though both of those things were in place almost before she had time to recognize they'd been misplaced for that brief space of time. There was no time to hold on to the idea of what that expression told her, though she could all but feel herself filing it away for later examination.

Brandon blanched so badly Alisha thought he might pass out, his gaze openly shocked and accusing, though Alisha couldn't tell who the accusation was for. "*Dead?* How? What happened?"

"A car bomb this morning," Reichart said. "In downtown Paris. We're looking into who knew he'd be here."

Narrowness flitted across Simone's eyes and disappeared again. "The Agency will find the responsible parties and deal with them, Mr. Reichart. You have no business here."

Reichart's tone went cool and clipped as he regarded the older woman. "I'll decide what is and isn't my business."

There were undercurrents to his words, telling of more emotional ties to the dead CIA director than Alisha would have imagined he'd permit himself in mixed company.

"This wasn't supposed to happen," Brandon said in a thin voice. "This isn't how it was supposed to go."

Sudden fury shot through Alisha, making her face hot and her hands tingle with anger. "Is it some kind of surprise to you, Brandon? After *you* used me to draw Boyer out fifteen months ago?" The anger was compounded by embarrassment, a link that Alisha herself hadn't seen clearly until she spoke. "The Sicarii have been gunning for him for years. Is that why you let us go? You knew I'd end up in contact with him somehow." And she had, despite her best attempts not to. *Send no one,* she'd told Erika, but Erika's protestation had been valid: how could she have stopped Boyer, her superior, from doing what he wanted? Alisha stalked forward, ready to take any kind of action that would relieve the rage that burned through her. "You son of a *bitch.*"

"Alisha, I never wanted—"

Alisha threw a punch that Reichart would have blocked, smashing her leather-wrapped fist into Brandon's teeth. He coughed and gagged, staggering backward with a hand cupped over his mouth, face full of wounded acceptance of her censure. His sheer pathos only served to infuriate Alisha further. It was Reichart's touch on her shoulder that stopped her from acting on her anger again, and he *did* block the second frustrated, furious punch she threw. "Leesh," he said, so quietly she thought no one else could hear. She closed her eyes briefly and inhaled a sharp breath, then lifted her chin in a reversed nod.

"I'm all right. I'm fine." Not even she believed the words, but they gave her a semblance of control.

"She's your problem now, Parker," Simone muttered in

the distance. "You deal with her. I don't care how much self-righteous fury she's riding. I don't want a loose cannon like that in operation on my field."

"She's had a shock, Susan," Greg answered. Alisha looked their way, staring at the two of them as Greg passed a hand through his hair in a gesture of weary unhappiness. "We all have. Alisha." He turned toward her, fingers spread in appeasement. "You're sure he's dead?"

Alisha wet her lips, taking a moment before she was confident of her voice's steadiness. Her elbow pressed against the black box's weight in her coat's inner pocket, and she nodded. "He had the—"

The double doors at the far end of the warehouse hummed and rolled open, rumbling and drowning out Alisha's explanation about the box. She turned, squinting against bright sunlight to watch half a dozen forms slowly detach themselves from the brilliance and become discernible.

Most were easy: the nauseatingly smooth gait of the Attengee drones came forward, flanking a human figure and bringing up the figure's rear. Above them, a few seconds later, came two Firebirds, hovering at a walking pace—so slowly Alisha could hardly believe they maintained altitude. The human, a woman from the size of her frame, walked comfortably among the drones.

"Who the hell," she breathed. Brandon, closest to her, lifted his chin.

"Phoenix."

The doors began rumbling closed, pinching off daylight behind the woman and the prototypes. Alisha passed a hand over her eyes, brushing away tears from looking into the brightness. Clarity of vision returned as she dropped her hand, still squinting toward the approaching parade.

Pale blond hair, soft and bright in the sunlight that

spilled through high warehouse windows. The veiled woman from the cathedral, Alisha thought, though she no longer wore a veil. Slender, taller than Alisha by several inches, her strides long and purposeful. Heels clipped on concrete in a cadence that lifted hairs on Alisha's arms. Footsteps, she thought, were not the kind of thing she expected to recognize.

Especially when she hadn't heard that particular stride in eight years.

Especially when the woman making them was supposed to be dead.

Cristina Lamken stepped out of daylight's glow and into shadow, smiling as her features were thrown into relief. "Hello, Alisha. It's been a long time."

Chapter 29

"That skirt you were wearing at the church must've been pencil-thin," Alisha heard herself saying. "I didn't recognize your footsteps then." She marveled at the casualness of her own voice, throwaway words no more than meaningless sounds over the turmoil that churned her stomach. So many questions boiled over she couldn't formulate any of them silently, much less aloud.

Cristina glanced down at the slacks she wore, and up again with another smile. Dazzling smile, Alisha thought; Cristina had always been pretty, but her smile lit her up from within. "I had to take very short steps," she admitted. "I didn't know you'd been there. Seeing you at the hotel was a shock."

"Imagine how I felt," Alisha said. She felt high flutiness trying to break through at the back of her throat, but her voice remained steady. There was pressure at the small of her back, one of the guns she carried suddenly feeling heavy there. The termination orders had never been rescinded. Alisha's palms ached with the impulse to pull the weapon and shoot, even though she knew she would never do it. There would never be answers if she did, but for one brief, violent moment she reveled in the vicarious satisfaction of the idea. Vengeance for a decade of lies in a single shot: it wasn't a pretty part of herself to acknowledge, but for a few seconds it consumed her. Rage, confusion, betrayal; too many emotions to name cramped her stomach, making her feel she could spit bile.

Worst, worst of all, were the expressions of those around her. Greg. Brandon. Even, most cruelly, Reichart. None of them were surprised. Unhappy, tired, tense, yes: those were all written on their faces. But not surprise, and for all their training, Alisha didn't believe for an instant that a woman supposedly seven years dead wouldn't at least garner widened eyes or lifted eyebrows. She knew her own voice was cool and steady, but it was a lie, a vocal facade meant to distract a watcher from the shocked color in her cheeks, the dilation of her pupils, the too-fast pulse in her throat.

They had known. They had *all* known. *Reichart* had known that her partner was alive, and hadn't told her.

"Base jumping, then?" Alisha heard her own voice again without having consciously intended to speak. Casual question, trying to make sense of the night she'd stood on a mountainside ready to pull a trigger on her best friend. Trying to understand how the suicide jump Cristina had taken had somehow landed her here, in a Parisian warehouse, seven years later.

"I was freezing," Cristina said. "All those mountaineering clothes were cover for the chute. Base jumping," she agreed with a shrug. "You remember our cliff-diving vacation? With Erika's suits?"

"Sure." Alisha's fingers tingled, as if blood had stopped flowing into them and was only now realizing its error. "It was a lot of fun." The bulky base-jumping suits made them look like flying squirrels, webbed along every stretch where limb separated from torso. Free-falling, with just enough break to keep from reaching terminal velocity. Alisha and Cristina had screamed the whole way down, sheer glee that erupted into howls of laughter as they staggered back to do it again, full of life and vigor and enthusiasm for dangerous pursuits.

"I had one made in white," Cristina said. Alisha closed her eyes briefly, remembering searching over the mountainside, staring in helpless anger and dismay at miles of moonlit snow.

"Well done." She opened her eyes again to find Cristina coming toward her, a broad, happy smile on her face, arms open for a hug.

There was no transition that Alisha could remember, no moment of thought or consideration. She slapped the gun from the small of her back and brought it up so quickly Cristina was still smiling and saying, "It's so good to see you again," when the weapon was pressed into the hollow of her throat.

"Alisha," Greg said, low and warning. Cristina swallowed, moving the muzzle very slightly as she met Alisha's eyes. Fearless, Alisha thought. Always fearless.

"Back up. I'm not really up for a tearful reunion just now, Cris. Back. The fuck. Up."

Cristina spread her hands, no longer offering a hug, and took several judicious steps backward. No fear. No anger, either. No surprise, but maybe a trace of disappointment, Alisha thought. Too fucking bad. "So it was a setup from the start, was it?"

"Alisha," Greg said again. He took one step closer, and Alisha dipped her right hand into the breast of her jacket, coming out with a second gun that she held on her handler as steadily as she held Cristina in her sights.

"This is a bad time for it, Greg. If someone doesn't start explaining very quickly, I'm going to go through with my termination orders on this woman."

"I'm your boss," Greg said, putting steel in his voice. "Those orders are rescinded, Alisha."

"Right now, Greg, nobody's going to walk out of here alive to tell on me, so forgive me if I don't really give a shit what you think my orders are. Cristina. Start talking." Alisha had never believed she had it in her to be a stone-cold killer. *What a surprise,* she thought without any humor at all. *Enough training and enough betrayal, and it turns out the last person you really know is yourself, Leesh.*

"It was a setup," Cristina said softly. "I'd been a triple agent since I was fifteen, Alisha. The FSB finally caught on to me. The only way to get them well and truly off my trail was for me to die."

"And I was the patsy who got to hunt you down and execute the order. You couldn't have told me, Greg?" Alisha didn't take her eyes off Cristina, fully trusting her peripheral vision to warn her if Greg Parker moved. No one else had. She could see rage on Susan Simone's face, and carefully held neutrality on Brandon's, as if he feared the slightest expression now would condemn his father. Reichart watched her with a mix of admiration and sorrow.

"We needed your responses to be flawless." Greg kept his voice soothing and calm. "Alisha, put the guns down. We have a lot to talk about."

"You know, I'm comfortable having this conversation just like this. Cristina. Keep talking." Alisha's arms ached, not from holding the weapons, but from keeping herself from squeezing the triggers. She would regret it if she did, she kept telling herself. It wouldn't be worth the momentary satisfaction of revenge.

If she told herself that enough times, she might start to believe it.

"I went to work deep undercover," Cristina said. "Being dead let me do that. I infiltrated the Sicarii, Ali. It's what I've been doing for the last seven years."

"You're royalty?" Alisha sneered. Cristina flickered a smile.

"You'd hardly believe me if I told you. I've been trying to ferret out the highest-ranking Sicarii in the CIA." She sighed a small, tired sound. "That's why the Firebird's black box is so important. We believe it has footage verifying a connection between the CIA and the Sicarii. Brandon, were you able to play back the tape?" Cristina glanced at him very quickly, eyebrows rising. He flinched, then stared at her.

"I don't know what you're talking about. The box never got to me. Alisha didn't deliver it. Reichart had it."

Cristina's mouth tightened. "Reichart gave it to me. I handed it over to Helen two nights ago. She was supposed to give it to you."

"Helen's dead," Reichart growled.

White surprise washed over Cristina's face and she shot a look at Brandon. "She never gave me anything, Phoenix," he insisted, sounding weary. "The box wasn't on her body."

Alisha's heartbeat rang so loudly, hit against her breastbone with such hard crashes, that it seemed a wonder that no one else heard it. She kept her breathing steady through effort, feeling the black box's weight in one of her coat's inner pockets. Sickness churned her belly, fighting to get out. Alisha set her teeth together and kept her eyes on Cristina.

Cristina. *Alive.* There wasn't even a single spark of joy hidden within the turmoil of emotions. No relief. Only cold, sickening anger. Alisha had imagined what it might be like to see Cristina again, one final time, and there had always been a sense of gratitude almost as nauseating as the rage she felt now, in those imagined scenarios. Seven years of clinging to a romantic idea that there might have been a good explanation were shattered: faced with one, Alisha could not bring herself to believe a word of it. "Who do you think is on the tape?"

"I know who's on the tape," Cristina said quietly. "I just need it as proof positive, so I can arrest Director Simone."

Silence rang in Alisha's ears, louder than gunshots. Not true silence: she could hear Simone's distorted shriek of outrage, the words coming too slowly to be properly heard. It was the silence of the pin being pulled from the grenade, warning that the irrevocable had been done and the only way forward was through sudden remorseless violence.

A thousand countable things changed in that silence. Brandon inhaled sharply, color draining from his face, and Alisha thought, *he's been taking orders from her for years.*

Illegal orders. That understanding came down over Brandon's expression like a curtain falling, and he gave one jerk of his head, staring at the combat drones that still hovered and stood behind Cristina. They were humming now, as if Cristina's accusation had triggered a fight reflex in their artificial intelligences even when Alisha pulling a gun on Cristina had not. Maybe they had. Maybe they were programmed to recognize the denunciation and to show a dominant hand as a way of preventing bloodshed. Their weapons compartments had clicked open in a precursor to battle.

Four guns, Alisha thought very precisely. She had four guns tucked into her clothes, and half a dozen knives. Reichart had at least that many, and the others were almost certainly armed.

The drones would obliterate them all if it came to weapons being fired.

Reichart. Reichart was rarely surprised, and showed little of it now, even as Cristina's accusation lingered on the air. He hadn't yet moved, taking in the situation in the split second of stillness, just as Alisha did.

No wonder, Alisha thought. No wonder Simone had wanted her out of Europe. She had been playing much too close to Brandon, too close to an agent being used for the wrong ends.

If that was what had happened, a warning whispered inside Alisha's ear. *If. Don't assume anything yet, Leesh. If.*

Greg. Alisha dared one brief look down the barrel of her second weapon, ascertaining Greg's expression. Like Reichart, he showed no surprise. No, Alisha thought: less than no surprise. A thread of satisfaction tightened the lines around his eyes and mouth, the same look she'd seen a thousand times when a job had gone well.

Who had done well, and to what end?

"—double-crossing *whore!*" Time resumed something like its normal speed with the end of Simone's outburst. There were guns suddenly, guns everywhere, in everyone's hands. Details still flashed through Alisha's mind, single points of importance that together made up the picture of catastrophe on the brink of erupting.

She didn't recognize Brandon's weapon, a bulky thing that looked more like a club than a gun. His face was still white, head bent over the gun, fingers darting over a pad on its side, too fast for Alisha to understand what he was doing.

And Greg. Greg, outside of the loop, somehow. Two guns, like so many of them now held, pointed steadily at Alisha and at Reichart. When did we become the bad guys? Alisha wondered, though the answer *when you started pulling guns, Leesh,* seemed blindingly obvious.

Only Reichart still looked cool, his targets curiously the same as Alisha's: Cristina. Greg. An odd wave of solidarity and relief swept through Alisha. The possibility of not leaving the warehouse alive loomed very large, but there was unexpected comfort in believing she wouldn't go down fighting alone.

Simone catapulted into Alisha's shoulder, less deliberate tackle than rage fueling a blind charge forward. For the space of a breath Alisha's aim was knocked askew, and in that instant Cristina moved.

Even now a spark of admiration flew in Alisha's breast. Cristina was a creature made for running, long limbs and slender muscle built for endurance races across enormous distances. Her actions flowed with the grace and bunching of a gazelle pushing away from the earth. Seven years of distance had taken the edge off Alisha's memory of Cristina's beauty in combat, but it came home again with the blond woman's deadly pounce and strike. Alisha was knocked to the side, Simone crumpling backward as Cristina's weight hit her. They tumbled together, Cristina coming out on top with a hand raised, fingers stiff for a killing blow.

Alisha fired, bullet whining so close to Cristina's head she thought she could see the other woman's hair stir with the metal's speed. "Stop!" Whether she shouted before or after the shot was fired, she was uncertain, but Cristina froze, hand still lifted.

A dozen clicks and whines lifted the hairs on Alisha's

neck, the too-familiar sound of the drones targeting. She imagined she could feel the heat of the lasers already, scoring her back, burning skin and muscle down to bone. "They're programmed to protect me, Ali," Cristina said in a low, tense voice. "With a shot fired, I can't turn them off. Put your guns down."

"Let Simone go. Murder isn't justice." Much as the temptation had held Alisha herself only moments before, she knew the truth of what she said. "She needs to be taken in and questioned, not killed."

"Put the guns down, Alisha," Cristina said, more urgently. "I don't want to have to kill you."

"I didn't want to have to kill you, either." Alisha heard her voice go light and thin again. "Funny old thing, life."

Cristina dropped her chin to her chest. "Protocol alpha seven nine nine—"

A buzz so deep it felt like it was bursting from her chest rattled Alisha, making sick shivers race over her body. She looked away from Cristina, guns still held steady, to find Brandon hefting his weapon with a grim expression darkening his face.

"—four one," Cristina went on, voice lifted slightly. "Termination program activated."

Brandon pulled the trigger.

Chapter 30

A physical wave of invisible power slammed into Alisha. She staggered, clutching her stomach against nausea that seemed to have no source. Electrical sparks flew, the scent of ozone burning the air, sickly familiar. Startled whines and bloops emanated from the drones, their firepower seemingly lost. In her peripheral vision, one of the Attengee's legs sprawled out from under it, turning it into a sudden mass of tangled metal. An instant later the Firebird above it crashed down, tremendous clatter making Alisha's eardrums ache.

She, like everyone, twisted at the sounds of metal crashing to the ground. Brandon, pinch-faced and angry, stood amongst the wreckage of all his prototypes, the weapon he'd held now lowered. "I didn't know," he said to Alisha, voice dull and flat. "Delivering you to the caves, letting you go again—they were Simone's orders. I didn't know you were meant to draw Boyer out. I'm sorry." He transferred his focus to Reichart, skin ashen. "I'm sorry," he repeated. "It's not enough, but it's all I can offer."

Cords stood out in Reichart's neck before he spoke. "She made her choices. What," he added, "the hell was that?" One short sharp nod toward Brandon's gun made the blond man lift it a little, then let it drop again.

"EMP gun. The drones can't be easily defeated by conventional weaponry. I thought there needed to be something to level the playing field." He looked back at Alisha. "It was your idea."

"Me?" Alisha stared at the lifeless machines littering the floor around Brandon, tension still pounding a beat in her temples. "An EMP? An electromagnetic pulse gun? I told you to build one?"

"You fried the drone back in Moscow with electricity," Brandon said with a shrug. "The EMP was the next obvious step."

"Of course." Alisha stared another moment, then turned away, voice growing cold. "Cristina, get away from her." She could see that Simone's chest still rose and fell, though the woman didn't otherwise move. Cristina herself didn't seem to have moved, arm still uplifted for the strike that would end Simone's life. "Cristina."

"Will you shoot me, Alisha?"

"If you make me, yes." Make me, Alisha thought, the idea distant. It was an inappropriate phrase; Cristina couldn't force her to shoot. At best, she could decide on her own actions, which would dictate whether Alisha chose to pull the trigger or not.

"I didn't think you could do it, you know that?" She turned her head, clear blue eyes finding Alisha's. "I'll never forget how loud that shot was, the one that went over my head. It seemed like it echoed in the mountains for a lifetime. I was honestly shocked."

"Then you should know I can do it again. Get up, Cristina."

Slowly, gracefully, Cristina unfolded herself from above Simone and stepped back, her hands lifted. "Could you? Could you pull the trigger a second time?"

"If you don't shut up," Reichart growled, "I'm going to do it for her."

Despite herself, Alisha found a little grin waiting in response to Reichart's threat. "Get Simone up," she ordered to no one in particular. Simone snarled and pushed up to her feet on her own, lip curled as Alisha followed her with a gun.

"Reichart, call one of your contacts. Get us secure passage out of here. We're all going back to Langley. Even you," she added to the challenging rise of his eyebrows. "I need somebody I can trust at my back."

Neutrality slid into place on Reichart's face so quickly Alisha knew it masked surprised pleasure. "What happens when we get there?"

"I'm locking all of them," Alisha said with a wave of her gun, "in protective custody until I can verify in God's own handwriting that every single one of their stories is straight."

"Who died and put you in charge?" Cristina wondered. Alisha's expression went icy, her voice full of implied danger.

"Director Richard Boyer."

"Actually—"

"Shut up, Greg." Alisha turned her head enough to see her handler. Former handler, she thought, with cold-crystal clarity. No matter what else happened, she would not work under the man again. There was too much she hadn't understood in the brief grimace of satisfaction she'd seen on his face.

"How," Simone said through her teeth, "do you expect to verify or debunk any of this?"

Alisha thought of the box in her pocket, weighing down the coat, and gave Simone a toothy, nasty smile. "Your behavior, for one." She would leave the box a secret—her trump card, she thought, until she had seen its contents for herself. "Reichart?"

He palmed a cell phone from somewhere inside his jacket and lifted it. "On the way." A few long strides took him away from the group, though Alisha could still hear his voice as he placed the call for their transportation. Dressed all in white and with his bleached hair, he looked like some sort of dangerous avenging angel.

"Alisha." Brandon's voice from behind her, sounding exhausted. "We'll need something big enough to discreetly get these drones out of here." He came up to her side, abandoning his awkward gun to rub his hands over his face.

"Reichart will handle it." Someone she could trust, Alisha thought, and found herself looking at Cristina again. No. She couldn't trust Reichart; he hadn't told her that Cristina was alive. But then, she reminded herself with an inaudible sigh, she hadn't told him she was carrying the black box that had begun the whole mess, either. There was no place in a life of espionage for the romance of utter trust. Even under the best of circumstances, she kept secrets and tried to ferret them out from others. Alisha shook her head and glanced down, tucking her second .45 into the back waistband of her jeans. All in white, she thought again. No good for sneaking around in, or subtlety. And somehow the outfit had gone unstained. A faint smile crept over her mouth. Maybe that would have to be enough.

One skittering step on the concrete was all the warning she had. Brandon crashed into her shoulder even as she looked up, barking a wordless alert through the sound of gunfire. Two shots, fired so quickly their reports were almost one.

Brandon jerked convulsively, full-body twitch that said something vital had gone wrong. Alisha put her arms out to catch him without thinking of her own safety, grunting as his weight went dead. She knelt with him, knowing without looking that she would see blood blossoming over his shirt. The crimson of her tank top wettened without staining, sprayed spots of blood bright and trickling on her coat, round and red on her jeans.

"Brandon." There was nothing to her voice, only a breath of disbelief. He forced a ghostly smile, eyes crushed shut, and whispered, "Maybe now you'll be willing to talk about Rome." The words cost him and he gasped, gritting his teeth together.

"Open your eyes, Brandon. Look at me." Fierce anger gave Alisha's voice strength. "I'm not losing somebody else this way. Brandon, look at me. Goddamn it, look at me." Even as she spoke she dared one brief glance up, and in a moment's look realized that she had miscounted. More than two shots had been fired.

Susan Simone's body lay barely an arm's reach away, pocketed with three distinct bullet wounds. There was utter silence in the warehouse, two men and a single woman standing over Alisha and Brandon's shivering form, each of them holding a smoking gun.

Epilogue

So I'm in therapy. For once even I think it's a good idea. Reyes is decent, for a shrink, and on the days when I just want to sit there and stare at the wall, she doesn't push me to talk. There are a lot of those days, to tell the truth.

The one thing I still haven't been able to figure out is why Simone went after me. The only reason I can come up with is that I was the only one she thought she couldn't buy. That's not an answer I like, but I don't think I'm going to get a better one out of a dead woman.

Every piece of paperwork was in place regarding Cristina. Eight years of undercover work, reports filed everywhere. They gave me the security clearance to read them, in hopes of convincing me to stay on. But they've made Cris the European director in Simone's place, and Greg's taken Boyer's job, and I…wish I could stay.

There I go singing again. Hard to tell when it's pen and

ink on parchment paper, but you'll have to trust that the words are music in my mind. The short version is I don't trust any of them, and I can't stay without at least some degree of belief in what I'm doing. Three people fired bullets to save my life, and a fourth took a bullet for me, and I don't trust any of it anymore.

It took two weeks for Erika to unscramble the box's tape. It's a nice system. The Firebird's got a video feed to go along with the audio reel, all burned to DVD under some kind of encryption code that Erika was alternately thrilled and bitter with. She kept saying she'd know Brandon's work anywhere, but it didn't help her unravel it much faster.

But I know this much now: Simone was dirty. I only watched enough to be sure of that, but whether it was Sicarii or arms dealing or terrorism, Simone looked like she had a hand in it. The Firebird had been on her for days, clips of all kinds of meetings saved on its DVD. It's a sneaky bird, or she'd have caught on to it earlier. Brandon did a good job with it.

He's out of the hospital and healing nicely, apparently. I haven't seen him. I don't know if I'm going to. *God, I don't know.* I'm not used to saying that so much, but it feels like the only thing I can say right now. He took a bullet for me, which is probably a sign that he's on the side of the angels, but I'm still not ready to trust that.

Which is probably why getting out of this business for good would be the smartest idea. When a handsome blonde takes a bullet for you and you still don't know if he's one of the good guys, your worldview needs some adjusting. And I can't get past that look on Greg's face. I still don't understand who'd done what right, there in the warehouse, and I'm not willing to ask him, because I believe he'll lie to me.

And I think I know what it was I saw in his face when

I told them Boyer was dead. I've replayed that moment in my memory a hundred times, trying to read it.

I think it was triumph.

I've lost track of Reichart again, but I can't imagine he's out of my life for good. Some days I regret that, and sometimes I hope I'll look up and see him leaning in the doorway with that cocky grin. At least I finally know what his agenda is. I told him I didn't have nightmares about the day he shot me, and it's true. Still, learning he's the man I always hoped he was helps me sleep better.

Boyer asked me what I would do if I wasn't an agent. The idea made me sick, then. Now...

Now I'm ready to walk away from a job I've spent more than ten years doing. I'm only thirty-one. I could have a whole different career ahead of me, a whole new life. I could become someone else, literally, if I wanted to—though that would mean leaving my family behind, and I don't think I'm ready to do that. But I might be ready to try that kind of life. An ordinary life, one that's not based on telling lies and deceiving people. There's usually a house up for sale on my sister's block, and it'd be great to spend more time with her kids.

I don't know if that's what I want, either. Teaching yoga, maybe settling down with someone who doesn't think shooting me is a good way to save my life, with no one from my past coming back from the grave to haunt me. It sounds boring, and boring sounds perfect.

I feel the past fifteen months have been a bad reflection of my life, like I haven't been seeing clearly. I think I'm ready to wipe away all the fog and take a good hard look in the mirror to see what's really there.

So this may be the last chronicle I write. I'm in Paris

now, and there's already a strongbox with my name—or one of them, anyway—on it. I've never gone back to any of them, but maybe just this once I will. There's something in that box I think I might want to have, if I'm starting over. Something to remind me that the past doesn't have to just haunt me, but can help define me, too.

I've always said *till next time* when I've finished these journals. It seems like what might be the last is a bad place to break tradition, though, so I'll say it even if I'm not sure there'll be one:

Till next time, then.

—Agent Alisha MacAleer

* * * * *

Will Alisha get her quiet life?
Check back in summer '06 to discover
THE PHOENIX LAW.

Is Silhouette Bombshell your favorite addiction?
Then get ready for more thrilling romantic adventures
featuring the most inspiring heroines on the shelves!
Turn the page for an exclusive preview of
one of next month's releases,

DEAD RECKONING
by Sandra K. Moore.

Available July 2006
wherever Silhouette Books are sold.

Late Monday afternoon, Chris lay on a catwalk stretched inches over oily bilgewater, a rough-drawn map of *Obsession*'s hull in one hand and a flashlight in the other. She didn't much care for poking around in the bilge, but necessity was a mother and there was no getting around it. Every through-hull—every hole in the boat that fed water into or out of the boat, through the hull—needed to be watertight. The last thing she needed was a hose to give way at sea.

At least her sister had called yesterday. Three minutes away from the bodyguard she called Igor was all Natalie could grab. While in a public pay toilet, no less. The disposable cell phones she'd bought were extremely handy. Chris just prayed she didn't get caught with one.

First things first.

The bilge's overhead lamps cast dim Vs along the catwalk. *Glad I'm not claustrophobic,* she thought as she shimmied on her stomach a little farther forward toward the hardest-to-reach fitting. One good yank and the clamp snapped. Another yank and the hose popped off the through-hull barb. She looked at the crumbling heavy-duty rubber. Were all the hoses this bad?

"Captain Chris?"

A man's deep voice drifted through *Obsession*'s dimly lit bowels.

Her stomach clenched until she realized it had to be a workman or something.

She leaned against the hull wall to lever herself back onto the catwalk. Nearly there, her hand slipped from the hull and plunged into the bilge. The flashlight clattered, then splashed next to her and went out.

"Dammit." She fished the dead flashlight out of the filthy water, trying not to use her imagination when her fingers touched solid, shifting objects near the bottom. God only knew what was down there.

"Chris?"

The man was close by, inside the engine room, and still calling her name. She crawled backward to the open door. Going ass-first into the engine room wouldn't be much of a greeting for the workman, but what the hey. He could learn to call before showing up.

She wriggled though the hatch, got to her knees, straightened and said sharply, "What is it?"

The first thing she saw was an astonishing pair of gray eyes, very pale irises rimmed with a much darker slate. The man squatted about a foot from the hatch. They were nearly nose to nose, and his gaze pumped every ounce of blood in her body straight to her core.

She registered all of this at once: he hadn't asked permission to board her yacht; he was in his late thirties; he wore expensive Italian leather shoes; she was smeared with grease and oil; he had thick black hair; her right hand was now bleeding; he smelled wonderful.

Not your average Galveston boat monkey schlepping down to a job.

"Special Agent McLellan?" she asked.

"Connor." His remarkable eyes gleamed at her, kicking her pulse into high gear.

"Smitty said you'd show up today."

"He told me you'd had some excitement." His voice resounded through the engine room. "He also showed me around a little upstairs."

Chris got to her feet, then closed the bilge hatch. "*Obsession*'s not much to look at right now," she said as she looked around for a shop rag to wipe off with, "but she's built like a tank. Come on upstairs. I'm ready to look at some daylight."

He followed her out of the port engine room into the lower deck passageway. "Will all this need to be fixed?" He waved a hand at the crumbling wall panels.

"Eventually. Have a seat." Chris waved at the bench seat in the salon as she threaded her way through the tables to the galley sink. "I'll wash up and be right with you."

"Smitty said there's a lot of work to be done." McLellan came to stand by the island counter. "He told me you were very resourceful—" He paused.

She glanced up at him and found his gaze thoughtful, considering. And admiring as it slid from her chin to her collarbone, then lower. She realized suddenly the threadbare tank top and satin demi-bra she wore for hot and dirty boat work showed almost as much as they concealed.

Then he murmured, "I see there was much he didn't say."

His masculine grace as he strode away reminded her of

the world her grandfather had lived in with his antiques gallery, his art, his clothes, his money. The world she didn't belong in and never would.

He looked at Chris for a long, somber moment, as if he could see past her tough facade as easily as he could see past the salon's water-stained wall panels to the strong framework beneath. Then he said softly, "We'll bring your sister home."

Sudden tears threatened but she blinked them back. She'd concentrated for the past five days on the effort, the plan. Keeping the schedule. It was all she'd allow herself to think about. Never beyond that. Never *what if Natalie's husband sends goons to stop them?* or *what if Jerome skips the island and goes straight to South America?*

Or, heaven forbid, what if he's killed Natalie already?

COMING NEXT MONTH

#97 LOST CALLING—Evelyn Vaughn

The Madonna Key

When a freak Paris earthquake plunged her into a hidden catacomb, museum curator Catrina Dauvergne made an amazing find—remains of the Sisters of Mary, legendary guardians of the Black Madonna. But this career coup made Catrina a target of powerful men set on destroying any trace of these martyrs. Now, as the suspicious earthquakes continued, could Catrina harness the sacred powers of the past to save the future?

#98 PAWN—Carla Cassidy

Athena Force

After testifying against her criminal father, Lynn White had been put to good use as a government agent. Her assignment to stake out Miami's Stingray Wharf was a cakewalk for someone of her special abilities—until she ran into ex-lover Nick Barnes, working undercover to bust a crystal meth ring. The feelings between them were explosive—only overshadowed by the *real* bomb Lynn discovered when her mission turned deadly.

#99 WHAT STELLA WANTS—Nancy Bartholomew

Between her partner Jake's demands for a special place in her business and her heart, and refereeing the romances of her agonizing aunt and New Age cousin, private investigator Stella Valocchi had way too many distractions. But then her high school chum Bitsy bit the dust in an explosion at the mall. Or did she? As Stella worked the case, she realized one thing—life was short, and it was time for her to focus on what *Stella* wanted....

#100 DEAD RECKONING—Sandra K. Moore

To rescue her sister from a drug-smuggling husband, charter-yacht captain Chris Hampton needed backup—bad. When two DEA agents offered to help, it was a godsend, and all three set sail for her brother-in-law's island hideaway. But then the "accidents" began—and when Chris nearly drowned, it was *no* accident. With a double-crossing killer on board, never mind her sister—could Chris save herself from being lost at sea?

SBCNM0606